Miriam Wakerly

No Gypsies Served

A NOVEL

Strongman Publishing

Published in Great Britain in 2010 by
Strongman Publishing
Woodland Edge, St Catherine's Road,
Frimley, Camberley, Surrey GU16 9NN
www.strongmanpublishing.com

A CIP catalogue record for this book
is available from the British Library.

ISBN 978-0-9558432-1-1

Printed and bound by Europa in Lithuania

Contents

Acknowledgements

I would like to thank the following people for their help and support in the writing of this book:

Basil Burton, Chairman of the National Romani Rights Association

Thomas Acton, MA, DPhil (Oxon), FRSA, OBE, Professor of Romani Studies, Greenwich University

Ann Wilson and Charmaine Valler of Surrey Community Action, and PC John Hockley, Chair of the Surrey Gypsy and Traveller Community Relations Forum, for welcoming me to their meetings.

Michael Smith, Editor O NEVO DROM, for permitting me to include Tom Odley's poem, for which he owns the copyright.

Erica Wakerly MA RCA who designed the book covers for both *Gypsies Stop tHere* and *No Gypsies Served.*

Thanks also to those who answered my questions so patiently in the early research stage; and to many writer friends for reading the manuscript prior to publication, providing valuable criticism and encouragement in equal measure!

What People have Said

Bridie Page, Derbyshire Gypsy Liaison Group
"Miriam has captured the essence of Romany/Traveller life managing to merge old and new seamlessly. A right riveting read!"

Sue Cook BA DLitt, Broadcaster and Writer
"Few of us even try to understand gypsies and their way of life. Our knee-jerk reaction usually goes no further than 'not in my backyard', as I discovered first hand when a family of gypsies arrived in a village near where I live last year. The immediate reaction among the residents was a mixture of alarm and resentment.

In Miriam Wakerly's Gypsies Stop tHere and its sequel No Gypsies Served, it's refreshing to see gypsies portrayed as individual people like the rest of us, making their way in life the best way they can. Reading this compelling story brings home the fact that it's perfectly possible for gypsies to be accepted successfully into our communities.

Wakerly's books do a wonderful job in helping to promote understanding where there is ignorance and tolerance where there is bigotry. I recommend them heartily."

Dr John Coxhead BA, Cert. Ed., M.Phil., Ed.D., FiFL, FRSA, Author of *Last Bastion of Racism*
"Miriam Wakerly's books Gypsies Stop tHere and No Gypsies Served are a window to the bigotry that a race of people in the UK still experience. Textbooks illustrating statistics of what racism is like are all well and good but what Wakerly adds is an accessible and readable 'way in' to the situation for the general reader, and the storytelling approach reinforces we are talking about real people here, not statistics.

I would recommend that people read these books as a reflection of the reality of contemporary Britain."

Thomas Acton, MA, DPhil (Oxon), FRSA, OBE
Professor of Romani Studies, University of Greenwich
"A vivid and imaginative interrogation of human relationships in the context of the relations between Travellers and English country people, and a worthy sequel to Gypsies Stop tHere."

Basil Burton, Chairman of National Romani Rights Association
"I read most of this book as it was being written and support it 100% - and may it help the Gypsy situation to progress further. What I like is that it is impartial and shows people as individual human beings."

John Hockley, Chair of the Surrey Gypsy Traveller Community Relations Forum and West Surrey Rural Communities Officer
"This sequel is no less gripping than Gypsies Stop tHere. The story has a number of threads as credible characters move in and out of a well paced series of dramas based around Gypsy/Traveller culture and lifestyle.

It is very well researched and does not shy away from tackling thorny issues borne out of prejudice and ignorance that still exist in all our communities"

Lynn Ede NUJ, AOI, Freelance Journalist/Photographer
http://lynnede.redbubble.com
"Miriam Wakerly draws us into the intriguing and sometimes prejudiced world of Gypsies and Travellers. She creates characters we care about, whose life experiences we learn and understand, having been educated in their life's journey, from tents to acquiring more conventional housing, a 'bit of earth' and everything in between. A compelling yarn, with a lifestyle education to boot in this recommended read!"

Michael Smith (Veshengro), Editor O NEVO DROM
The Romani Magazine by Romani for Romani

"This is another great book by Miriam Wakerly dealing with the subject of Gypsies and Travellers in Britain and this one may possibly be even better than the previous one entitled "Gypsies stop tHere". In fact I would say that it is a brilliant book and one that will have the reader spellbound.

The story is extremely well written and the information regarding the Gypsy persecution at home and abroad is well represented. The story has multiple strands that are all extremely believable and real and which will have the reader riveted.

Personally, I can identify with the figure of the Gypsy Dunstan in the story as growing up in a bender was also part of my childhood. Much has changed since and I am now, amongst other things, a journalist and living in a house.

In the end the story turns out well for all concerned and it would be so good if this book would lead to such things in real life too."

Foreword by the Author

No Gypsies Served is a sequel and prequel to *Gypsies Stop tHere* but both books can standalone. Like *Gypsies Stop tHere*, it is fiction, a story to entertain. So, someone asked me, "It's not the truth then?" This was a difficult one to answer.

The story, the characters, even the places are made up. Dunstan is not related to anyone with the surname Smith and Appley Green is not on any map! But certainly I have listened to real life anecdotes, read factual books and consulted web sites, all of which helped form the backdrop of the novel. Issues relating to social injustices, ethnic identity, opinions, laws of the land, alleged crime – the list is long – do exist, however. Some aspects are more factual than others: for example, the snippets you will read from O NEVO DROM are real. (Romani on-line magazine)

There again, reality can be dreary; a daily diary, recording raw, mundane detail, may neither highlight a meaningful message nor make compelling reading! Some scenes or events in the story have been inspired by what I have heard people say. Some have sprung from my imagination and I have striven to create these in the spirit of what I believe to be authentic.

For sure you cannot please all of the people all of the time, but I have tried to be fair and to listen to all sides. In *Gypsies Stop tHere* a divide lies between Gypsies and non-Gypsies. *No Gypsies Served* touches on a three-way stalemate between Romany or English Gypsies, Irish Travellers and non-Gypsies; although this is not meant to imply that harmony cannot or does not exist between these groups. *No Gypsies Served* also shows how history can throw light on current events.

I have heard Gypsies describe themselves as 'proud', 'secretive' and 'misunderstood' and must confess that the first two traits do stand in the way of attempting to rectify the third. I can understand, however, that because of past and present inhumanity towards them, many are mistrustful. I thank all those who have helped me.

No Gypsies Served is peppered with reminders of possible consequences of a Gypsy or Traveller leaving their community to join mainstream society. It is so easy for non-Gypsies to say that Gypsies and Travellers should all live in houses and fit in with everyone else.

Of course, there are many other happenings in both these books. The relationship between Kay and Dunstan is perhaps the vital theme and I know the various interconnecting storylines in an English village captivate a wide readership. I hope that includes you. Happy reading!

Miriam Wakerly

1

The letter had come in the post yesterday and now its contents awaited Kay's attention, a decision. How do people normally respond to anonymous threats, she wondered, even veiled ones? It was, after all, a very *ab*normal kind of communication to receive.

She looked at her watch. Nearly quarter past ten. If Dunstan were coming, he would be here by now. It had become an irregular but frequent event for him to join her for breakfast, usually at least three times a week. When her daughters, Suzi and Claudia, heard of this, there was much winking and nudging. 'Sharing breakfast' meant something else to them, but not for her and Dunstan. Their friendship had never gone that far although, she thought, with something between a smile and pursed lips, there had been times when she would have happily agreed for him to stay the night, with all that might imply.

Her gaze reverted to the letter now back in its envelope propped up in a toast rack on her windowsill between basil and parsley plants, in a pool of sunlight. My second shock of the week, reflected Kay. Some would say I've brought about this string of bad luck, inviting trouble all by myself. Perhaps they are right and maybe the easy option is to ignore it and trust it to go away.

Dunstan used to confirm his intentions by text. It was their little joke that she should always provide something different to eat – maybe fresh croissants from the village bakery, which meant an early start; rustic, herby sausages from the local farmers' market; her own orange-lemon-grapefruit marmalade; duck eggs; toasted cinnamon buns; crumpets with tasty toppings like Serrano ham and cream cheese, smoked salmon with scrambled eggs; or kippers with home-made oat-cakes. The list was long. Today she had been prepared to make a frittata but the ingredients were still assembled on the counter top. Somehow her appetite had drained away and she could not fancy eating a cooked breakfast alone. Making meals for one was something that had come hard after Marcus' death, once Suzi and Claudia had left home. Now she faced the same readjustment. Had Dunstan decided never to take breakfast with her again, she wondered? Feeling sick as this possibility seeped into her consciousness, she tipped a small quantity of muesli into a bowl.

For almost two years she had counted on him as her friend and ally, not merely a casual gardener. But perhaps she had totally misread the signs. She had tried phoning him, thinking at first that he must be unwell, too ill to reach for the phone for sure, or battling with some family crisis, presumably a matter of life or death. She remembered the summer before last, when their acquaintance was but a few months old. He had simply disappeared, for some weeks, and how she fretted, until eventually he spoke on the phone, calm and apologetic, only to tell her that his elderly mother had suddenly been taken ill. Had died, in fact. Then as if this was not enough, he had gone on to explain, "Some young people I know. Overdose situation, attempted suicide …" and she fell silent, humbled and guilty for being vain enough to imagine his absence had anything to do with her. She was not the pivot of his existence. She had learned that she should bide her time.

There were other matters scuttling around in her head. The inner turmoil she was feeling had been triggered last week by a phone call, the *first* bit of 'bad luck'. Fatalism was not her style as a rule. 'Life is what you make it', a truism her father would often bark at her; especially in those teenage years when it seemed the rest of the world was to blame for things going wrong or simply not happening as she would have liked.

That call had caused her stomach to heave with shock.

"You and me, we never really *met*, did we?" a man had said, speaking down the phone-line in a breathless way, slightly high-pitched. Anger was obvious, but more than that his voice was, she realised, snuffly, thick with emotion. "But I saw *you*. In court. You probably clocked me with the rest of our folks …" Kay sat down, feeling weaker and weaker as he went on to reveal his identity. "Gary's brother. Billy."

Kay felt she should say something. "Oh. Hello Billy. How are you?" Her response was inept, but she sensed she would find out soon enough the reason for his call. Until then how could she work out what was the right or wrong thing to say to the brother of the man who had murdered her husband?

"Thought you'd like to know he's dead," came the nasal voice, abruptly.

Kay paused, closing her eyes for a moment, to allow this to register. "Gary? He died?" she asked, softly.

"Bad enough 'im being banged up … You … you should feel bloody bad about this, now then, lady. That's the point. Uh? You! If it hadn't been for … you *know* what I'm gettin' at." His voice was getting louder now.

Kay had shivered at this, feeling the hairs rise up on the back of her neck and on her forearms. She swallowed hard, cleared her throat. Did he expect her to grieve for the man who had, without compassion, stabbed her husband to death in front of her, in their own home? "How did …? What did he …? What did Gary die of?" she asked huskily.

Her questions were bypassed. "You owe us, you do. That whole thing with your 'usband. Self-defence. Gary never went out carryin' no knife. Never meant to kill no one and now, gone for good. No chance to make good. All thanks to you, you bloody, fucking bitch!" Yes, she had been the one who had stupidly picked up the knife, but … what did he want from her now?

He slammed down the phone. Much later, too late, she collected her senses and dialled 1471, realising the phone had rung again since Billy's landline call, recognising the number given as her dentist who had probably called to remind her of an appointment coming up. So this man, this Billy, was lost. How had he tracked her ex-directory number down, she wondered? These practical thoughts struck her some while after the event. For hours she had simply paced up and down, shaking and crying, or lay hugging herself on the bed, just unable to cope with all the *angst* she thought she had managed to file away for good. Yes, she had done the wrong thing. She was the one who had, in fear, picked up that carving knife that had then been turned upon her husband by Gary, a man desperate for a heroin fix. But God knows, she had suffered enough for her error.

This, along with the totally unconnected letter, was something that even now, she urgently needed to talk about. She gazed at Dunstan's empty cup. His failures to show up seemed to be the third thing if, as superstition decrees, bad luck comes in batches of three.

The murder trial, four years ago now, had been mercifully quiet and swift: with past form, Gary was traced and, thanks to DNA forensics, convicted. How ironic it was that after moving from Richmond, London to her country idyll, Appley Green, in a bid to escape the past, she had actually opened up, baring her soul to the public in a confessional newspaper article. But this catharsis had helped her to then finally, finally, put it behind her as much as she could. The local community knew and had accepted the reasons why she had been the one who grabbed a knife …

But who would want to be reminded of these horrifying details now? A friend or neighbour? Suzi or Claudia? Her solicitor? To dredge up the circumstances of her husband's murder again would be like digging up a grave, dissecting a corpse, to say nothing of messing with her head. If tragic memories were to be stirred up, Dunstan was the only person she could think of who could listen calmly and help her through them. Somehow, he would know what to do.

Gary's brother, Billy, had not tried calling again. She wanted to believe that he had cooled off, that he had vented his rage at her in the heat of emotion, in the first wash of his grief, when he needed someone to blame. Yet it had a feel of unfinished business hanging oppressively over her, such that she felt a need to speak to him again to clear the air. A natural curiosity also caused her to persist with an unanswered question. How had Gary died in prison? She would not have wished death upon him in any form, despite his crime, but she was forced to wonder whether he had been violently attacked, taken his own life, suffered some terminal illness or simply been the victim of a random but fatal accident. How could her conscience allow her to hope that it might have been the last, and probably least likely within prison walls, of these miserable alternatives?

She cleared away the eggs, ham, cooked potatoes and other leftover vegetables, tidied up, and took a walk around her acre of garden, assessing how much work there was to do. For the last two years Dunstan had prepared the ground, grown seedlings or sown seeds straight into the rich loam of her substantial vegetable plot. He had undertaken most of the spadework, leaving her the lighter, less arduous tasks performed with hoe, rake or fork. It was her role to maintain the herbaceous borders while they shared chores like lawn mowing and watering. Come harvest time they would both delight in picking the produce; with Dunstan taking the excess as agreed, and she would then bustle about blanching, freezing, preserving and cooking. She surveyed the garden, now looking quite bare and bleak on this cloudy morning, and took in deep lungfuls of fresh air. Some early Aqua Dulce broad beans Dunstan had sown months ago would soon be thrusting out plump pods; soft fruit bushes were in leaf-bud; acid green, delicate pink clumps of crinkly rhubarb leaf were insistently forcing their way out of the dark mud, like some alien life-form emerging from primeval ooze. But where was the rest? She would go round to Dunstan's mobile home and see what was going on, perhaps after the lunch she had arranged to have today with Millicent, at the nearby Fox and Rabbit pub.

Before leaving the house, she took one more look at the letter, almost as intimidating as Billy's call. Would she tell her old friend about her various woes? Even now the words of this letter gave her a jolt.

Give up, demanded the writer. *Why keep on supporting these people who come along and upset everyone? Can't you see these Travellers are not wanted by most of the residents of Appley Green? Just because you managed to get a few cranks to gee up the council to provide this so-called transit site, it doesn't speak for the majority.*

What worried Kay, as she read it to the end, was that it was not a badly worded letter. These were sentences formed by someone who was serious-minded, in control, not blatantly aggressive in tone until the end, when there was a threat that was both frightening and difficult to fathom.

If you do not exert the considerable influence you seem to have with the council to get this ridiculous, interminable campaign of yours overturned, then clearly other people will have to do the job for you, by whatever means it takes. I don't imagine it will be a clean fight.

It had a very unpleasant tinge to it, this letter, this hate mail, particularly as some reasonably well-educated coward in the vicinity had chosen to send it anonymously.

There again, this person was as ignorant as he, or she, was arrogant! Whilst Kay had gained something of a reputation in the area for being in support of the Gypsies' case, she had been relieved to know it was all entirely out of her hands. Formalised consultations took place to obtain feedback from both the general public and the Travellers themselves and she had seen productive liaison work carried out by a network of community development workers. It gave some real hope for the future.

Dunstan would probably have an idea who lay behind this. She marvelled at his uncanny knowledge of the local community, all underpinned by the throb of healthy gossip. Despite facts often morphing through rumours into a thorough distortion of the truth, he always seemed to succeed in sifting reality from the delusions and fabrication that added colour to villagers' chit-chat.

2

Feeling even more wretched than when he had driven away from his mobile home, Dunstan drew up his camper van in the small plot in Hampshire where his old friend, Copper, sporadically hung out. Copper's shack and small patch of land were tucked away down a narrow winding lane. As Dunstan's vehicle had bumped and jolted its way over potholes, he winced at the gritty mud splashing up on its previously gleaming white bodywork, and growled at the thorny bushes allowed to spread out to scratch whatever passed through. His van was far from new but he took pride in maintaining it. Why didn't Copper clip back this undergrowth and get some mates to tarmac his drive? It made his blood pressure rise.

This was Copper's second home. Dunstan knew he spent less and less time here now. His main residence, where his wife, Sheila, and various family members lived, was a country mansion in Surrey with paddocks, stables, orchards – the whole package. Dunstan never felt any inclination to visit him there.

The grey-haired, elderly man with a face of scored leather, sporting a red and blue scarf around his neck, appeared with a wood-axe in his hand. He waved him in, beaming. His old lurcher, a greyhound-collie cross combining speed with intelligence, came bounding out from behind the shack, barking in a fearsome manner until he recognised Dunstan and his vehicle and began wagging his tail, playfully chasing the wheels. Dunstan parked a little way from an iron cooking prop from which hung a large black kettle. Ashes on the ground were damp from the light drizzle that had fallen during the night, but were fast drying out in the warmth of the morning sunshine. Stacked to one side against a wooden lattice fence were some calor-gas canisters, and against a wall to the left was a pile of logs and sawdust.

As soon as Dunstan stepped out of the van, Copper seized his arm and shook his hand, "Good to see yer *mush…*" he said, actually shouting without realising it, due to his own poor hearing.

"Hey, Bramble!" Dunstan made a fuss of the lurcher, that had served Copper well for all its adult life, both as hunter and guard-dog. He remembered it as a puppy, some ten years ago. "And you. Still not got that hearing aid then?" remarked Dunstan, resting a hand on Copper's shoulder.

"Bah! Nothing wrong with my ol' ears. What's goin' on then? You sounded troubled on the phone, my friend."

"You'll laugh when I tell you, you will."

"Will I? Will I? Oh, that's good. I likes a good laugh. We'll 'ave a sing-song later shall we?" He roared with laughter and Dunstan felt his spirits lift already. "Let I put the kettle on, *mush*, and then we can get to it … whatever 'tis, my ol' mate."

Who would think that this man had made a fortune from his scrap-metal business, thought Dunstan, as the old chap disappeared momentarily? He could just remember Copper as a young Gypsy man, when he, Dunstan, was a *chavi*, a young Gypsy boy. Apart from growing more bent and wizened, Copper never changed.

Dunstan sat down upon one of the old plastic chairs on offer and looked around the yard, overhung at the edges with elder and hazel trees. The small wooden building with huge windows that filled his dwelling with light, provided an escape to times past. The cramped kitchen area housed an ancient, wood-fuelled stove for cooking and keeping the place warm, but he had no mains drainage, no running water, no bathroom. Electricity came from a generator and was used sparingly. He had built this little home himself probably about fifty years ago. It was full of 'essentials' like books and paintings and once held Crown Derby dinner and tea services kept immaculately in cabinets that had belonged to his parents. The more precious items had been removed to the security of his modern homestead.

The sun was now struggling through the clouds as Copper appeared with his famous coffee pot on a tray with inverted cups and a jug of milk. Dunstan smiled at the memory of Copper gaining his nickname, his first name being registered as Ronald. As a young married man, an eighteen-year old *rom,* he chanced upon the coffee pot that was so tarnished it was bright green. It lay sad and forgotten amongst some other items in a house clearance sale. His first thought was that, once cleaned up and polished, it could make him a handsome profit, but days later, once he had it gleaming in the sunlight, he could not bear to part with it. His family teased him mercilessly for the fact that he had to have a 'proper cup of coffee in a proper copper coffee pot', the tongue-twister that some *chavvies,* Romany boys, had once learned at school. He had used it ever since.

Everything shook as he walked but Dunstan knew better than to offer help to this fiercely independent man.

"So?" said Copper, wheezing slightly as he settled himself in a chair opposite. Dunstan could see curiosity burning in his rheumy eyes but did not feel quite ready to unburden himself yet, secure in the knowledge that once he did, he would feel much better.

"How's the family? Come on, now, I want to hear all the craic."

"Could take a while now… So, our Mary-Ann, that's Jimmy's daughter, she's just had twins. Little peas in a pod, can you believe it and lookin' just like me, wouldn't you know it? Lucky for them they're boys! Hah-hah! So that makes … um …" he counted on his fingers, muttering to himself, "twenty-three grandchildren, and eight great-grandchildren at the last count."

"That's a lot of people – good job not everyone has *chavies* as fast as you and your folks, Copper!" Copper would not see things from the global perspective.

"They've all done well for theirselves, you know. Proper educamated they are, an' all. Little 'uns they read to me – they read better'n I can do myself, though thank God that's something I learned a bit of early on, unlike so many … them as never did the learning, well they never had the chance neither did they? Nah, they ain't done so good lately. I tell you Dunstan, the paperwork and stuff, all these Acts of Parliament, and rules and forms – the likes of old Billie, Humph' an' Boozy Lad – your generation, you remember 'em, they fall foul of the law so often they 'ardly have time to get over one spell in *stir* before they're back in again. They could come up with as good a bit o' scrap as the next man, a nice bit o' metal, but my God Dunstan, without they forms and the right weighin' and measurin' and all stuff like that, they're branded as criminals …"

Dunstan could see both sides. He had learned years ago that a degree of regulation was necessary to keep all fair and square. "And what about where they get it from? And how. All OK, is it? Nothing nicked uh?"

Copper's head rocked from side to side as if weighing up the question carefully. "Me own people. Can't ask too many questions. When you know they need to feed a family, to be back home at night with summat to show for a day's work, you can't. How would it be with the missus if they was to show up empty-handed, eh? You 'ave to take what they bring and not ask those things. Sometimes I'd tell 'em 'you take that back this minute, you daft what's a name,' 'cos they're mad thinking they nor I could get away with it. Like a copper statue there's only one of! Imagine that, the soppy *dinilos*. That might be recognised sooner'n you could say *gavver*! Hah-hah! No, mostly it were stuff thrown out, not wanted by the *Gorgios*, so … these days ordinary people is wising up and knows the value of their scrap, plenty of 'em helping theirselves I do know that, but still there's not many that can be bothered with disposin' of scrap the proper way, despite all their 'green' talk and recyclin' – all stuff we bin doing for centuries, ain't we? Hah-hah! More coffee, my good friend?"

At last Copper stopped to draw breath and Dunstan felt his whole body and soul relax. For Dunstan, Copper's nickname suited him – not because he was in any way like the police, the *muskerros* or *gavver*s, but because he was a sparkly individual, shining, in contrast to his more morose relations. He felt he could talk to Copper, or more often just listen, in a way that he could not with his own family. All the intervening years when he had been away from them had left a gap that had not quite healed. It was a rare and sad thing to have such a rift within a family in the Gypsy community, but then he had deserted them as a young man. He would always be regarded as a bit of an oddity, no matter what amends he had tried to make.

"You come 'ere often?" asked Dunstan, and they both chuckled as he spoke.

"Not as much as I did and that's the truth. No. Still runnin' the yard, from distance like. Sonny, Jake, 'arry an' Clem doing the work, but need to keep an eye on things. And what with weddings and funerals, there ain't much spare time for comin' out 'ere."

"What'll happen to this place when … well, eventually? Family interested? Your boys?"

"Nah. I don't reckon. Get demolished, someone'll be only too keen to get this plot and build a nice new country 'ome on it. Got this little bit o' land ... when were it? So long ago ... not sure. Weren't worth much in them days. Now? Fetch a fair few quid, I guess. Will you be stoppin' for a bit o' dinner? I got a fat rabbit bin hangin' for a bit, taters good for *tatti tatti*, onions, carrots, cabbage and turnips … a few cans …"

Dunstan smiled, looking at his watch, knowing this meal would take a while to stew in the old black pot by the time Copper had got the fire going and skinned the rabbit - courtesy of Bramble, whose forebears had excelled in keeping the pot well stocked, just like in his childhood days.

"I'm so tempted, but I'd best say no. Need to get back …"

Copper looked disappointed. "Not before you've told me whatever it is and given me a good laugh, though …"

"Ah, now, maybe I misled you there."

"I bet it's a *juval*." Dunstan hung his head. "Am I right?"

Kay's face, with its fine bone-structure and shapely lips, immediately appeared in his mind's eye.

"You old devil. Not exactly, but … well, the thing is, yes it's all on account of a woman, but that's not the problem now … oh, the truth is I don't know where or how to begin," he faltered, now wondering if Copper would be the least bit interested anyway. How is it, thought Dunstan, women are forever pouring out their problems to each other, listening, supporting, hugging … you see it on TV, and for real in cafés and pubs … He sighed. Men don't do this empathy thing so much, he realised, finding it difficult to put the words together. What chance do I have of writing an autobiography? About as much as a horse riding a bicycle.

"You see, Copper, I'm trying to go back in time, you know, to remember all those good times – and bad, when we were kids. Well, you were grown up and I was a young scruff of a *chav* … Mother and Father and the people we *jalled* with on the road ... but it's hard."

"You writin' all this down, are you?" asked Copper doubtfully, rubbing his chin.

"Yes, I am. Using a computer in fact. But, the problem is … well, two things. One is, do I tell all the truth when it's about people who are still alive now? Or at least their children are, grown-up and big enough to give me a battering. I mean, if they don't like what they read or hear about from others …" He paused. "And the other problem is getting things in the right order. You know I start off with one thing, like a scene in a film, that opens up in my head all clear and bright and then that sets me off with another little picture-story that goes back maybe ten years before and I can't seem to get any order or logical sequence."

"Mm. Hard." Copper looked bemused. "Don't reckon I'd know what to do with summat like that. How do other folks do this? Like it's a memoir, is it? A diary, 'cept you've got to do it all from memory? Oh, *dordi, dordi*! That's 'ard, that is …"

"Exactly. I've read others' life stories but they seem to have it all in order, one thing leading to another nice and neat, knowing exactly what people said and when, their style of clothes, hair colour … how their breath smelt, I swear! Honest to God …"

"Bah! They'd make it up, wouldn't they? Some of it, I bet. Who else would know any better?" A good point well made, thought Dunstan. Copper was looking at him, studying his face. He could feel his eyes boring through him. "There's more to this, ain't there? You said, a woman?"

"*You* said a woman!" replied Dunstan, laughing. It fell quiet for an endless minute or two before he threw his hands up in the air. "OK! This *woman* …" said Dunstan, eventually breaking the silence, "it was *her* idea and seemed like a good one at the time. I do some gardening for her – you know, the scheme I run for young lads in need of help …"

"'Course I do. You bin doin' it for years. Think I'm soft in the ol' 'ead? And who doesn't know 'bout your good works with the young ruffians? Specially since you became a bit famous. I got the press cuttin' somewhere …"

"That, in the local paper, was all her doing too, really. We had a good … friendship, something a bit sort of … special, considering our ages …" Dunstan stood up, suddenly feeling hot and lost for words.

"Oh-ah," said Copper, rubbing his hands. "Now it's gettin' interestin'."

"Well I think this whole life history thing has just spoiled all that. It brought out something in her that I never knew before … and because of it, my story … you see, I'm not too sure if we can ever be the same again. Something she said, or did, rather … We were going to work on it *together* but now she's made it *impossible*!" Dunstan felt so worked up, he was in danger of displaying tears in male company, tears of inner rage as much as any other emotion that may have been mingling with his embarrassment.

The following day Dunstan switched on his computer with a heavy heart, recalling books he had read in his 'literary phase' in his thirties, and in particular Marcel Proust's *A la Recherche du Temps Perdu*, or, as he read it, *Remembrance of Things Past* and he had recently come across a quotation from it: *We find a little of everything in our memory, it is a sort of pharmacy, a sort of chemical laboratory, in which our groping hand may come to rest, now on a sedative drug, now on a dangerous poison.*

Indeed. Well, he had started something he knew he must follow through but his reasons for trying to unearth memories, revisit his childhood and those troubled days as a younger man, had changed substantially. Initially it was to please Kay. How feeble and pathetic that seemed now. He had to chuckle. It was a poor reason to commit to such a massive undertaking.

Since dipping a toe in those turbulent waters, feeling their danger and strength suck him in, he could see it was no mean task to rekindle emotions and recall harrowing scenes of his life that he had conveniently tucked away for so long. Caught up in the contagion of Kay's enthusiasm, he had also imagined in his conceit that this *oeuvre* would be published and so he would be writing for the public at large! How naive was he? What were the chances of it happening? And how would people he knew like to read his reflections on them from a bygone age? Not at all, not one bit. He would be hated, far and wide and unable to hold his head up amongst his community, with whom he was not long reconciled ... Mm, he thought, reconciled maybe but still there was a separateness about him because of the life he had lived for so many years amongst *Gorgios*. He knew he was different. So now, he had to ask why he was doing this – and for whom.

On that question he had already done his thinking and knew the answer, instantly.

"For me," he said aloud, as the document he had begun a few weeks ago appeared on the screen. "For my eyes only." With a sudden spurt of energy and enthusiasm, he punched in a heading above what he had already written:

My first day at school

It was something of a cliché but now what did it matter? He was not out to impress or … please … anyone, not even Kay. It was an immensely liberating thought.

The bender was heavy with dew, the canvas quite sodden. I was glad to crawl out of it, though the air hanging over the roadside was damp.

As morning light, the colour of a pale egg yolk, began to break, I could see a silvery sky full of black, scudding rain clouds. Always the first thing I did when I got up, was to look up for signs of weather. If I beheld bright blue I was happy.

Mother had done extra hawking to get me fitted out with the right clothes. I struggled to get into trousers the colour of pine needles and a white shirt I thought were new.

"So smart you look," she whispered, squatting easily to be at my level.

She must've been in her early twenties but life's hardships had aged her. (At fifteen she ran off with our Father, she a country *Gorgio* girl, and him a young Gypsy man. I found out some years later they eloped in the Romany way and came back to the family regarded as married. Presley was born nine months later!) She must've had to learn a lot living on the road, *jalling the drom* as we would say, with Gypsies.

She had become fat round the waist – but then, of course, she was pregnant with the second baby she was to lose (I found out later she had a premature stillborn and a miscarriage after having me). I was her second attempt – and, as it turned out, her last – to get a child educated. My big brother, Presley, never took to school and later, I could understand why. "My littl' man." She held me close to her bosom and I felt safe.

He stopped, slightly embarrassed. Well, who would want to read this boring mundane stuff now, he thought? Then he had a chuckle as he thought of the saying, 'Safe as houses.' That would not apply here, but 'safe as home' could stand, he decided, since home was where you lit your fire with your family around you. Dunstan's spirit had flown back to that day now and he felt aglow with the memory … It didn't matter. No one else would read his words. He could feel the warmth of his mother's body close to him, smell the faint odour of her brown patterned jumper.

We had no running water where we were, no spring, stream nor tap, so Father had gone off on foot pushing a handcart with a bucket and a milk churn to the nearest garage to get them filled. Last place we stopped, the locals wouldn't give us any, so we had to move on. There was at least enough in the black kettle to boil up for tea. Mother already had a good old fire going and sausages sizzling in the skillet. Father wasn't doing so well as the main family provider then, moving from horse dealing into tree-lopping and hedge-trimming. He was still learning the trade and building up a kit of tools. So Mother had worked hard yesterday, out door to door with her bits of lace and stuff, to buy those sausages. I knew how hard it was as I'd done that with her some days. I liked knocking on people's doors. She said they were less likely to slam the door in the face of a child, but when folk saw her hovering at the gate they would do anyhow sometimes.

After Presley and I had eaten our *hoben* before getting off to school, some aunts and uncles and cousins came over to borrow our fire and while they were sorting out their food, Mother left off washing the plates in the enamel washing-up bowl. She sat down on a mossy old log, called me over, taking me to one side. I had to take off my shirt so she could splash some cold water saved from the day before, round my face, ears and hands. I wriggled and yelled as I always did but she held my arm with a firm grip until she was done. Soon the shirt was put back into place and a

knitted jumper several sizes too big was pulled over my head, my skin still wet.
"I'll miss you bein' around," she said and I can remember her chestnut brown eyes swimming with tears. "There's no more water till your Father gets back so you'll have to clean your boots on some long grass on your way. Now then, don't play up with the *Gorgios*, because if you do they won't let you come back." She said this, even though she was one herself, deep down.
She wiped my face with her sleeve, its woolly coarseness making me cry out again.
In case I hadn't got the message, she went on, "Behave and don't let us down. Just keep your head down and learn."
I nodded. I didn't know any other *chavi* who had been to school but I'd heard bad stories about schools, *Gorgio chavies* and teachers. Mother always said that some learning would help me get on in life and if I could read and write it'd make some things a lot easier. She could read and write a little herself, although she told me herself that even as a *Gorgio* girl her attendance at school had been poor. Living on a rough smallholding she'd had to shoulder domestic chores for her father and brother since her mother died when she was young. As far as my education was concerned, she was probably thinking of being able to read signs on the road, prices and labels in shops, warning notices and forms that would help me keep out the way of the *muskerro*, the *gavvers*. Father saw little need for it and always discouraged spending time on books.
With Mother's advice firmly planted in my head and sausages and sweet tea warm in my belly, I skipped off down the road with my *chavi* cousin from our makeshift roadside camp a full three miles to the village school. Part of me wanted to cry as I was leaving my familiar world for a whole day for the unknown but another part of me was so excited I thought my heart would burst ...

An anxiety began to build up in Dunstan and he stood up from the computer to get a can of beer from the fridge.

Questions had begun to spring up in his head. He had such a vivid memory of this special day, he could see it, feel it, smell it, but his thoughts were drawing him back further to the days when he was maybe three or four years old. They still had a wagon then, the fancy *vardo* that had belonged to his grandparents. It was beautiful, fitted out with carvings flashed up with whorls of gold leaf and bright, brilliant mirrors and neat little cupboards, shelves and drawers stuffed full of bone china and ornaments. With some effort he captured the image in his head and held it there. His Granf'er had been a successful horse dealer and there were pictures of horses, carved into the screen over where his mother and father slept. The type of wagon was a Dunton Reading … which prompted Dunstan to note down something else that just occurred to him.

How I got my name

"Did you call me after Granf'er's wagon?" I asked Mother one day when we were chatting, sheltering in the Dunton Reading from a nasty squall. She put her head on one side and mulled it over. I was probably about four and an ever inquisitive child.

"No, my darlin'. Just before you was delivered to this world, right here beneath this very *vardo,"* and she did not explain to me then that the rules of *mochadi* would not permit the mess inside the wagon, for at that age I just accepted it was normal for a woman to give birth on the hard earth outside, "we'd passed a church and because the birth pains were gettin' that bad we very nearly stopped in that church but your Father cracked on and got us off the road, not wanting to be accused of using a church for birthin' a child."

I got impatient, not understanding where all this was going. I had no idea at that age what Mother meant by 'birth pains'. "But how d'you choose my name? I never heard of no other Dunstans in this whole world, Mother!" I groaned. She ruffled my hair and laughed. "Why that ol' church was called St Dunstan's. I couldn't make out the sign as we travelled along, hurtin' as I was, but asked someone and they went and found out for me 'cos I thought, so long as it weren't St Mary's or something, it might gimme a good name for my new baby boy and there we are, so it did. So right away you was Dunstan, though maybe not so much the saint, I'd say." She tickled me and I fell about giggling. I loved my mother so much I would have fought for her, even at that age.

Many large families on the road with maybe 12 children or more would not have had a mother with the time to spare for talking like this, so Presley and I were blessed in that sense, though our lack of brothers and sisters must have caused much distress to Mother and Father. I can see that now.

He thought back to days when he was even smaller when they had this fine wagon. Thinking now as an adult he realised how lucky they must have been in those years of post-war austerity. Life for them had been easier, more comfortable than it was later to become. There were two blue and white piebald horses … what were they called? Magpie and Carter! What happened to them? He could remember watching the steam rise off their coats after a long trip and the smell; and was swept straight back to those early years. He recalled how important it was that wherever they stopped there would be the *poove* – grazing for the horses, the old *grais*. Then something else flashed up in his head. There was that time when they all got into some terrible trouble with a farmer and the *gavvers* because there was a sign that the men handling the horses could not read. They were told, too late, that it said, 'GRAZING OF HORSES FORBIDDEN.' Well how were we to know, he thought? As a child it just seemed so unfair to Dunstan, but now he had to concede that they had been guilty of trespass. But did it really need a car full of policemen, heavy handed *muskerros*?

He was allowed to sleep inside the wagon in a place under the big bed. So was Presley. That 'dog kennel', as they called it, was a lot cosier. Then sometime later suddenly they were all outside in the cold bender, no more than a bit of not-sowaterproof sheeting pulled over some long bent branches of hazel with some straw and a few rag rugs strewn on the ground inside. He had a picture in his head of his parents sleeping in another, slightly bigger one, very close by, that during the day was used for cooking on the Queenie stove if the weather was too wet for a fire outside. Then he made a connection in his jumbled memory, between a scene where there was much angry shouting and the sudden disappearance of the family's wagon. What was that about? He scratched his head, trying hard to remember but it was no use. He must ask Presley about all of this. Being that bit older, maybe *he* would remember; maybe it had all been explained to him by Mother and Father. He got as much typed up as he could recall and then stood up and stretched to rid himself of an ache in his shoulders.

With a sigh, he sat back on his cream leather sofa with what was left of his beer. Outside, he could see a couple returning to their mobile home, arm in arm. When neighbours walked past, so close you could reach out the window and almost touch them on a shoulder, it took him back to days on sites where big families lived together. You knew everyone. You helped each other and shared your last crumb when times were hard. On the mobile home park it wasn't like that. Most of the neighbours kept themselves to themselves, just like some people do in houses.

Then he thought again about what had happened the last time Kay saw the first page of what he had written, printed out ready for her to read. He could see in his mind's eye how she had picked up a pencil and, with a smile, lightly crossed out his title, which was quite simply ***"Dunstan's Life"***, replacing it with ***"Gypsy Turned Gorgio!"***. He had silently taken the pages back from her in a blind rage of which she seemed quite unaware. The fury he felt was so great he could scarcely breathe. Until that moment he had actually considered that they might settle down together as a couple.

3

"Such an awful shame," said Millicent, Kay's old friend who had come over from Richmond. Kay was not sure she liked her pitying look. Would she be able to confide in her and spill out her worries about the letter and phone call? And Dunstan?

"What?"

"All this build up! Your bloody hard work! People really making an effort to make this … what do you call it, transit site, happen? And no grand opening ceremony lined up for Saturday?"

"No, that would be … just wrong, somehow …" muttered Kay, pushing around a forkful of Brie and bacon salad on her plate. The committee who had organised the Appley Green Festival last autumn had thrashed this out and, along with the council, decided to keep everything low key.

"But you went to the trouble of getting it in the paper. Mm! I forgot to tell you!" exclaimed Millicent, putting down her glass and leaning forward. "It was so exciting, I suddenly heard this bit about it as I was driving along. Local radio! I thought, wowee! Kay, *my friend*, is behind all that. Mind you, I still find it hard to understand what prompted you. I mean … really, are these people worth all this support? You could be working for a children's charity or something worthwhile." Kay felt herself waver away from the possibility of Millicent offering a calm listening ear for her problems.

"I wasn't actually looking for a cause to work for, Millicent. It kind of drifted towards me, although I suppose I did grab hold of it with both hands as it passed by … but I've found it *worthwhile*. Make no mistake about that."

"OK." Millicent shrugged.

"Anyway," continued Kay, pausing to take a gulp of Rioja, "there are so many reasons why a big celebration wouldn't be right, I hardly know where to start." She hoped her friend would be satisfied with that. It would be tantamount to self-congratulation if she were to organise such a thing; and no one else had come forward to suggest or arrange any special festivities. No party, banner, speeches or cutting of red ribbon by a local dignitary. Kay felt sure people in the know would be of the same mind. The Travellers who happen to use the site first would not want the extra attention from *Gorgios* likely to ensue from any kind of flag waving. To apparently gloat could antagonise the anti-Gypsy element in the village and surely lead to 'trouble' … Kay felt a shiver of fear as words from the threatening letter filled her head. *I don't imagine it will be a clean fight.* Could she tell Millicent? Would she be sympathetic?

"I bet you've made yourself pretty unpopular in some quarters," remarked Millicent, frowning, it seemed to Kay, right on cue. "I mean, to be perfectly honest …" Already Kay was sensing she had her answer. As a friend who would urge her to surrender, to simply avoid putting herself in any possible danger for the sake of 'these people', Millicent was not the perfect confidante. Millicent did not complete her sentence, looking somehow embarrassed, but Kay could have supplied many optional ends to it.

They moved on to other things.

After Millicent had left, Kay decided to do as she had promised herself, before dusk. The spring evenings were getting longer now and there would be plenty of time. She would take a stroll round to Dunstan's home in an effort to catch him, after checking in case he had sent her an email.

There were a few new messages and, scrolling down, she found herself holding her breath, a voice inside her head warning that her enemy might have somehow obtained her email address. One message was a report from the local Neighbourhood Watch police constable, listing recent burglaries. These were common enough; people responding to relatively desperate economic times in the only way they knew how, though of course not to be condoned in any way, Kay felt very strongly, pursing her lips and shaking her head. The second email was from Amazon trying to persuade her to buy yet more books that would assuredly be to her liking, and another was from a company with an irresistible offer on printer inks, both of which she quickly deleted. Of more interest was a message from Max Leatherson, the Gypsy Liaison Officer with the local council: *No group has booked the site as yet – but they rarely do. Rumour has it there is a group moving up from the south-west on their way to Kent, likely to be here on Saturday. Thereafter would expect a steady stream that will need monitoring to ensure there's no overcrowding of pitches etc. Hope publicity has not reached out too far and wide, to be honest with you Kay, or the facilities will not be able to cope with demand. With around 6 pitches, estimate around 12 trailers, possibly more. Maybe you could get to work on getting another one opened up in Market Leaming, the next place in need! They could take the overspill!! Regards Max PS Perhaps see you at the site on Saturday?* There were, as she had come expect, no messages from Dunstan.

She quickly brushed her fair, wavy hair, finally pushing it into shape with her fingers, and applied a little mascara and lipstick. As she walked the two miles or so to the pleasant residential park where Dunstan lived, alongside mostly retired folk from the village, she reflected that Appley Green was probably almost as divided as it was when she first arrived, before she had embarked upon trying to bridge the gap between Gypsies and *Gorgios.* The more open-minded, liberal types were, perhaps naively, looking forward to the Gypsies returning with genuine excitement and interest. It was something of a landmark in history; the first time for centuries that their arrival would be, both officially and socially, welcomed by the community as a whole, maybe not unanimously, she conceded, but *on* the whole. They were entitled to be on this new stopping-place for thirteen weeks. She had learned from Max that the site manager, Molly-Marie, a Romany Gypsy widow, was already installed. Her four grown-up children had all, with gradual reluctance, moved out of trailers into houses for a more settled kind of life. After a year's residence in a council flat she was still yearning to return to her former way of life; so when she heard of the opportunity she undertook the training and was now a council employee and living in a trailer once more. Everything was organised. There was a group of 'green' local residents who, under Kay's tutelage, had given up their time voluntarily to help make the site ready, adding small touches, to greet the wandering families. They all regarded the project as a positive opportunity.

But as she walked past the Post Office and cut across the Green, Kay was acutely aware that there was a hard core of villagers still opposed, still ready to think and expect the worst. They were apparently in dread of the arrival of Travellers, openly expressing their views around the village without reserving their judgement until they were here. They were the sort of people who could actually spark off hostilities. A mere flicker of anger here or a simmering threat there could suddenly erupt into a flare-up for which the Travellers would get the blame, no question. Saturday should be a happy day, but if it all went awry then she, the instigator, would be made to feel she was the cause.

She at last approached Dunstan's home, which she jokingly once suggested should be called "Never Dunroaming". With his camper van parked outside, the overall impression was of its owner being on his marks ready to take to the road at any given opportunity, although in reality his living quarters, the mobile home, was a pretty permanent fixture. But the van was not there and she knew, without even knocking on his door or calling out to him, he was not there either. She felt tears coming as the sad acknowledgement overwhelmed her: he quite obviously did not wish to see her. It could not be negligence or forgetfulness that had stopped him from phoning, returning her calls, emailing, writing a card or calling by for breakfast.

And the garden! He had sent round one of his young helpers to do some planting and hoeing last week, which in itself was not unusual. It was a frantic time of year with many tasks to be tackled in time for the growing season. He would be working round the clock to maintain all 'his gardens', but normally he would attend to her garden in person at least once, more often twice, a week, even at the peak of the season.

So, she concluded, he has gone off somewhere without telling her and she must assume that he had business to attend to that was of no concern to her; he had no wish or need to keep her informed. To face the wholly unpalatable reality that he was ending their relationship in a very uncertain and, frankly, cowardly way was not something she was yet ready to accept.

Should I leave a note, she wondered, to at least show that I have made an extra effort to contact him? She rummaged around in her bag to find a scrap of paper and a pen and scribbled a couple of sentences, then at the last minute, suddenly awash with humiliation, she ripped it into little pieces, which she then stuffed in her pocket.

She marched home in high dudgeon. Why should I be the one to bend over backwards, she thought, angrily? She even began to have uncharitable thoughts about all those breakfasts she had gladly shared with Dunstan. Had he just abused her generosity?

In need of comfort, she called in at the village Tea Shoppe on the way home and indulged in a cream tea – freshly baked scones, sharp-sweet raspberry jam and proper Devonshire clotted cream. She knew the retired couple who owned and ran it as a kind of lifestyle business quite well by now. The raspberries in the jam were from Kay's garden, the teashop being one of Dunstan's outlets, one of the clients he supplied with the excess produce he took from her garden and others in return for his services. This was their business footing. How foolish she had been to ever dream that he was a friend

– a close friend. The memory of his warm smile, and what she took to be affection in his dark eyes, was becoming painful.

Once back home, she poured herself a large gin and tonic and turned on the TV, determined to involve herself in the second episode of a drama she had not watched before but had meant to. Frustrated at this, she went in search of some kind of trivia or escapism, flicking impatiently through numerous channels: a sitcom that failed to make her smile; a documentary about recyclable rubbish being shipped out to China; films she had either seen or avoided; a news story on the abduction of a teenage girl in Scotland; and the repeat of a programme on the world economy she had already seen. It seemed the television network was conspiring to provide her with nothing uplifting.

"Well, I'm really spoilt for choice!" she cried out aloud, turning off the television in despair. Even recorded and retrievable programmes could not tempt her. She would play some music and read a book. To just sit and think did not seem a good idea.

All her life she had never been sure about choice of music in times of emotional crisis. Should it befit the mood, or should it be jolly and uplifting? She stopped in her tracks for a moment. Is that what this is? An *emotional crisis*? For heaven's sake, woman, get a grip. She rather guiltily poured herself another gin and tonic, raising her alcohol intake for the day way over her norm, and decided to have a bath, with a view to going to bed with her book until she gently drifted off to sleep and floated into some exceptionally pleasant dreams.

Wafting around in an aura of herbal essences, her skin silky with unguents, she went downstairs in her purple and pink caftan to turn off the lights, double-check the outside doors were locked and bolted, and set the burglar alarm. It was only half-past eight.

Before she'd had time to do any of these things, suddenly there was a thunderous banging on the back door and she was instantly light-headed with fear. A man's voice called out clamorously, shouting something she could not make out. As both hands rushed to cover her face, as if this would somehow block out whatever was happening, old memories of Gary, the intruder who murdered her husband; the recent phone call from Gary's brother, Billy; today's email about local burglaries; the letter she had received from some unknown, clever, but possibly insane person in the vicinity – all melded together in one enormous surge of panic.

4

As Dunstan settled down again to record his memories, he seriously questioned who would ever read them. In theory, his struggle to remember was for his own pleasure and satisfaction. A double-edged therapy, he decided. But somehow he began to feel he needed an audience and, painful though it was, he found himself stretching the boundaries of his imagination. He pictured his grandchildren, perhaps teenagers, reading this, whilst also sadly acknowledging he would never have any. As a compromise he settled for a young, future generation, a mixture of Gypsies and *Gorgios*, who would probably know little about the old ways.

If they went at all, and most didn't, children from travelling families were more likely to go to school in the winter, than the summertime when there used to be more seasonal work on farms and suchlike. But we were travelling all year round, not always out of choice but sometimes because we were being moved on by folk. I'd missed most of my first year and my first day at school happened to be in the summer, not at the start of the school year, and I must have been at least six years old. It was not like for other kids, starting together pretty much on a level playing-field. The *Gorgios* already knew a lot, including how to poke fun and tease. It started with my clothes. My green pullover reached nearly to my knees and it was not really school uniform, which was navy blue. So one boy, called Richard, taller than me, started pulling at it in the playground, and I was worried the garment Mother had made to last would split and unravel.

I'd seen what can happen to knitting when Mother had unpicked jumpers and rewound the wool into skeins to make another garment. I'd seen her knitting it for months,

fingers flying, needles clicking, by the flickering light of the fire in the evening and in spare moments during the day. I cannot recall any of the other *juvals* knitting. It was something she had learned from someone when she was a young *rakli,* years before she joined the Gypsies. "It makes new things out of old, instead of just makin' do with the old," she used to say. I remember years later, before I left the family, I bought her some brand new wool – about six big balls all different bright colours and the way she clutched me, holding back tears ...
So back in the playground, "Stop it, get off," I yelled out to this Richard, trying to unfasten his fingers as they clutched a sleeve, stretching it out like it was a piece of chewing gum. He laughed and his friends came along to see what the fun was. This attracted a teacher who came across. Richard and his friends ran off. "Always bring trouble with you, don't you, you Travelling children?" I tried to keep Mother's advice and not annoy anyone further but it was hard. I told my cousin about this at dinnertime and he said he'd sort them out for me, for which I felt great relief. He was all of eight years old so should have no problem and I looked forward to seeing Richard squirming for mercy with his face flat in the mud!
A thing that happened on that first day was to do with a runner bean!

Well, for sure, no one would want to read about a runner bean, he thought and laughed aloud as he typed on into the night.

The Bean-Sprout
The teacher, Mrs Spencer, gave me a bean resting on a bit of white cotton wool in water in what I knew to be a jam jar. We used to collect jam jars. I took it and looked hard into her eyes. The fluff reminded me of the seed-heads of Travellers' Joy or Old Man's Beard. The bean looked hard and dry. Did she expect me to eat it? Or, perhaps, draw it using a pencil and paper, which I'd never used before in my

life? I was so worried I suddenly needed to empty my bladder and ran outside.
When I came back in she asked me where I'd been, probably knowing full well. At first I said nothing, feeling shy.
"I needed to piss," I said at last, politely, but staring at the floor. I raised my head and caught her as she winced. "Well, you must ask permission to use the lavatory," she said. "You've seen the others put up their hand, haven't you?"
"I ain't gonna to use the lavatory," I replied, plainly, followed by a swift rebuke from her. I was speaking literally. It was the truth. I needed to piss but not in the smelly lavatory, preferring the hedge! She never knew and I perhaps chose not to find out during the short time I was there what was required of me.
Then Mrs Spencer showed me some other jars and they had leggy looking plants in them.
"These have grown from the bean," she explained.
She wasn't too bad, actually, the teacher. Now green things to me were home – handfuls of lush grass to feed to the horses, hedgerow flowers, heather, gorse, wild daffodils in the spring, cowslips in meadows that we'd collect to make bunches, along with primroses, bluebells from the woods, violets and snowdrops to sell to *Gorgios;* ferns for making wreaths, holly at Christmas time - not so keen on those prickles - but things to eat? I knew about beans – in tins but more often dried that would need soaking before going in the pot. But I'd never really stopped to think about how things grew, or got started. I was spellbound. It was like being given a pet. It had what I thought at first was a name, but was told later the label was just **b e a n** with a number – I think it was **15.** Mrs Spencer then wrote something else which meant nothing to me but I realised later was actually **D u n s t a n**. I stared at these patterns, noticing **a** and the **n** in both lines of shapes, which I was informed were words made up of letters. I was off!
This was what Mother had meant about learning and I was doing it! I went home pleased and proud that I had learned

how to read already and might not need to go again – except I did want to see that bean grow.

Dunstan kept writing while he was in the mood, then suddenly yawning, he raked fingers through his thick greying hair and rubbed his eyes. He looked blearily at his watch. It was nearly one o'clock in the morning, which was late for him; normally a very early riser, he would usually be asleep by around ten o'clock. Throughout life he'd found there was more to do in the morning than most evenings, unless you were one for watching TV, reading books or socialising. He leaned more towards the pleasures of dawn, listening to the birds, getting his domestic chores done and planning his day before breakfast. Then, as soon as it was light, he would be outdoors, employed in tasks he loved best: planting, clearing land of pesky weeds, watching nature at work, seeing things grow and marvelling at the miracle of life, which never ceased to amaze and impress him even as he got older.

But he decided to continue just a little longer …

So I went the next day and the next and began writing a few letters of the alphabet and drawing and we learned to sing a song that I'd not heard before. I didn't make friends but I did keep out of trouble. I learned fast how to do that. My cousin's mother, Auntie Ada, was always telling Duggie, "If they hit you, hit 'em back!" and I think that was meant for the teachers too! Duggie was fearsome, with no fear – not on show anyway. (Later in life he took to bare-knuckle fighting, boxing without many rules as well as no gloves, as a way to make a living.) He said when his mother, Ada, was a young Gypsy girl at school – that must've been before World War II – she was treated badly with people calling her names and hitting her. These days they'd call it real physical and psychological abuse. They'd have the Educational Psychologist and the Social Worker called in now! But I reckon our people put up with things then even more than they do today. I am told Ada was a small, wispy child and at such a young age found it hard to defend herself and quietly suffered the insults. At that time, just a couple of days into my sporadic schooling, I wasn't sure what I'd do if kids pushed me around. Time would tell.

It was my third day at the school and we'd expected to walk back to our stopping-place as usual after the last bell, but Auntie Ada came to collect me and her two sons a bit early in the afternoon. With her dark looks and cast off clothes, she stood out a bit. People weren't so used to seeing dark skin as they are today. She held back, shy of being with *Gorgios* at the school gate, though there weren't many about as it was a bit before going home time, but as soon as we spotted her, she came rushing forward and grabbed bits of us, a shoulder here, an arm there, pulling and pushing, urging us to hurry.

"C'mon, I got the cart round the corner, hurry now."

Sure enough, there was their flat-cart and horse, called Flash, with Uncle Fortune minding them. We scrambled up, all shouting questions.

"Why're you here? What's goin' on? Where we goin?"

But neither Aunt Ada nor Uncle Fortune offered any explanation until we were well on our way, just yelling, "Keep your peace, won't you – you'll find out all in good time. We've had a difficult day, let's have some quiet now."

But as we realised we were heading off somewhere in a different direction – even at that age we had a good eye for roads and routes – we kept on hollering till they had to come clean. "All right now," and Fortune pulled up the horse to a halt, off the road where there was a field gate with a bit of space. These are the things you remember because they are big events in your young life. They stand out like streetlamps edging a dark, winding road and I suppose all my senses were heightened on that day. "We been moved on," he said. Well, we guessed that. It was nothing new. But, somehow, because I'd gone to school and Mother had got me kitted out in 'new' clothes, it came as a sudden shock, because we were moving further on, right away from the school and so soon.

"But what about my bean?" I wailed, distraught. What hurt was that the younger brother of bully Richard, a little runt called Peter, was my bean co-carer! I didn't trust him and feared my bean was in some peril, its future in considerable doubt. I can laugh about it now, but it was all I could do to stop the tears on the way to our new *atchin tan*, a field by a rubbish dump with pylons, which must have been about fifteen miles away from the school, because by the time we got there it was late evening, pitch-black. The sky was overcast, hail pelting like marbles. I remember the savage hunger I felt, with nothing to eat since my bit of bread and bacon at mid-day (I didn't have school dinner) and one of the small green apples Fortune had picked off a tree for us to have one each on our drive home. The breakfast sausages were long forgotten.

Dunstan rested his head in his hands for a moment. He felt this would be a good point to stop.

The thin walls of his home were far from soundproof and neighbours would be starting up their cars at the crack of dawn; so to ensure he got enough sleep to compensate for a late night, he planned to not only turn off his alarm clock, but also use earplugs. He would have a lie-in. But first, he just needed to round off this first day at school and the moving on episode …

Those pylons reared up against the night sky like monsters. The cables made a loud buzzing sound. I had no idea what they were and felt afraid. Despite my ferocious need for food, drink, dry clothes, warmth and sleep I pressed Mother for some facts.

"What happened?" I asked, once I had stuffed some potato into my mouth. "Were there lots of *muskerro*?" There were a few occasions before when police had raided our camps and sent us on our way, sometimes before first light. "Did you get hurt? Did anyone get into a fight? Where are we? Am I going to the school again?"

"Now don't you worry your head," said my mother, softly. She was a gentle kind of woman, yet so, so tough. I see that now more than I did as a *chavi*. "Your father and Uncle Fortune have the chance of some good work now, for one thing. There were no police, nor no fights, not this time."

She stroked the hair off my forehead, then pulled off my soaking boots, as I munched. "He's heard of some tree-cutting work on a big estate … and we're going to get a proper trailer for sleepin' in, with a motor car!"
My mouth fell open. "No! A motor? Us? You joking, Mother, you teasing?"
She saw my feverish excitement and toned things down a bit. "Well, I'm not saying like straight away, you know. But that's why we moved, see. To be nearer the work. We only got to hear about it today. So we can be a bit more comfy in the winter. And … anyhow, don't you tell your father I told you …"
How could I not talk to Father about this? "Why? Why mustn't I talk?" As a family we always shared things. Rarely did we keep secrets from each other, just from outsiders.
She paused, frowning. "Well, in case it don't happen, I suppose."

Dunstan decided to leave it there because he remembered that his mother's last comment barely registered, for by then the boy Dunstan was unable to fight off sleep any longer. It was the following day when he was sharply reminded of her warning by his father.

Once ready for bed, he glanced at his diary that kept track of all his gardens. His philanthropic business project was thriving; he had around twenty clients on his books and about ten young lads helping him at any one time with a fairly rapid turnover as they moved on to bigger and better things. Unlike more conventional workforces, their departure to new ventures was a mark of success rather than failure.

Tomorrow, there was a note earmarking the day for Kay's garden. He carefully drew a line through it.

5

Kneeling to keep hidden from view, Kay cautiously looked out through the landing window, craning her neck to peep round an undrawn curtain. Already dark, the evening sky was clear, studded with stars, a gibbous moon behind the branches of a silver birch in her garden casting an eerie light. She could feel her heart pounding; a dry throat made her want to cough. If whoever was at the back door would just step back slightly she might be able to catch sight of them without being seen herself.

For a minute it went quiet and she could hear footsteps going round the house – just like that other night when Joseph and his two brothers had come in search of his Gypsy wife, Lena, nearly two years ago. Then she had dialled for the police which, as it turned out, had been the wrong thing to do … but perhaps this time it would be the blindingly obvious and right thing to do! They had not attempted to break in – yet. If only she could make out who it was. Briefly her fear took her back to the night when Gary had broken into their Richmond home and she had thought they were being persecuted by animals' rights activists. She was convinced that the intruder was out to get Marcus and herself, not their money or possessions.

With all these horrors flooding her brain, she made a decision. If she could neither see nor recognise the man out there, past experience told her she should side with caution and dial 999.

The visitor must have seen the stairway light, she realised, more visible from the back than the front. There was a knocking once again, sharp and determined. She strained her neck just as a shape came into view, and a round face looking up at her became visible in the security light. The balding head and stocky build were familiar.

Seamus! Just for a moment she sank down onto the landing carpet, closed her eyes and put her hand on her heart, aware that it was still pumping away at a furious rate. Perhaps he had bad news about Dunstan …

Levering herself up at once, she called out, "Hold on Seamus. I'm coming," and feeling emotionally dislodged, was immediately rushing to the back door.

Once the door was open he unceremoniously strode in and sat at the table, as if waiting to be served. "Sure, now where's he gone? Jaysus, d'you have the least idea where d'old bugger has vanished to like a puff of smoke?"

It did at least add to her relief that he was not the bearer of bad news. Kay was used to his abrupt, bluff manner and knew it was just his way. In fact, she counted him as one of her friends. Though not related to Dunstan, nothing like him in looks, Seamus was a member of their family group and seemed like his older brother. She did not know too much about how this closeness had arisen but gathered that they had spent some childhood years together. It was going to be so fascinating to see this unfold in Dunstan's autobiography when she came to read it! He had been round to her house with Dunstan many times before within the past eighteen months or so, since the remaining members of Dunstan's extended family had come over from Ireland to live in Appley Green. Dunstan had helped to get them sorted out with a variety of accommodation until they could all be together again on a permanent residential site, which was their ultimate wish.

Kay switched on the kettle. "I should like to know myself where he is. Seamus, when did *you* last see him?" She expected him to say at least two weeks ago since he had blustered in demanding to know his whereabouts.

"Well for sure I saw him, I certainly did …" Seamus scratched his head, thinking hard. "'Twas when we went over to Mrs Hardy's to put up a fruit cage for her, so we did. For her raspberries and the like. And a grand job of it we made, to tell you d'truth, so much so that she asked for us to stay and have some sort of … hmm! Now what was it, what'd you call it? Like a kind of pastry pie so it was widout a lid. Not a tart, but full of eggy mixture and cream, it was, and actually not so bad as that sounds once you bit into it. D'kind of thing *you'd* make, for sure it was! D'you know, to be honest with you, Kay, the fourth piece was much better dan d'first …"

"Seamus, when? When was this …?" interrupted Kay.

His mouth snapped shut as if offended at being stopped mid-flow.

"So are you going to tell me what it'd be called – dis pie? T'ad bits of tasty bacon in it," he added stubbornly.

"I've not seen Dunstan for about two weeks. I … I've been wondering myself, where … I mean, he's not even been in touch. Is he ill?"

"No, no, no, not ill. Not at all. Top form when I saw him two days ago – at the Mrs Hardy's …"

Kay sat down ignoring the kettle that had boiled. "Oh! Oh good. He's all right then …" Kay felt a dark cloak of inappropriate disappointment wrap itself around her. "*Quiche* it was probably … *quiche lorraine*."

Seamus then ferreted deep into his trouser pocket to pull out a sheet of crumpled notepaper. He pushed it towards Kay, who stared at it blankly, still shaken and distracted.

"Well?" said Seamus, impatiently. "Can you read't to me?"

"What is it?" asked Kay, immediately hoping it might be something from Dunstan.

"Well, sure it's a letter." He looked at her askance. "Can you not see that?"

She tried to flatten the paper out on the table with the side of her fist. "Oh, it's from someone called Ruby-Ann," she said, looking first at the signature, "in the Republic of Ireland."

"That's it, you got it!" he cried out, as if amazed that she could work this out. Kay smiled. "I tought it would be. Ah-hah, she can write no more than I can, but wouldn't you know she'd be gettin' folks to write her letters for her?"

"OK. So this is someone who still lives in Ireland? Family, friend?"

"She is indeed a cousin. Of Dunstan's dat is. Not mine at all."

"Of Dunstan's? Really? How come she's in Ireland?"

"Well, our family and his they got all mixed up and dat's t'truth. This is going back many, many years, when I was a bit more'n a child. But t'bond was sealed, so you might say, when Ruby-Ann married one of our own, a Traveller named Edwin O'Brien. And sure enough they did have six little children one after t'other but just last year poor Edwin passed on, God rest his soul …"

"I remember Dunstan going to the funeral. It was a big event. He didn't tell me the details, though …"

"Near on eight hundred people at the wake. Sure it had to be in our Roman Catholic church but there were lots of people there who weren't Catholics, that's for sure ..."

Kay sensed a long funereal reminiscence coming on and stifled a disrespectful yawn, not from boredom but actually feeling tired. Another time she would like to hear more but just then she decided to cut to the chase.

"Right. It says, "*Dear Seamus …*"

Seamus settled back in his chair, looking pleased and pointing to himself, nodding. "Ah, but she's a lovely girl, is Ruby-Ann …"

"I hope this finds you well. Now then Seamus do you know this house is half-driving me up its walls, what with the bills and the neighbours who won't so much as say Hello how are you today? The children are all well, married and grandchildren coming along fast and furious as you can imagine. Most of them are in housing too now, warm and dry it's true, but far apart and not happy. Not really, not how we used to be even though living in those times was so tough."

"You see! They make you go into the housing and then wonder why people end up fair killin' themselves with the despicableness of it all. They do, you know, some of them, it's as true as I'm sitting here!"

Horrified by this, Kay frowned, shook her head sympathetically, then carried on reading aloud, "*I don't worry, they have shelter and food and their children are going to schools. But I do need to get away – to see people I know. So many have left. I am alone too much. It's not natural. Not healthy.* Poor woman," commented Kay, sympathetically, before continuing, "*So I am coming to see you all very soon. Tell Dunstan I still love him …*" Kay paused to swallow, raising her eyebrows and looking across at Seamus' smiley face.

"Well and this is the God's honest truth but I always thought she carried on carrying a torch for young Dunstan, sure I did, I'm not lying to you, but never dared so much as to ever say a word about it …" His face went grave, his tone of voice serious. "'Twould not have been right in the circumstances."

Kay resumed slowly, her voice becoming a little husky. "*… and have never forgotten him, though I loved my Edwin you know that, but Dunstan was my first love … till he left us all. You know that too. I'm as sure as sure that he will not have forgotten how it was when I was all ready to go with him … but he would have none of it. Imagine how I felt, it took so many years for me to forgive him.*"

"Is that the end, then?"

"Almost. Ruby-Ann just finishes to say that she'll let you know when she gets a ticket to fly to Gatwick and could ***someone*** come and collect her? The word 'someone' is … underlined. Quite heavily underlined."

Seamus was walking towards the back door now. "Oh, well I'll get old Dunstan to do that, I should tink. That'll be a fair old surprise for her, don't you tink, Kay? Now I must go and find him so's we can do a letter back. Or is there a phone number on the letter there? He must be somewhere. For sure, he'd've told us if he was going off somewhere. Wouldn't dare run off without leave – not twice in one lifetime!"

Before he finally walked out, away into the night, he turned. "Ah! I was that close to forgetting, we did hear that some families are travelling up on their way to d'new place here in Appley Green, but I expect you've already heard."

Kay nodded, barely listening to him at all now. "Yes," she agreed, vaguely, "I had an email from the Gypsy Liaison Officer, Max. They should be arriving on Saturday though no one can be sure exactly when."

"Right then. It'll be a good thing to see. Good-night to you then."

6

Kay had tried to dismiss from her mind the intimidating phone call from Billy, Gary's brother. As the days passed without her hearing more from him, its impact on her was ebbing as the memory faded. The letter coming as it did from a quite different, albeit unknown, source was more difficult to suppress. Its creator must be out there somewhere, possibly close by in the village and if he, or she, were to reveal an identity it was likely to be today, Saturday, to coincide deliberately with the arrival of the group of Gypsies. She acknowledged that she must be prepared for some kind of encounter. It could even be someone she knew! She sensed that she was no stranger to him – or her.

Early on Saturday morning Kay felt cheered by a phone call from Suzi, her younger daughter who lived and worked in London. "Frantic week. So busy, you wouldn't believe."

"But going well? Glad you made the change?"

It was about a year since Suzi had stepped down from the heady, ambitious world of fashion photography to simple, straightforward weddings, family and school portraits, babies and pets. Once disdainful of such prosaic products as decorative mugs, tea-towels and 'Cakes with a Face', she now voraciously sought out mundane but commercial money-spinners. Her own boss, she made her own choices and decisions and was revelling in it.

"Mum, more and more as it goes on. Even with the recession, I mean – well, market forces and all that, I just drop my prices and do deals. Have to work harder but I get the commissions and bookings … Best thing I've ever done. Love it." Just like Gypsies have to adjust, reflected Kay as she listened to Suzi effervesce, to move with the market, past masters at evolving to suit seasonal, geographical and economic changes. Opportunists prosper best, willing to turn their hand, chameleon-like, to something different if needs must. The principle is probably the same the world over. She remembered reading a saying by a Scots Tinker; *If you took a Traveller and set him in the middle of the desert he would find a living there. He would even sell that sand to the Egyptians.*

"Good, good, good! I'm happy for you, darling, and your father would've been so proud of you." She felt a lump in her throat as she said this. Suzi had shown guts to go it alone, climbing a precipitous learning curve from which she could have tumbled into further ruin so easily. She'd had a desperate time as commissions dwindled to a trickle, and advertising agencies shut up shop, leaving no option but to abandon her glitzy dream of fashion photography. Since then, Suzi had steadied her nerve and turned her life around. Some would say the safe option is to stick to what you know best, but in such a situation they could well be wrong, thought Kay.

"So what's on this weekend, then?" asked Kay. Suzi must have forgotten it was the opening day for the Gypsy site. But then neither of her daughters had ever understood why she had become so involved in campaigning for it. And would Marcus have been proud of her, if he had been here at her side today? Well, yes, maybe he would. He was a humanitarian, indeed he was. A compassionate man.

"Meeting a friend – yes male, don't get too excited but he's bloody fit, Mum, and his father is on his own so, well, you never know! No. No, forget I said that. I'm barking mad. Anyway, going to the Tate Modern, then lunch looking out over the Thames, quick browse in Borough Market we thought and tonight I'm out with a bunch of girls to a 'French chic' party, then on to a club. How about you?"

Kay hesitated. "Oh, not sure yet – nothing planned but something will turn up. If not I might take myself out to the local for some supper – bound to meet up with someone I know."

"But – what about today? It's the big opening isn't it?"

Kay was pleased she had remembered, even if only just. "Yes, it is and I must go. Maybe speak to you tomorrow." Kay was aware of the time. She must get down to the new Appley Green site.

Checking her mobile, she saw the briefest of texts from Max. `ETA noon`. That gave her a bit of a breather after all, time to do a few chores around the house, and all the while she was inwardly pushing out and away Dunstan's face, the twinkle of his eyes, the softness of his voice, his laugh that could light up her space … all with very little success. Had Seamus spoken to him by now, about the lovely Ruby-Ann? This was the question that was punctuating every other thought.

As she was about to put on her jacket, the phone rang. Her heart thumped, perhaps unsure of whether to leap or sink, her head full of conflicting expectations. Friend or foe?

"Hello?" she said, softly, still aware of the pounding in her chest.

"Kay! Oh, Kay!" cried a girl's voice, screeching down the phone. "You'll never guess what's happened?" Despite its pitch, she recognised the voice at once as it was young with a public school accent. This narrowed it down to Imogen, who lived with her two brothers in what might be fairly described as a fine country mansion about a hundred metres away set back off the road in wild, neglected grounds of about three acres.

"Imogen! Whatever is the matter?" She sometimes felt as if she had become their surrogate mother, being close to hand, retired with time on her hands, clearly short of nearby grown-up children and apparently in need of them.

Their mother had died when they were very young, the youngest child, Jeremy, just a baby. Her death seemed shrouded in a mist of secrecy and Kay saw no reason to pry. Their father, Bradley R Farlow, had been a famously successful entrepreneur with fingers in many pies, mostly overseas, so the villagers informed her. Few of the local people had got to know him though. Apparently he was often away from home and his three growing children, although she deduced that, though lacking parental care, affection and direction, the offspring wanted for nothing in the material sense. They'd had staff in the house, apparently, a cook, cleaner, handyman. Then about two years ago their father died, suddenly, from a brain haemorrhage. Her heart went out to them, when she then heard about the whole family saga and learned that they were, although almost concealed from the road, just a few minutes' walk from her house.

Since she first called on them and introduced herself she had certainly been taken into the bosom of their home and affections. They had decided to 'dispense with the domestic staff because really we can manage without them', they told her. Within the last month she had been called upon to help unblock a sink; advise on the purchase of a massive fridge-freezer, costing over two thousand pounds, and assist in booking a holiday for the three of them in Barbados. They had shown their gratitude by inviting her to a party, where she did not stay long, and buying her lavish bunches of flowers. Then there was the trouble they had with their now *ex*-gardener and handyman, where Kay's sympathies lay entirely with him, making her role as negotiator extremely challenging. Imogen, Timothy and Jeremy were a lovely, bright and bubbly trio and she had grown fond of them but, through years of neglect in all the practical things in life, they were, Kay decided, utterly hopeless and sometimes selfish.

So, what had happened now? Surely it could wait.

"The old playroom ceiling has collapsed," wailed Imogen.

Kay gasped. The 'old playroom', she recalled, in Victorian times part of the servants' quarters, was situated at the top of Cedar House, on the third floor. This did sound serious.

"What? Oh no! Is anyone hurt?"

"It just missed Tim. Well, the water just caught a shoulder but the actual plaster and stuff didn't land on him. Luckily."

"Water?"

"It's just pouring – it won't stop …"

"I'll come round right now – but, Imogen, I can't stay long – I'm just on my way out somewhere. We'll have to get help. You should turn the water off at the stopcock. Have you called a …?"

"See you," came the abrupt reply and the phone cut off.

To reach them speedily Kay jumped on her bike, which she had taken to using for short trips around the village. The grounds must have been beautiful once. Very Capability Brown, she noted briefly. Once at their imposing double front door she lifted the black iron knocker and rang the doorbell simultaneously; the household appeared to be either out or deaf, but certainly oblivious of her presence.

"I'm *here*!" she shouted, banging now with her fists. *For God's sake, I've rushed here for you not for the benefit of my own health*, she felt like yelling, thoroughly grumpy with the whole bunch of them. She was quite out of breath.

Eventually, the door was opened by Imogen, tall and slim with long, straight blonde hair, aged about twenty-two. Tim, a year or so older and Jeremy, just nineteen, rushed up behind their sister, wide-eyed. They all stood back to allow Kay to enter.

"Everything's *soaked*," grumbled Tim. "Now, how on earth do you think we are ever going to get the carpets and stuff dry? I mean, for Christ's sake!" He complained as if it were Kay's fault.

She heard the slosh of her shoes as she stepped forward on the oak floor of the large hallway and could see water dripping from above.

"It's still pouring out of the hole in the ceiling. From the attic where the tank is," cried Tim, he said helpfully pointing skywards. "Will it ever stop, do you suppose, Kay? Will it just empty itself?"

You stupid children! She bit back the unkind words. "Where's the stopcock?" she enquired, trying to be patient.

Imogen bit her lip and Jeremy, the youngest asked, "The stop what?"

"*Cock!*" shouted Kay, falling straight into the trap. She sighed, tempted to just abandon them to their watery fate. "Jeremy, call the fire brigade immediately – tell them it's an emergency." She knew there was an element of panic in this suggestion, but couldn't think of any other way to get out of the situation fast.

With eyebrows raised he stared at her and then grinned. "Really? What? 999?"

"Now. I'll look for the stopcock. We must turn it off to stop the mains supply. Oh, you useless lot …" she couldn't help but add. Imogen rolled her eyes, Tim thumped his head and Jeremy muttered, "Oops".

"Imogen," Kay cried out as she marched towards the kitchen sink, "Switch off the electricity. Look in the Yellow Pages for a plumber. Find one that can come out now. Tim, go upstairs move any valuables you can off the floors at ground level – good furniture, photos, electrical appliances, books, documents, things like that – and Jeremy, get mops and towels, whatever you have."

Soon everyone began to recognise their role and the fact that they could actually do things to help bring the situation under control, although after a few minutes, Imogen said she had called six plumbers so far but they were all busy or on answer-phone. "Well, it is Saturday, after all," she said, reasonably.

The stopcock was located and firemen were soon extracting water as best they could. Kay quizzed one of them on the availability of plumbers and was advised not to forget the insurance, take photographs, wait for the loss adjusters and so on. He was speaking to her, of course as if this were her property and her responsibility. She then found that Imogen, Tim and Jeremy had disappeared to admire the fire engine, and pose for photographs that someone said they would put on YouTube.

After a severe admonishment she told them, "Once you get hold of a plumber – and you'll need a builder and, later, carpet fitters and decorators as well – offer to pay him double-time to come out today. More, if necessary." Her last bit of advice before leaving was to get their solicitor to help them and protect their interests. She supposed they could afford his services and knew that he was by now a family friend, aware of the family history.

She looked at her watch. It was now late afternoon and she could hardly believe that, after two years of campaigning for the Appley Green Gypsy and Traveller Transit Site, she had missed the opening. Guilt niggled away inside her for treating the Farlows rather harshly. They were young, and the disaster was hardly their fault, but she had looked forward to seeing the first group use the new site so much and for so long that she was bursting with anger as she sped off in its direction. Life could be so unfair. This was not a statement of which her father would have approved, but it was true.

Determined not to let this rather major mishap mar a special day, she parked her car in a side-road and set off to walk the two hundred metres or so to the site entrance. As she turned a corner where the gates came into view, she saw many vehicles, mostly vans and trailers, blocking the way. She frowned. Surely the newly arrived group of families should all be safely on their pitches by now. Then she noticed the security gate barring vehicular access was still in place, which was odd. The closer she got the more she was puzzled and then alarmed. There were raised voices, dogs barking, engines revving in a way that sounded aggressive – she could smell the exhaust fumes – but nobody was moving.

She hurried down the road and as she neared she could see the site manager, Molly-Marie, a woman of slight build, trying to hold apart two men prepared to fight. Kay's heart sank, her legs turning to jelly with the sheer disappointment of it. What on earth had happened?

Molly-Marie did not possess anywhere near the strength required to separate the two who seemed ready to tear each other limb from limb. Kay stopped still. Would her intervention help? No way. Two camps had gathered to support each contender, egging them on. Her instincts told her to rush to help, while sanity urged her to call the police. But how could she do that, after all she had done to support the Travellers? They would never trust her again. But she could not allow Molly-Marie to get hurt. What would happen if she calmly walked towards them and appealed to their better nature to stop?

Much her surprise, as Kay became visible to the pugilists, they backed off each other making her feel suddenly gifted with some unfeasible power.

She'd heard Molly-Marie cry out, "Stop now! Here comes Mrs Brackenbridge!" Perhaps it was the urgency in her voice, maybe the respectful use of Kay's full name, but the man she thought she recognised from some event, perhaps a Gypsy and Traveller forum she had attended, stood aside first.

"Hold off, now," he said and Kay's mouth fell open when she saw the other man, a stranger to her, nudge the more familiar man on the shoulder with his fist, then fell silent and still.

Kay felt encouraged to approach.

"Can you call Max, Kay? Got a problem here and I can't see a way to set things right. I don't know what we're going to do about this." Molly-Marie sounded inconvenienced rather than distraught, as might have been expected in the circumstances. "This is *not* a dispute that can be settled fair and square by a *fight*," she added, glaring at the two men. Kay suspected she was a rarity in the community, a woman fierce enough to have some control over the men, Gypsy and Traveller alike, but there again, what did she know?

"What's going on?" asked Kay.

"I've two lots who want to use my site and there's no room for them both so one of them is to go," she stated flatly.

7

After scheduling his labour force in the area to ensure his gardening projects were adequately covered, Dunstan reread his last diary entry. His memories were fuzzy but the more he transcribed them the sharper they became. This drove him on to recall and record all he could. He wrote:

I was bursting to ask Father about the new trailer and car we would have. What colour, how big and shiny, how fast would it go? All these questions piling up inside me. For a few weeks we had been miserable surviving in those benders. No one would admit so much, but it was not comfortable when you'd known something better, added to which my parents must have felt not ashamed but left out, I see that now. Travelling people did not generally live like that, as far as I knew then, in the late 1950s – it was like turning the clock back. The wind would howl across the heath at night, the tent leaking and rain dripping on your face as you slept and no matter how much Presley and I huddled together, you lay shivering, you dreamed about somewhere warm and cosy like it used to be in the wagon. As soon as a fire was lit outside we would rush to it to bathe in its heat – that was a kind of heaven. Some of our extended family members still had rough wagons – post-war utilitarian jobs – and we gladly sought shelter in them when there was room. Families always shared as much as they could but there was a limit on what large families could offer each other. Spare sleeping quarters were a rare commodity, as I recall. As a six-year old, open to new ideas and change, the very thought of having a modern trailer like other folks stirred my imagination. To be able to store things, to jump in if you felt cold, to sit in there maybe altogether if the weather was a bit wild, and talk or sing, like

we would do outside which, looking back, did serve to keep our spirits up.
The summer sun rose as we ate bread with boiled bacon and drank warm, sweet tea. I kept quiet like Mother had warned me. Until about mid-day, Father stayed behind with others in our camp to make some pegs and flowers like chrysanthemums from elder wood. He was brilliant at doing this, paring down the wood to fashion the slender petals. Sometimes he would dye them with vegetable colour and I loved to watch. Boiling up onions or beetroot to make shades of yellow, pink and deep red was one thing, but he could do magic! He could cook up green peas to turn holly wood purple!
Anyway, Mother had gone to sell her bits and pieces in a nearby housing estate, eager to work the new area we had moved to. He worked quietly bent over his task, saying little. I wondered why my father wasn't doing the estate work Mother had mentioned – the reason for me leaving the school and for us all moving on this time.
"Mother says you got some good work comin' up," I said to him.
He looked up from his work, knife suspended in the air. "Nothin' definite," he replied, turning down the corners of his mouth. "Maybe. It's out there all right but who'll get it, now that's another thing, little fella." It didn't sound too good.
"Is it true we're gettin' a trailer and a car to pull it an' all?" I asked plainly, as he was preparing to go off with his hand-cart. Once he left for the afternoon, the question would be burning in my guts if I did not let it out.
He glowered and, though my father had never lifted a finger to me, I did flinch for a moment. I remember that as the first moment I briefly felt scared – by his reaction, not for my safety. There was a fleeting, defeated look in his black eyes that spoke of both anger and sadness. He stood up and towered over me, it seemed. I suddenly felt much smaller. "Who told you that?" he shouted. I could say nothing as he was clearly not pleased but he would have had to torture me yet never would I get my Mother into trouble.

Then he must've seen my desperate expression, my eyes searching his. He reached down and squeezed my shoulder.
"One day, fella," he said, hoarsely. "Believe it, if it helps. We don't want to spend winters like this. All depends on folk."
He clammed up then and moved away. He did not ask me if I wanted to go with him that afternoon and I sensed I would not be welcome.

It must've been at least a year before we were out of those tents …

Dunstan paused in his one-finger typing for a moment, wondering again what happened to the old wagon they had before. Why had he never thought to ask his father before he died last year? He'd always sensed that it was a sore point, what *Gorgios* would call the 'elephant in the room' that everyone ignored and stepped neatly around to avoid. He decided to give Presley a call right now, though he'd probably be out on a job, most likely supervising a small gang of two or three laying tarmac. He was getting too old and unfit for heavy labour but would lend his experience to younger, stronger men. When it became clear his older brother's mobile phone was switched off, he was not too surprised. Hot tarmac waited for no man. It had to be used on the same day and those who had obtained it had to pretty much guarantee, one way or the other, that someone would get their driveway tarmacked today. He would be taking that responsibility.

Dunstan wanted to ask Presley about the horses too.

I do remember us all crying when Magpie and Carter were sold. I couldn't understand why Mother and Father got rid of them, both like members of the family …

This reminded Dunstan sharply of another day, sometime later, when a dog he was given to look after as his own was run over by a lorry. He must have been about nine years old and yet he had forgotten about it. The stinging pain of this memory now caused Dunstan's eyes to fill up and he had to wipe them and blink a few times before he could focus again on the computer screen.

We'd stopped near a road as there was nowhere else to go. There were aunts, uncles, cousins, grandparents, about five trailers in all travelling along together on the way to Kent for some strawberry and hop picking. We'd all been in good spirits, looking forward to a few weeks of hard work and fun and, most of all, farmer's land where we'd be welcome to stop, as previous generations had likewise. But as evening came upon us, all feeling tired from travelling, we could find no proper stopping-place so we had to stop illegally overnight in a lay-by of a dual carriageway. It was dark and the traffic kept on coming. I'd let the dog's chain slip and I heard a thud, but no screech of brakes or howl from Barker, my poor dog. The stomach-wrenching anger at the lorry driver who had not stopped, maybe not even aware of what had happened, and the sickly guilt for being so careless was more than I could bear. I ran off, disappeared, and when the police came at dawn to send us on our way, there was hardly anyone there. Everyone had spent the night out combing the countryside for me! The telling off I got when someone found me curled up in a barn was something I shall never forget. You don't think of consequences when you're that young. I just had to be away from everyone to nurse my grief and kick myself for being so stupid.

It was close to lunchtime when he realised he had not even stopped for breakfast, which reminded him of Kay. He sat back, wistful that things had gone so very wrong between them. He read back what he had composed that morning and saw what a jumble it was. Random memories crashing in a chaotic stream. Good job, he thought, that he had no ambitions to get this published! It would be good to set it out in a more logical sequence of events but he would need expert help in this. Of course, Kay would be the right person for the task; she had experience as a wordsmith. She had once shown him some of the articles and brochures she had written in the taut, concise style needed for that kind of journalism and technical copywriting. But there was no hope of her assisting him. As far as his life was concerned she had demonstrated in letters writ large that she had no understanding of what he was about.

Painfully reminding himself of her irrevocable error he turned back to the opening paragraphs and the title, "Dunstan's Life", which she had seen fit to amend. Suppressing his rage, he decided to make himself a bacon sandwich, before making a few supervisory visits to his local garden projects.

Before settling down that evening with the intention of writing about his next school experiences, which he knew would be traumatic to recount, he tried again to get hold of Presley. Curiosity was becoming a compelling need to have answers. His older brother should be at home now with his mobile phone switched on. There was no landline in the small flat Presley and his wife Geena, now both in their sixties, shared reluctantly with two young *Gorgio* lads who worked for Dunstan. There were no spare pitches to be had on the local council sites and no more mobile homes available where Dunstan lived. His older brother's shared flat was a 'temporary arrangement', fixed two years ago when Dunstan had brought some of his family members over from where they were living in Ireland. The ultimate goal was to bring the family back together, living within spitting distance, but how they could do that was an unknown.

"'allo?" was Presley's response as he picked up Dunstan's call.

"Got some questions for you. Going right back. When we were little *chavies* …"

"I'm eatin', you *dinilo*!" Presley exclaimed, gruffly.

Dunstan realised his abrupt opening was unreasonable. He was just so keen to get to the point. "OK. I'll call you back in …?"

"Thirty minutes."

Dunstan stood up and began pacing around the floor of his home, thinking back to those times past. There was a picture in his head, like a scene from a film, of a stranger who was arguing outside with his father. He was loud with an accent that sounded different from any he had heard before. A *Gorgio*, probably. It was late at night and he could remember being tucked up in what they called the 'dog's kennel', his cosy bed of the old-fashioned wagon, beneath where his parents slept, but then he threw back the blankets, pulled aside the lace curtain at the window to peep out, to spy on the rumpus. He could see them, just the two men, Father and the outsider, standing around the fire, arms waving, fingers pointing, flickering flames lighting up angry looking faces. Then his head filled with something that happened the previous day. Recognisable by his resounding voice, this same man had called before! Yes, that was it, he was with a group of people – a family, two women, one older, three maybe four *chavies,* and they had been rude and disrespectful, climbing into the wagon, clambering over things, peering into cupboards. He bit his lip at the clear memory he now had of the wretched look on Mother's face who seemed at a loss as to why these folk were behaving so badly and with Father doing nothing to stop them. Normally he would have punched them for sure. It was just not done! Folks' wagons were private and personal inside, not open to strangers. Watching them from the outside, looking in, she stood silently wringing her hands and he stood by her side, wondering.

Dunstan paused to look at his watch. Just ten minutes had passed. He was feeling that all this had some connection with the disappearance of the wagon. Of course, that was it! Dunstan clapped his hands, feeling excited and frustrated in equal measure as he tried to piece this jigsaw of fragmented recollections together. His father must've done a *chop*, a deal, or just sold it. But why? Why did he do that when it left us with nothing but those old benders for sleeping? That was no 'lifestyle' choice!

He tried to think back to what happened after that man had left. It was a blur, as if the memories once etched in his brain had been planed away to become indecipherable. Presley was six years older. He might remember. He would've been more capable of asking questions than a four or five year old, who would be accepting of life's offerings. Things were not hidden from family. They faced things together.

Dunstan went to his desk and pulled out a tin box of old photographs from his father's side of the family. Tears filling his eyes, he ran his fingers over the lid. It had always held important documents like his birth certificate which one day he would need to obtain his passport. His mother was careful about such things and, having kept the box safe all her married life, had handed it to him the year before last. It was the last time he saw her alive. Following a stroke, her death was sudden, unexpected, yet this very deliberate act of giving was almost as if she had known her time was coming.

"Don't let these pictures go up in flames, son. These are history. You keep them safe and make sure your children …" and she had paused, looking at him sadly, acknowledging that he was unlikely to have children of his own now, "or Presley's … Let them have these memories and pass them on to their children."

Presley was happy for Dunstan to safe-keep them but one day his eldest son would have them to pass on down the line. They had agreed on that. Dunstan would peruse them from time to time but this stirred up such strong emotions, where he would feel tense and taut, unable to stop unmanly tears from blurring his vision, that he could not enjoy the experience of studying them. But now, if he could steel himself, they might help.

There was a family group that particularly fascinated him. It used to be on display in the old wagon and was still in its silver filigree frame, now tarnished through neglect for which he felt guilty. He wondered who the photographer was. Why had they all gathered and stood so still for him or her? His gaze wandered around the picture of people, standing or seated, all in their best finery. It had the formality of a wedding photo but there was no sign of a bride or groom, or other evidence that this was the occasion. It was occurring to him that he should really have these precious records of the past professionally copied. Kay's daughter, Suzi would do that, if only ...

He stared at the backdrop, unable to believe his eyes. Why had he never realised before? It was the wagon. *The* wagon, in all its glory. It was very high, imposing. There was an elderly gentleman, with neatly trimmed white whiskers, dapper in the extreme in tall leather boots, who Dunstan knew to be his father's grandfather, so his great-grandfather. A horse-dealer he was, well respected and successful in his trade. Then at his side was Dunstan's Grandf'er, who had followed his father's trade. Dunstan analysed his features, seeing a likeness to himself. He was dressed in a coat with a yoke and patch pockets; trousers high-waisted and drop-fronted in the traditional style, a silk *diklo* around his neck. He wore a soft black velour hat at a jaunty angle.

The women looked so stylish! Wrap-around paisley shawls caught by brooches, heavy gold rings and horse-shoe buckles, tortoiseshell combs, embroidered aprons and *pinnas.* All of them, including his grandmother, had long hair in a central plait pinned up at the back. Dunstan could just remember this enduring hairstyle from his early 1950s childhood ...

His phone rang, making him start and bringing him back from his reverie.

"Did you know Seamus has been lookin' all over for you?" were Presley's first words.

"Ah, no. I had no idea. What does he want?"

"He has some news for you – from a long lost love?"

Dunstan twitched with embarrassment. Surely, his family would not regard Kay as his … Their acquaintance was not *that* long and could scarcely be classed as love; and who else but him knew that whatever their relationship might be, it was lost?

"I'll call him," said Dunstan, fully intending to avoid him. "Now, do you remember us sleeping in that fine wagon – the one that's in the ancient photograph that Mother passed on to us, with all the old fellas and Father's relations?"

"I do."

"Well then, suddenly we were roughing things in those bloody benders – in the winter not too hot. What happened to that fine *vardo*? Was it sold?"

"It was."

"You remember anything about that?"

"I think I do. I remember Mother and Father talking about that sale for many a long year afterwards, an' all. None too happy about it, to say the very least."

"So?" Dunstan felt this was like extracting water from a stone.

"'twas a poor deal. This antique dealer *mush* who specialised in Romany artyfartyfacts came round and offered to pay a good price for it for his shop – wanted it to stand prettily outside to attract interested customers, I would reckon. Wagons were becoming pretty rare and much sought after," yes, thought Dunstan, because many were traditionally burned with their contents as a funeral pyre, "but it all went 'orribly wrong."

Dunstan was by now desperate to know what happened to the money. It must have fetched a fair sum and it seemed their father was lucky to find such a keen buyer. Actual travelling people would not by then be so interested, despite its beauty and true value.

"How?"

"Well, I'll tell you. This *Gorgio* gave a price that was enough to 'lift our family out of the past and see us right for the future'. That's what Father said after he'd gone, his eyes glitterin' like wet coal they were – you know that look he had. He was goin' to buy a truck or some kind of vehicle so's he could get more work doing trees and all that, and the plan was to get a shiny, new trailer to replace the wagon. For us all to live in like, big enough for Granf'er and Nan an' all. So Father went off right away and did a deal with someone – slapped hands on it, for all the new stuff he'd had his eye on for months, even though he couldn't drive a motor. This *Gorgio mush* come back the next night and said he'd now seen the state of the undercarriage and woodworm and all kinds of rot, he reckoned, and dropped his price to a third. Said it was the best price our Father'd get anywhere. So much work would be needed for it to be fit to display, let alone use. Said it were a 'death-trap' – I shall never forget the look on Father's face when he told us - and 'we'd all probably meet our Maker in it one of these fine days'. He was an unpleasant fella, to be honest."

"So he sold it? And, on behalf of Granf'er I guess, as it was really his wagon?"

"Yep. He did – and the money he got might have stretched to a small trailer or a used car, but not both!"

It was all becoming clear. "So they decided to earn and save as much as they could, live in tents until they had enough and then – two years later it would be – they would have their much used trailer and truck. When they got it, it was bloody heaven, though. I can remember that."

"Yes, so do I …"

"Right. Cheers for now – don't forget old Seamus."

8

On hearing Molly-Marie's brief assessment of the situation, Kay felt furious and stood hunched for a moment, hands thrust deep in her pockets, as it sunk in. Why do things always go wrong? So *very* wrong? She felt the burden of responsibility crushing.

"How did this happen? Who got here first?"

This provoked a loud chorus of replies from all sides, from anyone who heard her. Kay somewhat ineffectually raised her hand.

"Molly-Marie, tell me."

Molly-Marie looked nervous and was hesitant to speak. "You'd better speak to Max. He knows," she shouted finally, above the hubbub. She had respect for their Liaison Officer, now with the council; his family were partly of Gypsy stock.

Kay nodded and quickly found his mobile number on her phone. She would be lucky to get hold of him on a Saturday; she knew he had greeted their arrival earlier on as an out of hours duty, a one-off event. She saw, with renewed amazement, that the two men had raised their fists again, circling round, as if confronting each other for a prize fight.

Molly-Marie jumped in and put an arm between them like any well-seasoned referee. "No! This is not the way. You wait for Max and mind your manners." They shrugged meekly and nodded. It was all beyond Kay's understanding.

"Max, we have trouble at the site – there's two groups here. One appears to be already installed …"

"I heard. My spies are ahead of you! On my way – be five minutes."

Kay looked around as they all waited for Max, their saviour and only hope as far as she could tell, to arrive. One group was clearly in already although she could see through the gate that barred free access that there was a little space left. The transit site was not full to capacity.

"There's no room for all the second group, but couldn't some of them come in?" Kay asked Molly-Marie, who simply pursed her lips and raised her eyes to heaven at such an absurdity.

Once Max arrived the crowd surged and squeezed, converging on Kay, Molly-Marie and Max. Just to help things along, two police cars turned up at the end of the road, beyond the long string of trailers and trucks, as near as they could get to the scene.

Another man stepped forward to speak to Max. "Sure we've been on the road for forty-eight hours or more, travelling from the north. *We* have to stop. We *have* to stop! There's sick old folks and new-born babies here!" he declaimed, loudly.

"But am I right in saying Appley Green is not one of your usual stopping-places? I'm Max Leatherson, by the way, Gypsy Liaison Officer. What's your name, anyway?"

"O'Donnell, sir. The stopping-place we usually go to near Reading is all blocked off …"

"Not an authorised site, then."

Mr O'Donnell shook his head. "You know there's few enough of dem. We tought we'd do the right ting. Heard of this new one so came around this way, at once, sir!"

"Well, I'm sorry, but you've missed the boat, mate. The other group got here this morning."

A representative from that group said, "We've paid, put our deposit down, signed a licence and everything, so scarper you …"

Max intervened quickly. "Let's keep this civilised, shall we?" With a twitch of his eyebrows, he indicated the approaching policemen.

"That's all we need. *Muskerros*!" came a cry from someone.

"It's true, the first group of Romanis have agreed the rules and been processed."

"What about the spare pitches?" asked Kay, trying to be helpful.

"You've got to be joking!" replied Max. "I'm afraid you'll not find Gypsies and Irish Travellers mixing."

Kay frowned, thinking of Dunstan's family and how they got on together compatibly and had done for years, as far as she understood it. But Max was a Gypsy by birth so he should know what he was talking about.

"But there's more of us – and babies an' all," cried out a young woman, carrying one of said babies in her arms. "We'd fill the site, sure we would. You should let us 'ave it! We need the water and 'lectric and ..."

"Yeah, yeah ..."

"And turf this lot out ..."

"YEAH."

"What's going on here?" asked a police officer, forging a passage through with an arm. "Trouble, Max?"

"Nothing we can't sort out."

"There are two spare pitches, could take six trailers in all at a pinch – those with infants or elderly can take those," called out Max to the crowd of Irish Travellers but specifically addressing their spokesman.

There was uproar from the Romany Gypsies.

"If they set foot in our camp, we'll go!"

"Well, go then," shouted a young Irish man. "Fell for dat one all right, didn't you?"

"No, we're here already! Anyway, where would we go?"

"Well, just so matey. Now, where would *we* go? It'll be gettin' dark before so very long."

Now a reporter-photographer arrived from the local press. Kay's heart sank for sure this time, and she felt as if she had just slipped into a nightmare, even blinking to make sure she was not actually sleeping and wishing with all her heart that she was.

Max cleared his throat. "Look, everyone. I'm sorry this has happened. The first day of our new site. This morning's group is signed and sealed. It stays. The second group to arrive must move on. That's it."

This was greeted with grim resignation. "So we'll go up the road then, won't we, and take our chances, uh?" Max simply shrugged and looked away, perhaps pretending he had not heard lest he be later accused of condoning the proposal. Kay empathised. He had no magic wand to wave.

A sight then impressed but puzzled Kay for she saw the two fighters step forward, shake hands and clap each other on the shoulder. It seemed they'd coolly agreed not to go through with the fight, as if it were some cancelled boxing fixture.

Still bewildered, she was then seriously knocked back anew as the significance of what had just been said properly sunk in. The second group, then, will have to stop off on the patch of hard standing on the Common where Gypsies have stopped illegally for many a long year. In other words, nothing had changed.

The Irish man continued to speak, despite the uncertainty of who was listening to him. "We'll be gone by tomorrow evening, "Don't you worry. For sure, we only needed the overnight stop."

When Kay got back home, all three Farlows were hanging about in her front garden awaiting her return.

"We lost your mobile number. It was in my phone which got basically saturated," explained Tim, still sounding as if some gremlins had just done this thing to them.

Feeling in low spirits, Kay nodded, forcing a smile. "Look, I'm sorry for being a bit cranky earlier on. It wasn't you … it … was something else going on. Nothing to do with you. Just unlucky timing." She had never mentioned to them her role with the Gypsy site, thinking they would not be particularly interested. They tended to be preoccupied with their own lives and now did not seem a good time to explain where she had been.

The three of them shifted about uneasily, looking down.

"What's the matter?"

Imogen spoke up. "We're all right. We've booked in to a hotel for a few nights. We can't stay in the house." It struck Kay that in such a crisis her daughters would have turned to friends to put them up.

"Surely there are some dry spaces downstairs where you could curl up?" Kay remembered how in her younger days she was able to sleep anywhere, anyhow, through thunderstorms and gunfire, probably. A wet bedroom would not have required total evacuation.

"It's just too miserable," said Jeremy, looking forlorn.

Kay put an arm round his shoulder, as if he were a child. He did not seem to object. She was afraid they were just escaping, unwilling to face up to the work, the responsibility of putting things right.

"We called Jeff, our solicitor. He's been round to see us, already," said Imogen. Oh, I bet he has, thought Kay! "The plumbers have done something and say there'll be no further trouble, but the burst tank and pipes and stuff will need to be replaced. The ancient plumbing system has basically had it. They advised not to turn the water back on until it's all checked out thoroughly, so ..."

"I see. So you have no water. That is a problem."

"Anyway," Imogen continued as spokesperson, "Thanks for your help, earlier."

Kay knew they had no relatives they could call upon. Although they did have friends aplenty their own age, they were nonetheless alone in the world at times like this. Jeremy resented the family solicitor, appointed to guard his interests until he had passed eighteen, supervising his life.

They began to turn around and walk off to Tim's car, parked in the road.

"Where are you staying, then?" asked Kay.

"The Abbey Lodge Hotel," they responded at once, in unison.

Of course, they wouldn't consider a Travelodge or a pub with rooms. It would have to be a fine country hotel with spa, gym, *haute cuisine* and acres of grounds. This is what their father would have taken them to. It was all they knew. They would have a great time, indulge themselves thoroughly and run up a frightening bill, Kay was thinking. Should she offer to have them stay with her? Should she? She might enjoy their company, in a strange sort of way. Would this be a good idea? They could keep an eye on the wreckage at The Cedars … But she was tired, and deflated by the day's events. She'd had enough to contend with …

"You could stay here," she heard herself saying. "I mean, if you like, although I expect you'd much rather …"

Imogen was the first to rush forward, her eyes brimming. "Oh! Could we? Could we? Are you sure?" She hugged Kay. Kay assumed that, in the absence of any parental affection, she had acquired this friendly gesture from friends. Kay hugged back with both arms, feeling touched by the strength of Imogen's unequivocal, unilateral response.

Tim was smiling broadly. "You don't mind? We did wonder. We'll pay you and everything, but …"

"Oh, don't worry about that," protested Kay, mildly. "You can probably help me out with a few things though …"

She could not imagine anything where they could be useful, but … maybe she could set them to work in the garden. Heaven knows she needed help there, with Dunstan apparently vanished and his team of workers patently overstretched.

It amazed her how fast the three of them could move when sufficiently motivated. By dinnertime they were settled in, each having unpacked a large holdall in the spare bedrooms. Now assembled downstairs, Tim presented Kay with a crate of Dom Perignon. How practical, thought Kay, with a chuckle!

"We could have a party!" shouted Jeremy, punching the air.

Pictures of young people crowding through her home, behaving badly in numerous ways, filled Kay's head.

"Maybe not," she replied, smiling. "But thanks so much for that. You really shouldn't. These will be for special occasions of course, but … let's open a bottle now, then we can decide what to eat …"

Dinner proved to be interesting. Imogen was a 'veggie', Tim told her he had "always had an aversion to vegetables, certainly an intolerance, possibly an allergy." Such rubbish, thought Kay. Jeremy would eat anything but in large quantities. Eventually, after much discussion and opening and closing of fridge and freezer doors, a menu was agreed upon.

Although exhausted, Kay felt cheered to have company as they sat together round the dinner table to share, according to preferences, vegetable lasagne, a platter of mixed grilled meats with a chilli sauce, baked potatoes with soured cream and a green salad. It was a long time since she had catered for four.

She gave Jeremy the task of keeping everyone topped up with wine, lager, water or whatever they wanted, within reason. He took his responsibilities seriously, she noticed.

"By the way, Jeff, our solicitor, and strictly speaking Jeremy's guardian, you know, he asked us a load of questions about our 'financial status', all so boring to be honest," said Tim, draining his glass. "But he said we need to procure the services of a bloody financial adviser to help us, to … well, what was it he said, Imogen?"

"To 'manage our *affairs*'. I wondered what he meant at first! He gave us a name and number to call."

"He's after our money, that's what he is," put in young Jeremy wisely. "They're probably in it together. In cahoots, isn't that what they say, Kay? Co-llab-o-rators."

"Collaboration is not always a bad thing, Jeremy," Kay pointed out, a memory flashing like a light being switched on, back to when she and Dunstan had collaborated: in the garden, in their pursuit of Lena the young Gypsy woman, and in the crazy chase after Tibor, the Czech Roma immigrant ... They had shared so much in their wonderful collaboration.

"Anyway," continued Tim, "seems we need help with sorting out our budgeting and that sort of thing. Should look at ways to make our money work for us."

"Sounds like an excellent idea," responded Kay, relief and alcohol causing her to glow inwardly, and probably outwardly. Two professionals would now be actively supporting these young people who really had no clue how to balance their household books or keep stock of their shares, which she knew they had inherited. She hesitated to even think of how they might be using and abusing their several credit and debit cards; failing to check their bank statements; spending money without thinking; putting themselves open to all kind of identity thefts and fraudulent goings-on by other people. It was not as if they were incapable; they just lacked guidance and had never been shown that taking responsibilities was part of adulthood. They were a strange, vulnerable trio and she did not feel equal to the considerable task of protecting them.

Sunday was wild, wet and windy when anyone would be thankful to have a sound roof over their head. In such weather, Kay always spared a thought for the homeless on the streets, or indeed for Gypsies and Travellers weathering the storm in less solid trailers, and their dogs kept outside in all but freezing conditions. It was how they preferred to live, to keep extended families together and to preserve a certain kind of freedom, she understood that, but she knew that some of the permanent council sites were prone to flooding where drains would overflow, making life unpleasant and hazardous to health. But what really stretched her imagination was how previous generations coped with such foul weather when they were managing in those old bender tents. Families with twelve children! She had seen photographs of Irish Tinkers on the roadside and at first thought the images must be as old as photography itself, but was appalled and astounded to see that they were in fact a snapshot of life in 1969 – when she was in her teens.

She pictured the Irish Travellers who had been forced to stop on the Appley Green Common yesterday and wondered how they were coping, with no facilities. Perhaps if their stay was very brief, their water supply would last and they could somehow dispose of domestic rubbish and other waste without causing complaints from the local people.

The Farlows' Sunday was mostly taken up with clearing, sorting and ditching things outside that were unrecoverable, ready for a skip. They assiduously took photographs, already looking forward to following through the 'before and after' effect, as if they were on a makeover TV programme. Kay was pleased that they were taking it on as a project and taking it in their stride. They took pit stops at Kay's house and ate meals together with her. She almost felt obliged to cluck, she felt so like a mother hen. Her bedrooms, and indeed most of her house, took on a distinct air of occupancy but she tried not to notice the muddy footprints, half-empty mugs deposited everywhere, damp towels left on beds; or complain at the lack of hot water in the morning, the television left on overnight and the debatable websites that had been visited on her computer, resulting in some emails she was at first shocked to receive until she increased the security levels to filter such spam. After all, it was only for a couple of days and nights …

On Monday morning, after another night of severe winds, the sun shone brightly and steam was gently rising from the ground in Kay's garden. She showed Jeremy and Tim around her fruit and vegetable garden trying to spark some interest in a particular tangle of weeds where she would prefer to see a line up of spring cabbage and root vegetables and signs that her artichokes could breathe. Imogen then offered to take a stroll round to The Cedars to see if anything had changed while her brothers went indoors for brunch. She had not been gone for long when Kay's phone rang. It was Imogen, speaking huskily in barely more than a whisper.

"Kay, there are these men at the front door – they're scaring me. You know we have those stickers warning off door-to-door traders? Well, I've told them, but … anyway, I've called the police. Maybe they've got their eye on the stuff we're throwing out. Not that we want it, obviously, but they look like Gypsies to me."

She put the phone down, tried counting to twenty before setting off. Just as she was about to close the front door her phone rang again.

"Hi Mum! Just a call to see how you are," came the voice of her older daughter, Claudia, who had moved to the Midlands where her husband's job needed them to be. "Not getting bored or lonely, are you? Suzi said you were stuck in on Saturday."

9

Late evening found Dunstan still struggling to assemble his memories in chronological order, but he knew there was an aspect of his early life he must extract and commit to paper before he could progress to other events and people that shaped subsequent years. Unsure if pouring it all out into his computer would make him feel better or worse, either way it would be an emotional challenge. Might it prove to be useful therapy? Would it be cathartic and purge him of the enduring resentment he held, enabling him to deliberately forget, maybe even forgive? Or, would it remind him and serve to underline all the pain and rancour that the young boy, Dunstan, felt and kept bottled up and that Dunstan, the man, met with all over again. It might tip him over the edge.

Though loosened up with red wine, he drummed the desk with his fingertips, feeling oddly charged with nervous energy, as if about to face a stony-faced panel of interviewers for a job or go on stage to act or sing, which he had never actually done so could only imagine the butterflies. Replenishing his glass, he wondered why he needed Dutch courage to face this. Surely it was all so long ago, he had lived a life – a double-life, for nearly fifty years – and successfully *moved on* ... He reminded himself that no one else would see this account of his life. He could delete selected blocks of text at any given moment, so what had he to worry about?

Feeling small and different

We 'Traveller children' as we were called, were separated out and sat at a table in a corner. This was because, at the age of eight, we were way behind the other kids in reading and writing. Maybe that was the teacher's logical thinking. It

might've made sense if we had then been given some extra teaching and attention to enable us to catch up.
But we were more often forgotten about. I had been told so many times by my mother not to make trouble with the *Gorgios*, but to stick it out and get what I could out of it. It was a lesson for life, as she saw it, I guess.
In no time at all, though, this logical arrangement worked to our social as well as educational disadvantage. Playtimes put a tight knot in my stomach. The other boys would be in small gangs playing 'tag' or football; girls, in twos and threes, with skipping ropes or mostly with linked arms, fell in and out of best-friendships. Our little group stuck together, defensive, quick to react, almost moving as one organism, like a small flock of starlings or six-strong army of ants. We felt like sitting ducks, prime targets, but looking back, as we patrolled the playground practically joined at the hip, we might have looked a bit scary to the other kids! We found ourselves excluded, so we stuck together, often taking care to speak in Romany *jib* so we could not be understood. Again, this may have given us an air of mystery. Plotting little connivers!
They did not seem frightened by us though.
"Thickos, thickos, look at all the thickos," some would chant, poking out their tongues and running off together laughing.
"Dirty gyppos. Don't you ever wash? My Daddy says you don't. And your fathers are all thieves and tell lies."
"Smelly, dirty gypsies. Stupid, smelly, dirty gypsies." In those days the word Gypsies was used as an insult, whereas today many Romany Gypsies are proud of their Gypsy heritage.
Then it would build up. "Stupid, thick, stupid, dirty pikeys ... my mother says you never *should* play with gypsies in the *wood*!"
I remember when one sweet-looking, little girl with blonde curls looked me in the eyes and said this and I thought why? Why should you never play with us in the wood? It was a while later when I found and was able to read the well-known rhyme in a book. Then I just asked myself why would anyone write this in a poem?

I had scrubbed my face and hands with fresh water from the jack can that morning and my Mam had taken care to wash and dry my clothes. That water had not been near food or animals or *Gorgios*. It was not contaminated in any way, so why were they saying that?

Dunstan swallowed hard as he read through what he had written. He could feel the hurt he felt then and had a little walk around to cool off, transporting himself back to those days when he had felt like a pariah.

Becoming Gorgiofied

During lesson time we were given much time for drawing and playing with bricks, jigsaws and Plasticine (the smell takes me right back there), anything to keep us busy. Perhaps the teacher thought we were incapable of learning and not worthy of her time. There was no knowing how long we'd stay, anyway. One minute there, the next day fled to another part of the country. Later I worked out that we were probably set apart so as not to hold back the other children, *Gorgios*.

It was hard enough anyway, sitting still indoors without talking, when we were used to being outdoors in all weathers, either playing, running and shouting, exploring or helping with tasks like collecting firewood or, when we still had the wagon, feeding the horse or sweeping up. The girls would help their mothers cook meals and look after any babies in the family group. We mixed with people of all ages, from newborns to great-grandparents.

So the classroom thing was a big enough shock, but it was even harder for a small child to be pushed away like a wicked dog, to be spat on and reviled in so many ways. Some *chavies* would lash out and fight back, as their older brothers and sisters had probably done before them, and they would get into terrible trouble. Others would take to stealing and lying since they thought that was what people expected of them anyway so they might as well derive the benefit. They lived up to their name – and would also get

into terrible trouble and not be allowed back. Or, their parents wouldn't send them again.
I was a quiet child, a bit shy. Mother was gentle, unlike some louder and more forthright Gypsy women I knew. They would stick up for themselves but were usually forced to be deferential and respectful to the *rawnies* in their *hawking* or else how could they be expected to sell their wares? And *dukkering*, they would usually tell folks the fortunes they wanted to hear. Who would pay them for telling them that in the next month they would be ill, have an accident or lose all their money within the coming year?
So I would hold back and watch, listen and maybe I did learn more than the others. On those odd days at school – and there weren't many of them - I grabbed every chance I had to learn my letters and asked the teacher for a writing book and some readers like the rest of the class had. I was quiet but I had nerve. Then I could curl up in a corner causing no trouble. Sometimes us *chavies* were told to clean or tidy up after the others. Perhaps the teacher thought this might help us with practical skills for our way of life (I'm being kind); that we would feel we did have a purpose after all; or that it might save someone else having to waste their precious energy. The day a *Gorgio* child was sick on the schoolroom floor and the teacher was overheard to say, "Stand clear children, I'll get one of the Travellers to clean it up," was the day I felt a sense of injustice churn inside me as all groups of ethnic minorities must have felt throughout history when they are labelled and treated badly. Anger and hatred were kindled on that fine sunny afternoon in the late 1950s.
At the next school I knew the score. I had practised my reading and Mother was helping me a bit too, when Father wasn't around. I showed the teacher what I could do. Already I was pulled out from the other Traveller kids and put with the *Gorgios.* I found a fairy story with pictures called Jack and the Beanstalk (thinking of my bean-sprout and looking at the enormous plant that was growing up into the sky) and asked if I could read it to the teacher because I was so excited and wanted to make sure I could read it properly. Then she asked if I would like to read it to the

class and I was accepted. I had proved something to them and crossed the line, but I was no *Gorgio* and never would be. My mother had done such a thorough job of taking on the Gypsy ways, even despising *Gorgios* for the most part, I did not even know at that age that Mother had come from *Gorgio* stock.

Some would say I should have stuck with my own and been loyal to them but even at that tender age I began to see another way ahead. This was during the school day. Back with my people I was a Gypsy lad through and through to my very bones, with no intention of ever leaving them, no matter what.

Teachers seemed intrigued by the fact I was making more progress than my Gypsy peers. It reflected well on them to have this kind of success so they were encouraging and in some schools I got more than my fair share of attention.

My father knew I had learned to read by the age of ten, but he did not know how well I could read or what I was reading. There were no books in our trailer and I had never seen him read so much as a newspaper. There must have been things going on in the world of which they were unaware. Did they know anything about the nuclear bomb threat and the Soviet Union testing, what CND stood for, or that Russia had launched Sputnik the previous year? Had they heard that the rest of the nation was in mourning for Manchester United football team, the 'Busby Babes', killed in a tragic plane crash? Things that might affect their existence directly, like the opening of the first motorway in Britain, or new brands of car they would hear about by word of mouth, but their knowledge of current affairs did not seem to extend much beyond this. They would have thought the Common Market was a row of stalls. Though Mother would only read if she needed to, Father could not. I could read and found out facts they knew nothing about, at which point things got difficult.

My father would say, "Get your head out of that schoolbook of yours now and come over here and help me. You'll never grow up to win the heart of a Gypsy girl if you can't earn a living."

And in his company, even Mother would warn, “If you keep learning *Gorgio* stuff you’ll turn into one!” Father and Presley would laugh at this and give her approving glances. Soon I was hiding my books and looking at them only in secret. And at one school I went to nobody knew I was a Gypsy and I felt what it was to be a *Gorgio* and how different it was. I joined in with games and sport and was invited to other kids’ houses. I had to decline the offers, as my mother and father would have put their foot down, maybe because they would not have liked to ask them back, or simply because they did not want me mixing with *Gorgios*, whatever their reasons. I had the chance to go and see the film ‘Ben Hur’ but this never happened.
But I was accused by *Gypsy chavies* of becoming *Gorgiofied*. I was already torn between two worlds.
The schoolbook that first captivated me, when I was about eleven, was *The Secret Garden.* I loved that book! Even though *Gorgio* boys teased me. “That’s a girl’s book, that is! You should be into *Robin Hood* and *Treasure Island*.” But the teacher had started us off by reading it aloud and I was enthralled.

The Secret Garden
First published in 1911 (I just checked my copy) some kids found it quaint and old-fashioned. Maybe that was why I took to it. Even the little girl, Mary, whose British parents had died in India, I felt for. She came over to England, without any family, to live a lonely life in a huge, huge house with a hundred rooms. I could imagine nothing worse. She was teased. She liked to make little gardens, ‘making heaps of earth and paths.’ I liked that – it was our kind of play. She had ‘nothing to play with’ by way of toys, just like Gypsy children in those days. There was nowhere to keep them and no money to buy them!
Then there were descriptions of the Yorkshire moors, similar to the New Forest in Hampshire that I knew well. Heather, gorse and broom. I liked Martha the young woman whose job it was to care for Mary. She loved the moor and she came from a rough and tumble large family that was

always hungry. I could imagine Ben Weatherstaff, the old gardener and found it exciting to read about 'green spikes stickin' out of the black earth' with the coming of spring.

I did not fully realise that Mary was odd, not a normal *Gorgio* girl. She was haughty, giving people orders because of the upbringing she'd had in India, but I enjoyed the idea of her being a pale, thin house-dweller and the way fresh air built her up, got the blood flowing colour to her sallow cheeks, giving her a hunger and brightening her 'dull eyes'. All this was telling me that the Gypsy life was far superior to life in a house. It made me feel very good about myself.

Then came along talk of Dickon and I was goggle-eyed! A boy, like me, whose name began with a D and ended with an n! His older sister, Martha, said he had saved a half-drowned fox cub and a crow and he was out in all weathers. He got seeds for Mary to plant in the 'bit of earth' she had been brave enough to ask for and ...

The teacher had started us off by reading the book aloud and then we were supposed to carry on reading ourselves. That was problem number one – my reading needed to improve fast! So I had to make that happen – through a great deal of practice and concentration. There were several copies of the book for pupils to share. Problem number two was that I knew our family was likely to be moving away very soon; the summer fruit picking season had started, an important and good part of our lives.

At this point, my hero Dickon had not yet appeared in the book for real. It was like waiting for a celebrity to appear on stage. I had to 'meet' him. There was a lot of talk about magical forces of nature later in the book, but by this time the magic I had discovered was that of the printed word, how it could take you to other worlds, expand your knowledge and I could see how people within pages could come alive in your head. And I learned more about secrecy. I must have my own copy of this book to take away with me, and keep it hidden.

So a first big step had to be taken; one of disloyalty. I had to collude with the teacher who agreed to purchase the book for me and then I had to find the money to pay for it. I helped my Dad as much as I could and he would slip me the odd sixpence which I kept until I had enough.

Somehow he had veered off at a tangent, Dunstan realised, as he paused in his writing. With all the other things going on in life outside of school: hawking with his mother, learning how to handle horses and later, drive a truck, hack down a tree and knock on doors to get jobs lined up with his father, that book stood out as being important, a crucial milestone and he had to document it. Had he not come across it, his whole life may have taken a different course. He would never have gone on, much later, to pour over Plato's *Republic*, Aristotle's *Politics,* Schumachers' *Small is Beautiful* and many works of fiction …

But he had been bracing himself to write more about the bullying, leading to the day that even now stirred up a powerful loathing for certain *Gorgios*. He knew he must not lump all *Gorgios* together for then he was no better than folk who did the same with Gypsies.

The day of the fight

Some schools were worse for teasing and bullying than others. People didn't talk about 'victims' like they do today and did little to detect or prevent it in schools. Kids will fight – it was seen as natural. Teachers would sometimes turn a blind eye – I've heard it said they were scared of Travellers' big families coming along mob-handed to sort out differences.

There was a particular time when I was singled out by a big lad called David. He would lie in waiting, pounce on me, taunt me with words, then poke and punch. The usual jibes. I did my best to avoid and ignore him.

But one day, he started to say things about Mother. Now she had been unwell and not able to do any hawking or help Father, not even cook or clean. She was mysteriously laid up for a few days and I would guess now that it was the loss of a baby that might have caused this illness.

I was watched over by aunts and cousins. Families would always help each other out in such times. But I was thirteen, old enough to pretty much take care of myself and to worry about Mother and wonder what life would be without her. I acquired a real sense of mortality. Although I'd been to many a funeral as a child, sometimes unsure of who the person in the coffin was, I'd never before really considered that someone close to me would at some point die. It was a bleak time, and how was I to know that she would recover and live to see her seventy-first birthday?
Then David ambushed me and started his usual disgusting name-calling, but added a new one to his list.
'Your mother is a Gypsy slut.'
I threw myself at him, pounding his chest and stomach with my fists, heart pumping, fired up, kicking and fit to stamp him into the ground if only I could floor him. I found a strength I did not know I could call upon. By taking the bully by surprise for a change, I winded, then actually injured him. Blood poured from his nose and his hand rushed to his right eye as he yelled with pain. The damage was, it seemed, quite thorough and extensive.
This resulted in his parents coming to the school to ask for an investigation; my parents plus about six other family members trooping along in my defence for I had told them truthfully what a nasty piece of work this David was. Loyal to me, their support was loud and united. I was then banned. Well, we were moving on anyway but I had probably done no favours to the next lot of Traveller kids who went to that school.

Dunstan stopped at that point realising that he was seeing the event in a different light, now as an adult after so many intervening years. At the almost farcical picture he had conjured up – small boy in temper lashing out at yob, complete Traveller tribe terrorising schoolteachers – he could not help but see its pantomime-like humour. He actually had a smile on his lips, despite the fact that it was such an emotional event at the time. He thought of all the times he had bitten back the words he longed to utter, turned the other cheek, beaten down the anger that rose up in this throat from his very boots ready to explode out of his mouth. That was the first time he let rip! And, he thought wryly, much good did it do anyone.

It felt good to dissect himself, to remember the fascination he had for growing plants he learned from books he went on to after *The Secret Garden.* He started to make a list of the ones he could remember, for he did not own all of them now. This new-found know-how led him to experiment.

Growing food for the family

The women would say, "Now, we're out of potatoes, or we could do with a cabbage or two ..." and we would have to find them from somewhere. Taking care to remove a cabbage head and leave the outer leaves intact, or dig up potatoes and stick the leaves back where they were, we somehow never felt this was *choring*, that is stealing, even though it was. We had to eat. Some farmers knew about it but turned a blind eye. Out of a whole field, it wasn't much to lose.

Instead of taking from fields, begging or buying vegetables from shops, the whole idea of growing edible plants had a great attraction. But Gypsies on the move could not do this, except I did remember an uncle telling me he used to plant potatoes in a secret patch of land where he knew the family would return to harvest the crop. I built on this simple idea and managed to provide a few root vegetables and onions for our cooking pot. Into the 'Joegray' they would go – a stew full of surprises. Without any care the crops were poor, by any standard, the plants stifled by wild plants, disturbed by animals, afflicted by pests and suffering drought or flood, whatever the climate threw at them. But if some of them survived I could scarcely contain my excitement when I found I had grown almost free food.

The range was limited, although I was forever trying new things. I would save the seeds from a tomato, dry them out and one hot summer they did take and grow. Peering amongst a tangle of grass and groundsel and other wild plants, I leapt in the air and shouted, "Look, Mother, these

are ours!" They were green, but I kept moving them around with me putting them out for a sunbathe whenever I could till they turned a wonderful bright red.
When I studied packets of seeds I once discovered in a village shop I found the instructions included all kinds of tasks like 'thinning, potting, fertilising, spraying, feeding, watering, training ...'. If only I had a 'little bit of earth', like Mary in *The Secret Garden.*
One glorious summer we didn't move from our pitch. I'm not sure why – I think we had plenty of pea-picking and suchlike where we happened to be for some weeks so had no need to travel. My Uncle Fortune saw my keenness for growing and built me some wooden trays and a terrace-like structure woven out of twigs and branches, like he would fashion a basket. I could keep the seedlings off the ground, away from snooping dogs, foxes, chickens or pigeons, swapping the trays about to make sure they all got their fair share of sun.

Dunstan decided to stop at this point, thinking about all the people in his childhood he had not even mentioned. They were now milling about inside his head in a colourful throng. There were so many. Family, friends, people they met on the road from time to time, like Copper, who was father of several children when Dunstan was still a child himself, and the fairs and festivals with the big get-togethers.

He turned to a poem in a book he had once found in a second-hand shop by Tom Odley who he'd heard had sadly now passed away:

Trials of the Traveller

When you're travelling the road with no fixed abode,
Your trailer hitched on to your truck;
When 'Calling' is hard or they've closed down the yard,
Hard times when you're down on your luck.

When it's pouring with rain and you've pulled down some lane,
When you're bogged down aside of the road.
When the Chavi's be ill and you've just got a lil
For some lova the law says you've owed.

At night cars come by, at your trailer let fly,
When you're lying asleep in your bed.
You're rudely awoken, find your window's been broken;
Thank the Duhvi the baby's not dead.

A gavva comes by the next day to as "Why?
You're still here; why haven't you gone?"
With your tongue in your cheek, you tell him, "Next week,
For then, sir, I'll be moving along."

He then dikhs the glass, lying there in the grass,
And says, "Now what's all this mess?"
You tell him the facts, but he only reacts
By saying; "You can't expect less."

"You've no right to be here, so surely it's clear,
House-dwellers, their anger will show?
They don't like your kind, so always you'll find
Such treatment wherever you go."

You mention the Jew, on the cross who they slew,
And how He'd travelled the road.
How He'd been forsaken. His life from Him taken,
And how He's no fixed abode.

The gavva replies, with the same well-worn lies;
"I can't help that, I've my job to do.
Just orders I'm taking; they're none of my making.
The choosing of way's up to you."

You ask, where to go; he says, "how should I know?
Just move on and leave the place clean."
This mush dressed in blue, and his treatment of you,
It's the same at each place you've been.

The stops you once knew, now left, are so few,
Those places, where once you could stay.
That roadside now which is cut by a ditch,
Or blocked by huge heaps of clay.

That place by the wood, where the living was good,
That corner of untended field.
How many the lane, when you've gone back again,
It's entrance to you is now sealed?

The Travellers all dreading, the spider-web spreading,
Of factory, motorway, town.
Our movements restricting, our life-breath constricting,
On sites they say, "settle-down".

Destroying our beauty, in the name of their duty,
To help us, they claim, is their wish.
By forcing their way and making us stay,
They're making us 'land-dwelling fish'.

The life on the road was ever our mode,
Living the life, hard but free.
Though some call us 'lazy', and others just 'crazy',
Sane, hard-working people are we.

Though rogues we may be, consider with me,
Does the Gohja not cheat twice as much?
Though 'Gyppo' you style us, and often revile us,
In secret you envy our touch.

Though sometimes you're needy, more often plain greedy,
But ever you're seeking for more.
You despoil all Creation, and, in contemplation;
What 'Gyppo' has ever started a war?

Think On......!

Dunstan closed the book pensively. He must give Copper another visit. He would ramble on for hours! All those weddings, funerals and horse-fairs .... they were the good times. But he knew he must write about his early teenage years when his family met with the Irish family. For this he would need to talk to Seamus about *his* childhood, especially before the families first met, before they had even emigrated from Ireland to England looking for a better life. Now that is something about which he knew so little and would dearly like to learn more.

10

As Kay approached The Cedars, walking this time, determined not to rush or panic, she noticed firstly a white Ford transit van parked in the road, with ladders. As she turned to pass through the open gates, the next thing to strike her was what must have been a very tall slender silver birch lying across the driveway. It was posed at an angle, since it had crashed down into a thick clump of mature rhododendron bushes, providing what must have been a relatively soft and peaceful landing. Strange that Imogen was in such a state of terror that she had not mentioned the tree on the phone. Good thing she had not driven round.

A fresh-faced young man, smartly dressed, was striding out towards her, whistling. She had spotted him examining the fallen tree before continuing his way back towards what was presumably his van. There was a pile of leaflets in his hand. Now, she thought, what should I say? *Are you a Gypsy? Did you know the young woman who lives here has just called the police?*

"Mornin'," he said as he came nearer to Kay, just nodding as he was about to walk on, but then he turned and added, "Do you live 'ere by any chance?"

"Hello, there," replied Kay, catching sight of two men in workmen's clothes who appeared from the direction of the house and followed in the wake of the first man. She wondered why they were lagging behind. "No, I'm a near neighbour. Delivering leaflets?"

An awkward grin spread across his previously rather solemn face, eyes almost twinkling at her. He had the look of a salesman, Kay decided. "Certainly am. You live in this road, then?" He handed her a well-produced little flyer, offering in straightforward terms the services of tree surgery and garden maintenance work with a mobile phone number to call.

She pointed in the direction of her house and nodded. "Well, there's one job that looks as if it needs doing," she said, looking at the silver birch. "Could be more like it in the area. Quite a gale we had."

"Huh! Well, try telling that to the young lady here," he said, gruffly. "Course now we have to let people think about it, allow a week's cooling off and all that, but a job like this, well, it's obvious it needs doing now. Right here and now."

Kay nodded agreement. "So long as you agree a fair price."

"If we could get that far. To speak to 'em! There's two cars stuck on the other side. How are they going to get 'em out? And we saw a fella trying to deliver a skip but 'course, he couldn't get through so had to reverse back out. None too pleased! It'll need chainsaws and heavy equipment – surprising how much wood there is in a tree!" He laughed, then added with a sigh, "Ah well, you can't win 'em all. She's got our phone number." He shrugged and was about to leave her, when Kay heard the sound of a vehicle behind her and a look of surprise on the man's face. The other two had by now caught up.

"Enough work here to keep us busy for the week," said one of the two men who had come along, also staring through Kay, it seemed, to what lay beyond. "Bah! Here we go again. Another job lost."

"We'll maybe call back – see if she's had a chance to talk to 'er Dad."

Kay jumped in. "The three youngsters here have no parents. They are the house-owners."

"Ah." The young man nodded but then frowned, clearly distracted by what was going on behind her. She saw that two police cars had now stopped in the driveway. "Right. OK. Well, we'll maybe try her again in a few days' … what's all this, then?" This was not the reaction of guilty men.

"You just stay put there, would you, please," ordered one of the policemen who had turned up in the first car. More police disembarked from the second car. Kay could not believe her eyes. This was, frankly, ridiculous. "Want a word. Had a call from this house. Harassing these people, I understand. Demanding they give you work? Mm?"

Kay stayed put listening to the three young men account for themselves once the police had gone through the process of getting names and addresses. It struck her as very demeaning and their calm responses were impressive.

The police seemed to have made up their minds that the allegations were true once they admitted to being Gypsies. Kay felt stirrings of anger rise up inside her.

"We'll need to talk to Miss Farlow who made the call. You can come with us," said one of the officers. Kay supposed the possibility of them disappearing in true elusive Gypsy fashion was a reasonable assumption, though who could blame them for that? She kept quiet for the moment, following the group of three Gypsies and four policemen. This was so out of proportion it was beyond belief. She held herself in readiness to speak up at the right moment. "See what she says," the officer went on. "Then we'll decide whether to call the Trading Standards scambuster team, eh? They're up to their necks at the moment, otherwise they'd have been here with us."

Kay saw a dark, angry look that spoke of resentment in the faces of all three men at this threat. She saw jaws clenched, eyes narrowing, as they ground their teeth and held silent.

Before rushing off from her own house, she had briefly urged Jeremy and Tim to finish their bacon sandwiches and coffee, playing down the 'emergency', actually thinking she might do better without them. While hanging back slightly for them as they caught up, Kay took the opportunity to call Imogen, warning her that this rather alarming gang was trooping its way towards her front door. By the time they arrived – all ten, including Jeremy and Tim – she had opened the door to greet Kay who had now taken the lead.

"Kay, I freaked. I thought they were going to force their way in, get violent with me. I mean, three of them! But … did

I over-react?" She appeared very young and naïve as her big blue eyes gazed at the four policemen in complete bewilderment.

"You did the right thing," one of them assured her.

"But why so many of you? Are they … I mean … are they criminals? Wanted men or something?" Her face had turned even paler than usual.

"No," replied Kay, before anyone else could speak. "These are people offering a service. They have leaflets and are operating completely within the law. They saw your immediate need though, Imogen, as well as a skip haulier unable to gain access, and wanted to speak to the householder, assuming that you had parents. No offence committed or intended, and no reason to be worried. I'm sure they'll discuss a reasonable estimate with you and it'd solve a very real problem you have, wouldn't you agree? Perhaps the money you saved on hotel bills could be put to good use on getting your neglected grounds in order."

She paused to draw breath, her heart pounding, realising that everyone was standing, some tight-lipped, others with mouths gaping open, gazing at her. Still shaking with anger she wondered if she had overstepped the mark.

During the next week or so Kay felt as if she were meandering through a murky fog, unable to see things clearly, afraid of what might suddenly loom out of the enveloping mist. Another anonymous letter arrived through the post. As before, the postmark was local and she wondered who in the neighbourhood could be so vindictive. What sick kind of mind would want to intimidate her in this way? She debated with herself over and over again whether she should take the letters to the police but she suspected they would simply stare at her blankly. What could they do? No hint of sex or violence or psychotic behaviour, nothing that would warrant valuable police time in investigating the identity of the perpetrator. She needed to talk to someone but could only think of one person able to discuss the issue sympathetically and come up with a sensible course of action. He still had not put in an appearance or even been in touch.

A police officer had taken her to one side after The Cedars incident to explain that there had been a number of distraction crimes in the area and anyone knocking on doors and causing trouble required a quick response, "... especially where Travellers are concerned," he whispered, conspiratorially. She just glared at him, feeling that the comment was racist and unnecessary.

No, she wouldn't get much sympathy from the police. The letter was snide, referring to the *unfortunate double-booking*, offering her *congratulations on the popularity of the new accommodation provision for our friends.* As ever, it was couched in good English but what did he or she hope to gain by pouring scorn on what had already happened?

Then there was the splash in the next issue of the local newspaper. ***Gipsies Fight it Out*** was the front-page headline with a small write-up emphasising how it had all gone wrong with negative terms like *double-trouble* and a big photograph of the two men apparently engaged in combat surrounded by an unruly crowd. No real, impartial explanation or sympathetic understanding for what had happened and how, when families have nowhere to live, that must feel. No sense of the desperation, the disappointment or the physical hardship. If these had been black people these reporters would have been wary of breaking discrimination laws in some of the comments they made. But these were 'just gipsies', and journalists, like the rest of the population, seemed to be able to get away with it.

The culture clash that occurred at the site could at least be discussed with Max, now that the dust had settled somewhat, with the Irish Travellers fled to some other part of the country.

Like a cat that had found the sunniest spot, she settled herself down one afternoon on a warm, conservatory sofa and called him.

"Was there anything that could've been done to prevent this happening?"

"Not really, Kay. Of course, if there was a network of temporary sites with proper facilities across the length and breadth of the country, and well publicised contact details then this would go some way to stop this kind of thing happening. It goes on all the time – situations arising from the shortage of stopping places and sites in general. Years ago these warring groups, or families even, would have simply avoided each other, but now …" His voice trailed off as if weary of listening to himself.

Her gaze abstractedly followed a band of dark cloud that started to move across the blue sky. The tops of Scots pines and silver birches within her view began to stir. "Mm. Many of my friends, even my own daughters, would say that they should just give up anyway and take up any chance of going into housing and be done with it! Move on!"

"I'm sure. Easy enough to say. But – well, my family were on the road in times past, you know that. I was brought up in a house, went to school and university, and don't know much different, but my grandparents were in wagons and trailers and to have been put into a house – well, it would have killed them, I reckon. They once had a useful way of life, and a different way of thinking, of being."

As heavy raindrops began to thump down on the glass roof above her, Kay could understand why people struggled to see why anyone would choose a caravan over a house. Nonetheless, she agreed. "Absolutely. Understood. I've visited enough sites and talked to enough Romanis to know that. I guess it's the same for the Irish Travellers, although I don't know so many of them."

"Exactly the same. They have a different but parallel history. The way of life they struggle to hang on to is very similar. And folks surviving on the road tend to develop the same ways and traditions. Of course both groups would say they're nothing like the other, on the whole. But we shouldn't generalise, should we? People are individual human beings."

"Indeed. They seem to be lumped together with a nasty label slapped onto them all too often," agreed Kay. "Now, to get back to Appley Green, is there anything more we can do to prevent this kind of thing happening again? We really don't want it to … happen again …" she said, her voice cracking as she suddenly became emotional, thinking of the letter as well as the Travellers who were disappointed, the conflict she witnessed and the arrival of police, "… do we? Oh Max, I feel I've really failed. I mean, I helped to bring about the transit site by getting the locals … well, most of the locals … to buy into it, as it were, and actively support it. But, tell me honestly, has it made things worse? Or, at best, no better?"

She heard Max chuckle down the phone. "You're just playing with words now, Kay," he teased. "Look, what you did should be an example to the rest of the country. Those pieces you wrote for the local paper – many of them have been picked up by other interested parties. I've seen stuff on the Internet that must've been lifted from your articles! And the good thing is that regional assemblies are trying to get councils to spread responsibility more evenly for providing Gypsy and Traveller accommodation needs." As he spoke, the wording of the last hate letter came thundering back to her. She also recalled what a Romany Gypsy had revealed to her, claiming that some councils were reluctant to accept taxes from itinerant Gypsies as this would legally make them responsible for their accommodation. So many different viewpoints! It made her head spin sometimes.

She sighed. "Well, Max, I hope the system is beginning to work in their favour, then we shall all benefit. No one wants to see illegal camps continue and presumably grow even bigger."

"Nor do we want Travellers to be in a situation where they have to set up permanent homes illegally without planning permission. That's not the way forward either. It just makes *Gorgios* understandably aggrieved and the Travellers stressed and insecure, permanently living on the edge."

"So, there's nothing we can do then, other than what is being done by officialdom?"

"What you've done – getting local residents to see things differently, reducing the prejudice, and to work towards getting more transit sites in other areas. One new site is good, better than none, but in reality little more than a nice gesture."

A nice gesture. It sounded weak, ineffectual. "Well, that – getting other sites – ah Max, no. I couldn't do that. Way, way beyond me. And I don't seem to be doing much of a job with the locals these days, either ..." She sighed.

"You're doing fine, Kay. Don't give up."

Max urging her on made her question what she would give up anyway? Exactly what would that entail? If she relinquished her support of the Gypsies' and Travellers' pursuit of places to live, in keeping with their residual traditions, then she would no longer attend forums and events; visit permanent sites where she had become friendly with residents; or write the articles that the local paper still printed from time to time and had helped damp down local antagonism to a degree. She would stop giving talks to groups of resistant people, who sit doggedly fuming with arms folded. If she gave up doing these things what would be the outcome, she wondered?

Word would get out that the non-Gypsy campaign associated now with Appley Green had fizzled out. She and the Gypsies and Travellers were defeated! Other councils would hear of this and sit back, relieved that there would be less encouragement for such agitation in their catchment area, for – well, *look at Appley Green*, they would say, *a flash in the pan.* Then she could truly say that her actions had done more harm than good – empirical proof that taking action led nowhere and achieved nothing!

Moreover, whoever was writing the letters would think they had won their battle, she realised, incensed with the notion. This alone was enough to spur her on.

As she lay in bed that night, she reflected on her conversation with Max. Why did I not think to ask after Natalie? How remiss of me, she thought. Were they still together? She somehow doubted it. She had lost touch with Natalie since her graduation, when she journeyed abroad on anthropological assignments. Such long absences must have put a huge strain on her relationship with Max, but for sure, Natalie and Max were at one time very close. Kay had also been close to Natalie, too.

Kay would never forget how, soon after her move to the country from Richmond, Natalie had enlisted her help, her fervid leaflets causing more division than reconciliation. She would always remember the first time she heard Natalie's father, Ted, so outrageously outspoken against his own daughter in his diatribe against Gypsies and Travellers on the radio! It was pleasing that she felt responsible in some way for bringing him round – one of her small achievements in life, she felt.

It set her thinking. Would Ted Devonish lend his support in any way now if she called him up, she wondered? He was always such a gentleman, so attentive and reliable, so solicitous of her welfare in the old-fashioned way. Natalie was disappointed that she and her father had not in fact 'got it together', as she once said quite openly. But Natalie was possibly the only person who had worked out that Kay's affections lay elsewhere; so one day Kay hinted that she should convey this truth discreetly and delicately to her father, without mentioning any names. It occurred to her, too late perhaps, that Natalie was not well known for tact. For over a year she had not heard from him at all. Nursing his wounds perhaps.

Maybe she could confide in *him* about the letters. She so desperately needed someone to listen and understand. As these thoughts were rolling around loosely in her head, she suddenly opened her eyes wide and felt her heart thud.

Could Ted have felt so spurned? *Could he …?*

11

Dunstan's head was spinning from his last chat with Seamus. He had expected it to be a challenge to get him talking about the distant past but words gushed from his mouth in a torrent. His recall was total, delivery unstoppable.

"Nobody's ever asked me to talk about those old days, you know. But it's all here," said Seamus at the outset, pointing to his own head. "Fresh as the day it happened. Fresher dan what I did just last week, to tell you the honest truth …" and he was off, veering down a network of memory lanes at a cracking pace, filling in every last detail of colour, smell, tragedy, joy, hurt, injustice and triumph.

Ruby-Ann, Dunstan's cousin from Ireland, was now sitting in the passenger seat as Dunstan drove her away from the airport in his camper van.

"I knew it would be you waiting for me here," she said, as she made herself comfortable, slipping off her shoes and checking her appearance in the vanity mirror. "Isn't this fantastic now?"

"It's good to see you," responded Dunstan. "And looking so well. The others are planning to show you the sights, and putting on a bit of a shindig, I hear. A welcome party. Kind of a reunion, eh?" He gave her a tentative smile. She was regarding him radiantly, her round cheeks flushed. Dunstan vaguely and with some private embarrassment, assumed it to be a symptom of the menopause, but his knowledge of this was slight.

"I've waited so long."

"When was the last time you came over?"

"Not since Edwin passed on. Not seen many family since the wake last year. Even my own children are that spread apart and busy with their own lives."

Dunstan nodded, focusing on the traffic as the van slipped onto a motorway and he increased his speed. Soon it would be evening rush hour and he hoped to beat it. He needed to get the seething mass of facts Seamus had given him onto his screen before they began to fade and distort in his head. He had taken no notes nor recorded his stories for, had he resorted to either notebook or tape, Seamus would have clammed up as if he were being televised live to the nation.

She went on, "Terrible though isn't it? Takes a funeral to get friends and family together. I see less and less of people as the years go by."

"So how's the estate where you live?"

"The house is good enough but neighbours not that friendly. *Gorgios* mostly. You know, Dunstan …"

He knew from Seamus that she held grudges and felt himself to be a rather captive audience so decided not to prompt a stream of grievances. Perhaps she would ask him a question about his life, his work or other family members now living in or near Appley Green.

"While we're just here together, you know, the two of us I just want to say, Dunstan, that all those years ago when you were sixteen and I was just fourteen … you know I hated you with a passion for just walking out on me like that … well, for leaving all of us, your Mam and Dad, everyone. You abandoned everyone! We couldn't make any sense of it …"

Dunstan shifted uneasily and focused hard on his driving, checking his wing mirrors. "At the time. Mm. I know. But you do now, so … there's no point in dwelling on what a villain you all thought me at the time."

"But … you see, my point is, when we realised the truth, you suddenly became a hero. All over again. Dunstan …"

He was aware of her reaching down for her bag, pulling out a tissue and … oh no, now she was wiping her eyes. He was not good with women who cried.

"Now then, don't be getting yourself upset. That's all in the past now." Even as he said this, he felt a hypocrite since most of his waking hours these days were taken up with digging up the past – instead of gardens, which, if they had feelings must also be feeling abandoned.

She sniffed. "I know, Dunstan, but surely didn't you realise that once the air was cleared and we understood why you'd disappeared, everything changed? I mean, how we all felt about you." Actually, thought Dunstan as he heard her speak, he did not realise. For so many years he was sure he would never be welcomed back by his family.

She went on, "Even though I'd been married to Edwin for so long, with already four of our six children, my feelings for you were still as fresh as they were when I was fourteen …"

"Why the divil did not you warn me, Seamus? I bet you knew what was going on inside her head! Tell me you didn't!" Dunstan roared down the phone that evening. "Playing about with people like this. No good will come of it. Now she's convinced I'm all good and ready to propose to her and live in Ireland with her for the rest of our days! She's set on it! She thinks I've just been holding back all these years – *so many years* - even through my marriage to Margaret, and waiting for Edwin to pass away to leave her free. I mean, the whole thing is obscene, ridiculous and too sad to credit."

"Oh. That far. She's gone that far has she? This is the God's honest truth I had no idea she was quite so fixed on you, Dunstan."

"Well, nor did I and that's for sure."

"So, now, what should we do, do you tink? You'll have to … let her down gently, so you will. Spend a bit of time with her, in a friendly kind of way, and then softly, softly, softly, push her away back to Ireland."

"It won't be easy."

"No. It will not. I was thinking though she'll have some memories you could put in this diary thing of yours. Maybe talking some more about her younger days will get all the nonsense out of her and then she can be more at one with the world and go home a happy woman. What do you tink, Dunstan? I'm telling you the truth now, you can't be too direct. You mustn't be hurting her. It could be the straw to break the whatsit's back – she's had the terrible depression, you know, living in that house with no friends or family about her."

Dunstan sighed. "I know. Don't worry. I'll be gentle, kind, tactful, all those good things, but … anyway, I have to go now. I've a lot of writing to do."

He was not sure if he wanted too much extraneous detail. After all, this story was really supposed to be about his life, not the world and Ruby-Ann. Sure he wanted Seamus' story because this would help him to explain a few things about how the families met.

Leaving aside the problem of Ruby-Ann, who was lodged for now in a Bed and Breakfast close to where Presley lived, Dunstan switched on his computer. In the old days this kind of accommodation would have been unthinkable. Surely someone will squeeze her in, double up somehow or the other. But Presley and Geena had no space in their shared flat; some second cousins lived in basic cramped trailers on a site a few miles away and another cousin was, unfortunately, missing on a flying visit to see some old friends up in Yorkshire, taking his small tourer with him. Dunstan could feel the pressure mounting already …

He would have to make himself busy, get back to his gardens, not spend so much time on his computer locked away alone, and lonely looking, in his mobile home somewhat isolated from the hub of Appley Green.

He brought up the notes he had made after a couple of previous sessions with Seamus and began adding a few bullet points. He would write up the whole thing tomorrow but, before retiring for the night, he decided it was not too late to call up some of his notoriously unreliable workers for a progress report.

He enquired about various clients and their gardens.

"They keep askin' about you and questions I can't answer, but I'm keepin' things tickin' over. …"

"Runnin' out of seeds and other gear … I'll send you a wassaname, requisition slip."

"Think we may have lost a customer …"

"Wheelbarrow broke yesterday …"

"Mr Taylor may've died …"

He also checked on the welfare and progress of his team members, for whom he cared a great deal. Finally he spoke to a lad called Scotty who had been assigned to Kay's garden.

"She had three other guys working in her garden the other day. She wasn't there herself but …"

Dunstan raised his eyebrows. "OK. She must've found alternative labour then. That's fine. Fine. Just leave that one. I'll have a word with her myself and sort it out."

He gritted his teeth and sucked in a sharp breath through them. She had not even had the courtesy to tell him.

Dunstan could not help but admire Seamus for his amazing memory that enabled him, with much arm-waving and head-scratching, to tell his story sequentially. Now he must capture the luxuriant verbiage before it withered or befuddled in his own head. He could not write it down for Seamus to check through as Seamus could not read well enough. Indeed all his life, just to survive, he was used to retaining huge amounts of information in his brain since he could never make notes. No address-telephone book, jottings, diary, or lists of any kind! Dunstan could see he would need to read it aloud back to him, but his immediate task was to get down as much as he could.

Going first right back to his childhood on the roadside in Eire, he described the years his huge family spent in shelter tents. Dunstan reflected on how mothers would raise ten, eleven, twelve children in conditions that would make a cave-dwelling look like the Ritz.

I asked Seamus how his Irish family came to be living by the side of the road. He said for generations past they had always been Travellers. He knew this from stories handed down. Some had been horse-dealers. He believes, from what learned folks have also told him, and I have read the same thing, that Travellers have been in Ireland for untold centuries. Whatever his origins, he says the group of people he grew up with, his wider family, were separate from the rest of the Irish people, earned their living by moving from one settlement to another, but never made much money. Settled Irish people in general shunned them. Seamus knew folk who would live off their goats, cutting turf in the bog, and plying the tinsmith trade up until the time when the law changed the demand for tin. Dairy farmers were legally bound to use plastic or chrome buckets, with no seam and more hygienic for the milk. And so a way of life was lost.

I've read about this in books but it was different hearing it from someone who had lived it. Some people were starving. Seamus' eyes filled up as he told me this. Women were arrested for hawking and begging, just to try to make ends meet, just to feed and clothe their children, no more than the basics, to keep alive. They'd survive eating rabbits and potatoes from fields and cook them in clay. His face brightened as he recalled happy, carefree days they would go off fishing for eels and hunting for rabbits and hares with their lean, lurcher dogs. Those crossbreeds that do a good job with both catching dinners and guarding your home seem to be common to both Romanis and the Irish. How did that happen? I don't know. Managing and surviving challenges presented by life on the road, it seems people end up with similar ways and traditions.

'When times were really hard, poor people in houses would go to the workhouse in the truly olden days,' says Seamus, 'but at least we Travellers could live off what the woods and the green pastures could offer ...'

Dunstan paused, realising that he could not emulate Seamus' accent in print – it was no good to even try.

'Some of us fared better during the wars than non-Travellers. That was the good thing about our life, for sure. We'd never have gone into a house in poverty, it would have been so much worse in a slum than in the open air, we all thought.
So we did anything to bring in a little money to keep us all fed – sugar-beet and mangel picking. Some of the women, if they had a handcart, would pull scouring stone. For many years we Travellers were most useful for bringing news – before the days of radio, TV and the newspapers – and that what'd'y'call it Internet and all that ... People would look forward to us coming to their village to tell them all the craic but we're not so welcome these days, and that's the truth.
But it was hard, honest to God,' Seamus told me, 'with too many deaths and sickness. So the keen ones decided that life might be better across the water in England; we thought for the sake of our babies and children, and their future, we could maybe find a better living doing building work. Those with barrel-topped wagons and horses had real problems in Ireland finding anywhere at all to halt.
But of course when we got there, when I was near enough a man, we found some new rule stopped Travellers from camping by the roadside so each time we stopped, we'd be pushed off by the police, so we would. We had nowhere to go. The English Gypsies did not want us taking their places or working their patches.
We did not know the country; we spoke a different language – our Cant. To tell you the truth, we did not know how to build, though we'd learn the skills, sure we would! But meantime we had no money, no food, nothing. We would do the scrap iron picking. Sort it and separate the hard (the 'nipple' he called it) from the scrap, get it clean and take that along to dealers and get a bit of money that way. And rags.

We could find work but the big problem now was that – well, d'you know, no one wanted us! I mean, no one. Everywhere, be it pubs or lodgings, there were signs we could not read but it was clear by people's faces what they said and sometimes they would read them out to us. Things like: *No Dogs, No Irish …, No Animals, No Gypsies, No Caravan dwellers, No Blacks and No Irish need apply …. No Gypsies Served* was displayed in the window of a café.'
By 'Dogs' people often meant 'Gypsies' – oh, yes, Seamus assured me on that.
'We found ourselves getting into fights to stick up for ourselves. Then some took to the bare-knuckle boxing as a way to make a career of it.
If we were selling door to door, say lino or carpets, like some of us did, trying anything to see what could work, we had to do a bit of price-cutting to compete and sometimes what we sold was not the best quality, to be honest with you. But what else could we do? It was hard to make even a few pounds a week. Meanwhile, we still had nowhere to live, no ways for keeping clean, couldn't even get drinking water sometimes, always being moved by police who were ... well, they were horrible to us in those days. Mean. Terrifying. Violent even, kicking over stoves, bashing down our homes, assaulting our children. Sure it was bad. We struggled to just exist.'
Seamus could remember how in 1964 in Ireland, he heard of a terrible thing that happened. He told me a school had been built in Dublin just for Traveller children, and the council workmen, not Travellers themselves, burnt it down!
'What were we supposed to do? Some of our people behaved badly to get folks' attention, to try and get them to realise how rough we were being treated. We were desperate. But the newspapers and all that, they were always against us and this did no good with how others saw us. Some became careless about clearing up when they were moved on. Why should they bother to please those that hated us?'

Dunstan stopped for a moment, hoping he was doing justice to Seamus' emotional real-life tale. He reached for the local newspaper cutting he had kept about the Irish Travellers and the Romany Gypsies fighting over the Appley Green site. Still, after all these years trying to share the same pockets of land in this country, there were times like this when they could not live in harmony! He wondered if the press had been fair in their report. He suspected probably not. He knew first hand how press photographers had in the past sought out piles of rubbish, junk that was often dumped by local people, deliberately to make the worst impression. More likely to sell papers and feed people's righteous indignation.

How disappointing this clash, and the reporting of it, must have been for Kay. But then, as a *Gorgio*, her understanding of the Gypsy and Travelling community was pretty limited, after all. She had proved that.

12

Kay sat down after a hectic day in London with Millicent. She had enjoyed the change of scene but now, with aching feet, she wanted nothing more than to sink into a hot bubbly bath. They had taken in an exhibition at the National Gallery, a lunchtime concert at St Martin's in the Fields in Trafalgar Square and then, after lunch in Chinatown, browsed and scoured Regent Street in search of shoes, bags, belts and frocks. She could not discuss her problems with Millicent, nor indeed with any of her friends or family. It had been good therapy to get away, to escape the unshakeable black mood that sometimes gripped her these days.

Tomorrow was a clear day, she thought, as she flicked through her diary. Good, she would attempt a few tasks in the garden. But where to start? How can I ever catch up to get even the basics planted before the growing season is done, she wondered? Why does it matter? Why? On a global scale it ranked as big as a mote of dust … but matter it did.

The young Farlows could no longer be expected to help out there, anyway, that's for sure. The novelty had worn off – as novelty for them indeed it was! And, since having talks with the financial adviser, they had worries of their own to face, she suspected.

At least she could sow seeds to provide a variety of leaves, lettuce and radishes, ready for the table in no time, and she would throw in a few potatoes. There would be some satisfaction in that. Some of the early soft fruit varieties were ripening by now. She began leafing back in her diary to see how long it was since she had seen Dunstan. As she counted back the weeks, so her heart sank further until she felt faintly sick. To have had such trust, and felt the warmth of true friendship, only to have it blanked out as if it never existed … well, perhaps it never did. Maybe he was just using her and now she no longer suited his purpose. She swore mildly under her breath, cursing her own naivety for having believed in him.

A few days before, she had overheard a conversation in the Post Office confirming that, if he had actually felt anything for her, in the way that a mature man might feel for a woman of similar age, then she had been well and truly supplanted. It was as if she had stepped into a scene from *Lark Rise to Candleford* or *Cranford.*

"Seen Dunstan lately? He's got a new friend by all accounts."

"Well, it's about time he found a good woman in his life, if you ask me …"

"He's spending a lot of time with her, walking around."

"Where's she from? Not round here, is she?"

"Ireland, I think. Has a touch of the brogue. You heard her speak?"

"No."

"Oh yes. And you only have to be within earshot to know she does most of the talking. But, I have to say, he seems pretty happy to be doing the listening."

Then the two heads got closer and voices became small. "Bit more than talking and listening I heard. Seen coming from his caravan early morning – if you get my drift."

"Oh good for him!" There was some, what Kay could only describe to herself as, tittering. "Oh listen to us, talking about folk behind their back like a couple of gossips …"

It had been almost farcical to hear. Just able to see the funny side, Kay stifled something between a laugh and a cry as she pondered over an array of greeting cards. She managed to stop herself until she emerged onto the pavement only to find tears trickling down both cheeks, which she hastily wiped away with her fingers, trying not to draw attention to them.

Telling herself there was no connection, she decided she really must get around to face Ted, to rap on the head with a final blow the absurd idea that it could possibly be him sending her the vile letters. Walking home that day, she'd vowed she would invite him round for a light supper – a chance to catch up. She wondered what he would make of such an approach, if he supposed she and Dunstan were a couple. Perhaps he knew, like the rest of the village, that Dunstan had found someone else. This would pose a slight risk that he might get the wrong impression; rejected woman on the rebound!

So she would first go through Max, she decided, and find out what Ted was doing with his life these days before contacting him direct. She could then use Ted as a sounding board, get his opinion on the latest incident in the village. Soon time would be up for the Romany Gypsies to move on but – same old problem – they had nowhere lined up to go. The site they had planned to travel to after their allotted number of days at the Appley Green transit site, had been closed off to them. The council had some other plans for the land and had not yet sorted out an alternative temporary stopping-place for Gypsies and Travellers.

The village incident involved a teenage girl who had picked up a piece of Crown Derby in the small antique shop by the Green. The owner of the shop later recounted to Kay what had taken place.

"The girl walked around the shop with the figurine to show it to her friend, you see. I asked her to put it down, because someone might think she was going to steal it and then the police might be involved and it would all become so unpleasant. I was polite, and knowing she was a Gypsy, not wishing to cause offence. Well, if looks could kill! The girl didn't say anything and went off quietly but she seemed … defiant, you know? Half an hour later her whole family came back, demanding to know why their daughter had been accused of stealing!"

Of course, another letter to Kay had followed, referring to this shop incident that had got into the local paper but, so typically, was completely misreported, with a headline that gave the impression an offence had indeed been committed. Kay pulled out the cutting she had pushed into her bulging file of newspaper articles. Yes, this would be a talking point for Ted. She would scrutinise his face intently as she whipped out first the article and then the corresponding letter.

The Farlows came round to see Kay at the weekend; saying they needed to talk to her about something. She was on the point of going out so invited them round for a mid-afternoon Sunday roast so they could do it properly.

She did not push them too hard to discover the burning issue but rather allowed the conversation to take its natural course and come round to it gradually.

As they gladly accepted portions of upside down rhubarb and ginger cake with custard and cream, Tim remarked, "Those … er … Traveller guys, Gypsies, what do they like to be called?" He shrugged. "Anyhow, whatever, they did a pretty good job for us, you know? Not that we know that much about gardening and stuff. It always used to be … sort of taken care of. But, hats off to them, hedges all clipped back, stray trees removed. Worked their backs off."

"Good. I'm glad it worked out. I'd've felt guilty if it hadn't!" replied Kay, feeling genuine pleasure from this news, an increasingly rare sensation these days. "You could recommend them to others in the neighbourhood, offer to give them a reference they could show to people. That might help them."

Tim hesitated. "Oh. Don't know if they'd want that sort of thing. Do you think?"

Behind the superficially cocky manner, it struck Kay how lacking in confidence this young man actually was. You would think becoming head of the family in his late teens might have forced him to grow up fast, of necessity, but to Kay he seemed tentative and immature.

"They might not think to ask, but, believe me, it could be very valuable to them. Especially as the project they did for you was sizeable and they made a good job of it, as you say."

"OK. I'll do it." Tim nodded, surprisingly suggestible.

"We need to get ourselves sorted out," put in Jeremy, suddenly, leaning back so his chair teetered on its back legs, Imogen and Tim glaring at his interruption as if he were a naughty seven-year-old. "Apparently."

"What, the house? The repairs? I thought it was all coming along OK. You seemed to be doing so well last time I was round ..." Kay wondered if she sounded patronising, but they did need encouragement. Of that she was certain.

He sat forward, earnestly. "No. *Us*. Our *lives*. We all need to get *jobs* and earn serious money."

"Of course you do. At your age, everyone should be earning a living, or preparing for it in some way ..."

"We're NEETs! That's what our financial adviser says."

Kay smiled. Maybe she was a NEET herself! After all, she was not yet drawing a state pension, but lucky enough to live comfortably on Marcus's estate and her own savings, investments, with employment pensions lined up to drop down. Funny and arguably wrong, thought Kay, how that term 'Not in Employment Education or Training' tended to conjure up an underclass, what even now is called a 'dole queue', some of whom were, presumed to be work-shy squatters, scroungers living off the state, pulling benefit scams. Yet with the recession, many clever, hard-working people had dropped helplessly and headlong into the ranks of the unemployed. Maybe there would always be a virtually unemployable minority, but these three were well-spoken, able-bodied, well-cut young adults, with all the advantages of an expensive education, without careers. Tall, majestic ships with no rudder between them. Was it their lack of caring parents that made them unaware of adult responsibilities? Was it because they were so used to having everything done for them? She wondered what it might take to stir their interest and motivate them to get stuck into something worthwhile.

"We never really saw the urgency before. Always meant to – eventually, of course," Tim went on, languidly. With him being the eldest had he perhaps set the trend, such that Imogen and Jeremy had thought this lack of ambition was normal? She thought of her own daughters, Suzi and Claudia, and how different they were from the Farlows.

"Well, do you have careers in mind? Or plans to get qualified?" asked Kay, her gaze embracing all three of them, hoping she could be useful and willing to open up the discussion. This was clearly the basic reason for their visit.

Imogen, who had been quiet over lunch, perhaps worried, spoke up first. "I want to do something with horses or fashion, that involves travel," she said.

Kay bit her lip, beating down a bizarre image of Imogen wearing Galliano jacket, Alexander McQueen trousers, Marc Jacobs shoes, astride a mustang galloping across a Mexican desert.

"That's ... interesting. Specific, in a way. What about you, Tim?"

"Well I do actually have a degree in Business Studies," he said rather grandly, and Kay was astounded to hear this. Perhaps he did have a brain after all, with his focus on theory rather than household practicalities! "So I would hope to move straight into senior management within a blue-chip company. Or, possibly run my own business. Haven't quite made my mind up yet." The corners of his mouth turned down slightly with his head inclined thoughtfully, as if his indecisiveness was the single obstacle at stake. Kay was almost unable to speak. Where do you start to gently knock false arrogance out of someone without stripping them of hope? And had they heard about the 'economic downturn', going on 'depression'?

"You Jeremy?"

"He's the really brainy one!" put in Imogen, and Tim looked as if he would explode. It was a strange kind of sibling rivalry, without parents to impress, just each other. "Straight Grade As all through school, without ever even trying, so utterly unfair. Always the teachers' favourite," she added, with more scorn than envy.

"Like you would know," muttered Jeremy, poking her arm.

"So what do you want to study at university, Jeremy?" asked Kay.

His mouth fell open. "Me? University? No way! A fucking stoodent?" he exclaimed, affecting a glottal stop, 'estuary' accent which he clearly believed to be the epitome of cool.

Kay blinked. She didn't like to hear him swear and she would have expected him to hold back in her presence, out of courtesy. She tried to reserve choice words for impact in moments that truly warranted them. These days it was just another everyday word – she mustn't show her age.

Deciding to ignore it, she asked. "Well, what's your inclination? What kind of work have you in mind?"

"I … I shall live on me wits!" Jeremy pronounced with a broad smile.

Kay clasped her hands together, arms forming a steeple, and rested her chin on them. Then she unclasped her hands and stood up. "Well, I … I'll go and make coffee and … this will need some thought," she said, calmly, racking her brains for the name of a reputable recruitment agent who could give all three a sound reality check.

She was surprised that their conversation over coffee reverted to the Gypsies who had acquitted themselves so honourably. Jeremy seemed to find the whole concept of knocking on people's doors to find work extremely attractive.

"Must be so cool. Doing something like that."

Imogen laughed. "I never heard you offering. I mean you could've …"

Jeremy grinned good-naturedly. "Not actually doing *that* – too much like hard work. But I mean being your own boss. Freedom!" He punched the air theatrically. "Control! Yeah!"

"It's good when it works, Jeremy. Can be very daunting though, being responsible for getting your own work, especially when you're a family man with people dependent on your income, just to survive," pointed out Kay. "I was self-employed for a number of years. Loved it. But hated the paperwork, and at least half my time was spent on the phone, or on sales visits, giving presentations – all financially dead time."

"But then you win a commission and charge enough to profitably cover all those overheads, presumably?" said Tim.

Kay nodded. "That's right. But imagine if you never get the work and the bills pile up. Imagine if you have children and there is no food to put on the table."

They all reflected on this for a moment. "You think it's easier to be an employee then?"

Kay put her head on one side. "It depends. Take a sole-trader who runs a shop. He or she could do well all day every day if they were selling the right things at the right time to the right people!" It seemed to Kay she was stating the obvious, but the three appeared to be soaking it all in as if she were a celebrity business guru proffering great wisdom.

"Supply and demand. But if you're an employee you have different rights …" and Tim drifted off into a learned exposition much like an academic essay he had perhaps once written, or obtained on the Internet, thought Kay fleetingly, almost at once repressing such an uncharitable suspicion. He had never come across to her as capable of obtaining a degree, but swiftly recognised her own shortcomings in reading people correctly.

After a few minutes, Jeremy stretched his arms up into the air and yawned. Kay empathised and gave him a wink. "What do those Gypsies do if they can't get enough work to live on?" he asked Kay.

"I think they help each other a lot."

"They claim benefits, of course, you idiot!" put in Tim, addressing Jeremy.

"Only as a last resort, I'm told. They're a very proud people," said Kay. "The man should provide, or other family members will come to the rescue. Then in better times, they would hope to reciprocate. But, generally, travelling people have always been flexible and if things aren't working out, they look for new ways to make a living."

Tim laughed. "You bet they do!" he scoffed.

"Wow," exclaimed Jeremy. "But, but … why do they carry on like this? I mean, why don't they get jobs like most other people have? Not tossers like us, obviously," he added and they all laughed at themselves, which Kay saw as a rather healthy development.

"They have a different outlook on life that's been handed down." Kay tried to think how to explain. It was always difficult, especially in the company of seriously bigoted people. At least Jeremy, bless him, simply wanted to know more. He seemed genuinely interested.

"I guess before industrial and agricultural revolutions, before huge cities, railway and road networks had grown, people lived simple lives," began Kay, trying not to sound like a teacher. "Well, obviously you've all studied history and maybe seen period dramas on TV?" They looked at her blankly at the TV suggestion, shaking their heads. She was reminded that not everyone settled down to view documentaries and historical drama as she did; perhaps they were too busy 'living'. "OK. Anyway, ordinary folk really *needed* occasional services of skilled people like knife-sharpeners, blacksmiths, tinsmiths, and maybe some entertainment – dancing, singing, fortune-telling – you see where I'm going. Travelling people provided all these things and more, peddling all kinds of stuff – brushes, carpets, baskets and little craft items, and hawking bits and pieces like wooden pegs they'd make themselves out of things they'd find in the countryside. They'd travel to do seasonal fruit picking, mending things too, all work that was valued in villages. A bit like me providing a marketing service to companies that couldn't justify employing a permanent, full-time marketing specialist. Only more useful! Just the same principle, though."

"But all that traditional stuff, we don't need that. We go shopping!" put in Jeremy, "or order online."

"You're right. Plus the fact there's so few places for them to stop. Laws have been passed to put a stop – ah! no pun intended – to that." She smiled and went on, "But these people have handed down from one generation to the next a way of living, traditions and values that mean everything." Kay paused, holding back from citing a current example of Roma women in Italy who were willing to set fire to themselves rather than be split from their husbands or have their children taken from them. This might be too much for the Farlows. "So, a house on an estate just doesn't feel right for many of them. They feel confined and long for freedom. Restless. And they stick together in large, extended families to help defend themselves against the rest of the population who historically have treated them shamefully. It would be hard to get that kind of togetherness in housing … Look, it's a big subject, I could go on and on, but I can see Imogen and Tim getting fidgety now, so I'll look out some books for you, Jeremy."

After they had returned home, Kay turned to her computer to check out some websites she thought might interest Jeremy. She came across some disturbing articles via an online magazine called O NEVO DROM: ***UN refuses to include Romani victims in Holocaust memorial event***; and yet Kay knew already around a vast proportion of the Romani population had been gassed or otherwise murdered, just as the Jews had. The problems going on in Italy now made her shudder. She found an item entitled ***Italy is a xenophobic and racist country.*** At first she warned herself that this kind of article was in danger of being racist itself, against Italians. But the research and evidence seemed thorough. It concluded:

… the percentages of inmates of Roma origin … become grotesque: there are some prisons in which the inmates from the Roma ethnic group

amount to over 30%, while the Roma – now less than 60,000 in Italy – barely amount to 0,1 % of the total population.

Maybe, thought Kay, trying to get her head round this, the dire situation in which the Roma find themselves, forces them to crime, but the more she read the more she suspected these outrageous figures might be the result of institutional racism. She found many more reported incidents and individual racist attacks where civilians and police seemed to be joining forces:

A few hours after the media had given the news of the attack, gangs of racists destroyed some makeshift shelters in the Primavalle Roma camp. The police immediately completed the operation and bulldozed the camp leaving 50 people homeless (including many sick people and 20 children). As always, their only sin was being Roma and happening to live near the scene of the attack.

No way was Kay going to give up her campaign to help. No way could this kind of extreme violence be allowed to infiltrate across Europe. She gave herself a little shake; it could never happen in the UK, of course! But then she reminded herself of things she had heard people say, even in rural England. She read further:

Neapolitan magistrates recently sentenced a young Roma girl called Angelica to 3 years, 8 months' imprisonment without any proof and on the mere evidence of an Italian mother who had accused her of trying to kidnap her baby. EveryOne (Groups) had already demonstrated that the charge was unfounded at the time. Angelica's lawyer has made an official protest against this unjust verdict …

The likelihood of a young Roma girl needing another child to support, or holding rich parents to ransom, seemed highly remote to Kay.

… the "Roma racket" where, according to the Milanese authorities, children were forced through torture and threats to carry out thefts

amounting to millions of euros every year. The truth of the matter was that they were children from families living in conditions of terrible hardship who were involved in petty theft ...

Let us remember that intolerant movements have often, throughout the course of history, attributed brutal and ferocious crimes to unwelcome minorities in order to justify their repression. It is no coincidence that in the years when the Nazi-Fascists were in power Jews and gypsies were described as negative stereotypes whose rehabilitation was considered impossible ...

Kay became drawn to these articles she was finding, unable to leave them alone. Her personal worries tapered into something as small as a single grain of sand. Racism on this scale was a seemingly insurmountable problem no individual could hope to solve. Some crime was inevitable in such dire conditions of poverty, but how do the people climb out of it? Thank goodness, thought Kay with a sigh, that our country seems to be heading the right way, but progress was slow for the people involved, and fragile. Compared with this kind of horrific persecution, UK problems seemed relatively mild, but for sure she would never give up.

Max was right. She would call him tomorrow and, as a first step towards finding out who her particular persecutor was, enquire about Ted's well-being.

13

Had he been a bit harsh on Kay, Dunstan wondered? He flicked back in his diary and was dismayed to see how many weeks had elapsed since he last saw her.

As the sun rose that day to warm the fresh morning air, they had ambled round her garden together, planning new raised beds for a neglected area that lay in the shelter of an old shed. As a cold frame, it could be a veritable suntrap, they thought, opening up more opportunities for aubergines, peppers and cucumbers that had singularly failed outdoors last summer. Little did they know then what a grey, wet summer lay ahead! A blue-tit was singing its heart out high in the treetops and there were signs of collared-doves nest-building in a young Scots Pine.

They had eaten eggs Benedict, followed by blueberry muffins, a mighty fine breakfast that had cancelled out lunch completely, he seemed to remember, with a fond smile. Then he had shown her the start of his life story …

I've been so pre-occupied, he thought, so taken up with my memories, neglecting the passage of time. But how can I just brush her insult under the carpet, even if it was perhaps unintended? That was the very point, she was unaware of the significance of what she had written when she scored a line through his story title and replaced it as if she owned it.

It could be rather embarrassing now, he thought doubtfully, after such a long gap. In one way, he felt a need to see her again that was strong and urgent. Doubtless, they had become soul mates, able to anticipate what the other was thinking. More often than not, they would laugh or be appalled at the same things. Their conversations could flow like a poem, full of rhythm and resonance, each listening and responding such that he wanted to pull her close and tell her that maybe it was not too late for him to find in her what had been spectacularly lacking in his mixed-up life. It was not her outstanding hospitality, he reflected, which was a lucky bonus he did not repay anywhere near adequately. He should return her generosity, take her out, take her away perhaps, and his eyes misted over as ideas developed in his head ... No, what he cherished was her company, their shared enthusiasm and laughter, those soft grey eyes and the way her gaze sometimes wandered over his face as if ... They had undoubtedly formed an attachment, of one sort or ...

But there we are, she's clearly managing fine without me, he reasoned. She's secured help for her garden, without even letting on. She has made no attempt to contact me, well, apart from a few calls I missed on my mobile. I was full of anger at that time, as I recall, returning calls to nobody. Have I neglected her more than she has ignored and forgotten about me?

He was a little unsure of how to move forward. To turn up casually would in fact be a statement now, after so long an absence. It would announce *Kay here I am. I'm sorry I've kept my distance – now can we make up? I forgive you.*

But had he forgiven her? Not really. But he didn't want a debate about it. There would be no point. You can't unsay things.

But something had changed; he felt less hurt and outraged. Now his feelings were turning to guilt and he questioned if he should be the one asking for forgiveness. He would need to think of some specific reason to see her, to test the water, so to speak.

Hoping some inspiration in this direction would strike him soon he decided to carry on with his writing, which activity was capable of removing him from everyday life into his own private world. After a full day's work back in his clients' gardens today he now had a couple of peaceful hours before he would call it a day. He had more of Seamus's recollections to write up, but there was his own story, and all that trouble Presley had with the police and the actual day he left his family. There was so much he wanted to trap on the page so that it was there, done, over and he could move on with his life. With a smile on his lips, he put in a heading to get him going, to dive again into troubled waters.

Getting myself 'educamated' (as Copper would say)
In some ways my education just happened. One thing led to another. I ate my way through all kinds of books. For me they held the key to open doors into other worlds, and inside other peoples' heads so I could learn from them and their lives and mistakes they had made. You could travel around the world or feel what it was like to be a vet, lawyer, spy, footballer, bigamist! Oh yes, I found all kinds of reading matter so that part of me began to drift away from my own people. I will admit that, but I would always be loyal to my family and all the Gypsies and Travellers I knew because they were blood-relatives or friends like kin.
After the *Secret Garden* with all its talk of the wind wutherin', I was attracted by the title of *Wuthering Heights* and, struggling a bit with the Yorkshire accent, I ran off with Gypsy Heathcliffe on the moors as if in his tracks. I felt his pain. Then as a teenager, I got into more weighty matters, beginning to ask teachers awkward questions like, *Where did human beings come from? Is there a God?* They put me on to *The Holy Bible* and Darwin's *Origin of Species* and I guess my reading abilities had really gone up a few gears as I struggled to digest their content, eager to fathom some meaning. For what could be more important?
Still a child, months would go by sometimes when I had no school to go to. As ever we were moving around the country in our trailer that Father finally purchased through a *chop* with an old friend at the Appleby horse dealing fair.

Dunstan paused for a moment in his typing. He was flying now – so many memories crystal clear as he emerged out of his childhood like a butterfly! But, although he had more of Seamus' memories to write up, he must get things in order. I am not good at this, he sighed.

Meeting the Irish family

I was nearly 12 when it happened. It was a fine, good evening and I remember everyone feeling happy. We'd been having a singsong round the fire, our stomachs full of hot rasher puddin'. The younger men had been out doing hedge trimming, the older ones staying on the site making baskets, minding the little children. The oldest women mostly helped prepare food, cleaned up inside the trailers and wagons, wiping and polishing to keep everything gleaming but some, the grandmother age-group, had gone out with the younger women hawking different sorts of colourful flowers made of paper or wax and those wooden ones that looked like fluffy chrysanthemums.

We formed a fair-sized family group but had set up camp in an old traditional stopping-place, a beech wood clearing where we could stay out of sight for a bit. Such places were becoming an increasingly rare thing but here we felt safe for a few days. There was grazing in a nearby meadow for the horses, shelter from the wind and a stream to provide fresh water. Perfect. We were talking about how we would travel to Stow on the Wold. We'd missed the spring horse-fair and would go to the autumn one to meet old friends, mostly from Father's horse-dealing days. We had no idea if our usual *achtin tans* for breaking up the journey would still be there for us and would it be easier or more difficult to halt with motors and trailers? But we would do it somehow in a couple of days' time and were not unduly worried. In fact, we were all feeling mellow and cheerful – and then we heard the sound of unfamiliar voices coming towards us. Irish accents!

It was quite a small group, just a young man and wife with three elderly parents and five or six children, two of them older teenagers, one of whom was Seamus. They were on foot and, as they loomed up in the dusky light, to say they looked travel-weary would be an understatement. Each of them was overloaded, bedecked with rolls of blankets and all manner of ironmongery and things necessary for survival.

Father stood up to look at them. His expression was blank, not welcoming. These were outsiders, unknown to us, and we had no knowledge if they were of good character. Their pace slowed down as they gazed at our large group that formed a circle of trailers and wagons. They appeared to have no mode of transport whatsoever, not even a flat-cart, which did seem odd for Travellers, but they would have seen the wood-fire smoke curling through the treetops and heard the sound of our jolly voices.

"How are ya?" cried a man with a head of white hair. He wore cord trousers, a shirt, jumper and jacket which did not look too old but were in need of a wash. The whole tribe looked dusty.

Greetings were slow and awkward at first, with eyes darting around nervously.

"Could you tell us of some place where we might lie down for the night? Is there a sheltered spot or someting like dat?" The man's gaze moved slowly round our vehicles as he spoke. "Y'see we don't know these parts at all, not one bit and have no idea where to go."

Of course, the small group could have just pitched in a field corner or on the roadside but they would know from hard bitter experience this could incur the wrath of a farmer or the strong arm of the law, possibly even before daylight.

I saw a flicker of compassion cross my mother's face, especially as her gaze swept across the faces of the children. They wore layers of clothes and turned to face us inquisitively, the tiny ones clinging on to their mothers' legs. She must've been thinking, "They're tired and hungry and have no place to go," so she was the first one to approach, ahead of my Dad.

Soon they were sitting down round our fire, telling us their story, eating some bacon pudding we had left over and drinking tea. They had come across from Ireland months ago to get work but could find no place to stay … and I heard them talking on into the night before, by the light of an oil lamp, they put up their basic shelter tents, what we would call benders. They had thought, on leaving Ireland, they had left all that behind. I was too sleepy to hear the full extent of their tale, which is why I needed to get it from Seamus.

"Will you be tipped off here soon then?" the white-haired man called Mick asked, to which my mother replied, "We're going to Stow in a couple of days. You can have this bit o' ground here till we get back." It was typical of Mother. "I'll speak to the others – there's a few that are staying, so you'd have company." No hesitation in helping those in need and I knew even then that the memories of living in benders by the side of the road were still raw. Of course it was what happened after this that really bonded our two families.

14

Jeremy came round to see Kay one morning on his own.

"Have you a minute?" he asked politely, when she opened her front door to him.

She had only just showered and dressed and was about to have a solitary breakfast before tackling a long list of tasks.

"Of course! Bacon sandwich?"

His eyebrows flashed up approvingly and with a grin on his face he quickly followed her through to the cosy kitchen. Having put bacon under the grill, she turned to find him spreading out some papers he'd brought on the table.

"I've found out a few more things – you know, about Gypsies and all that. More of the today stuff. It's scary!" He thrust towards her some web pages he had printed out. "The way they're being treated in parts of Europe. It couldn't happen here, could it Kay?"

"I would hate to think so."

"But councils are having to find double the number of, like, plots, in lots of places and other people don't want them!" Resting his elbows on the table, he put his head in his cupped hands and looked at Kay. "Don't you think it's all just terrible?" He seemed different from his brother and sister. She could not imagine either Imogen or Tim expressing concern over social issues that did not affect them directly.

"One of the problems, Jeremy, is that some, not all, live in poverty on sites badly maintained by the councils, on rubbish sites – I mean, literally near rubbish tips, by motorways, sewage plants, marshy flood plains, anywhere that nobody else would choose to live. Unhealthy places – and miles from schools and hospitals! Then we see pictures in the media and the general public think that's how they choose to live! 'It's their choice!' I've heard people say. Well, they want to retain some aspects of their traditional lifestyle but not in squalor. And why should they? It's ironic, you know. They have such strict rules of cleanliness. They had to, to survive on the road. Elderly Gypsy folk have told me they never used to get these tummy bugs like people in houses get! Leftover food would go to the dogs, or the chickens or even Mr Fox down the road. It was never left hanging around and nothing was wasted …" Kay paused, looking at Jeremy, thinking she had spoken for long enough. She found herself getting carried away but it was good to find someone willing to listen. "I'm sorry, Jeremy – I'm going on a bit …" She rose from her seat to put the crispy bacon between thick slices of bread.

"Yum, thanks," he said, as she placed the sandwiches with a bottle of brown sauce on the table. He sat forward in his seat. "No, no. Go on. It's cool, honestly. Better than any history I did at school – because it still matters to people living today! It's still relevant. It's … political."

"Well, the authorities want to provide, but … the problem is that people generally have little good to say about Gypsies and Travellers unless they've actually met them and then they think 'Well these can't be the real ones, these are really nice people!' Councils have the power and the legal backing now but no councillors think they'll get re-elected if they say they are in favour of increasing the size and number of sites in his borough. Public opinion is always against."

"But if people knew and could understand better …" he urged, genuine concern etched in his young face. He reminded her of 1960s student protestors, activists - CND, Vietnam … independent thinkers who really cared. Now there were climate change protestors striving to do their bit for the planet. "Anyway …" he bit his lip and gave her a sideways glance. "I have a plan."

Kay chuckled. "Ooh. Is it a cunning one?"

"Extremely. Devious like you wouldn't believe!"

Kay sat down with a fresh pot of coffee. "Well, I'm sitting comfortably. You'd better tell me what it is."

Jeremy had to slip off for a moment to take a call on his mobile, giving her a few minutes to reflect on how her days rarely turned out the way she expected. *Her* plan today was, first of all, to do some gardening – there was so much that needed attention (including herself but that, she knew, was another matter). Pigeons had been attacking her brassicas which, annoyingly, always made people laugh when she told them, but it was sorely frustrating. All the sowing of seeds, tending, potting, transplanting, watering, fertilising, weeding, and finally netting them only to find the cheeky birds settled down on the net, pecking away through the holes as their own weight caused the net to sink like a comfortable hammock for them. She wondered why she bothered. "There are shops that sell vegetables," Millicent had recently dryly reminded her, possibly with just cause.

Today she was also determined to make contact with Natalie, the young person who first led her down the road into the world of Gypsies and Travellers. It was about two years ago when Natalie first knocked on her door, just a couple of days after Kay had moved from Richmond to Appley Green. Now she was thinking it might be best to contact her through Gypsy Liaison Officer, Max, (they were she believed an 'item') but this seemed convoluted, so she would at least try Natalie's mobile number first. Had she graduated by now? Was she even living in this country? Her uncertainty told her how long it was since they had last spoken. It would be good to catch up but, more than that, she needed to find out more about Natalie's father, Ted. It was so long since she had seen him and they had always rubbed along well enough, once she had persuaded him to be more sympathetic to the Travellers, as his ancestors had been. Indeed his farming family had always provided seasonal work and a place to stay in centuries past, but no longer able to sustain this tradition, he held views that had turned caustic and sharp over the years, until she had softened the edges. Until she had won him over!

Perhaps Ted was unwell, or had taken an extended holiday away somewhere. After they met a couple of years ago, when she was actively campaigning for the new transit site in Appley Green, he would call her up for lunch now and then. But, as had crossed her mind before, perhaps he now thought she had a significant other, which she knew was far from the case. Dunstan had totally abandoned her for no good reason and, she felt with a wave of sadness, would never be forgiven for that.

The letters, although purporting to be threatening, were like an annoying background noise – as she imagined tinnitus must be. The irritation needed to be cleared up and if Ted were the guilty party, she needed to know. If he was innocent, then at least he could be eliminated from her enquiries and she could move on. She had not identified any other local suspects but she would take one thing at a time. The first step was to get hold of Natalie, once Jeremy had left.

She was impressed with the digging around Jeremy had done, drilling down into a variety of websites and blogs, unearthing one or two she had never come across. He had begun to spread the word through Twitter and other social networking sites, too.

"I've always wanted to be a 'double agent'," he said, reaching for his mug of coffee and half-eaten sandwich.

Kay pulled a face, sighed and closed her eyes. "Oh Jeremy, what? *What?*" Too many films, too many computer games …

"You know, undercover reporter more like. I'm going to pretend to be a Gypsy!"

Kay pushed the hair from her face, sat back in her chair and folded her arms. "Mm. Go on." It was strange he should have said this, for it had struck her earlier on when she was drawing comparisons between him and his brother and sister, how his swarthy skin did make him look rather Mediterranean or even Asian. He could actually pass for what some people termed a pureblood Romani.

"By the way, I forgot to say before, Nathan said to thank you for sticking up for him and his mates. They were given quite a few jobs around here and it was all down to you. *He* said that – and I agree. It was. They bought some safety gear, helmets, goggles, ear protectors and all that stuff, with their profits. He showed me."

Kay shuddered that they were managing without before.

"Really? I'm glad. Sometimes you have to stick your neck out a bit."

Jeremy stretched his neck and laughed. "But, anyhow, yeah, word got round. Nathan's great – he's got a fantastic looking sister …" He took a deep breath, as did Kay, for different reasons. "Now! My plan! Like a fly-on-the-wall TV documentary," Jeremy continued. "We looked at them in media studies," he added as a brief aside.

"So what do you hope to gain from this? They won't like being filmed, I imagine," Kay pointed out, feeling slightly uneasy at her sweeping generalisation. Some individuals might relish being in the frame! What do I really know, she thought?

"No, no. This will be investigative journalism. I'm going to pose as a Gypsy and go job-hunting. Have you read this?" He rummaged amongst his pile of printed web pages, soon producing something about discrimination in the workplace and how Gypsies had difficulty in finding employment in the *Gorgio* sense, say an office job, a contract with the council, work in a shop or a bar.

"But this is complicated," warned Kay, handing the article back to him. "Often a travelling person would not be considered because their education has been disrupted or cut short …"

"I know. I get all that. But my plan is to apply for jobs that any school-leaver with no qualifications could do. Even kids who are still at school. I have friends who are students – yes, effing stoodents, and they do this kind of thing in the vacations – in warehouses, stacking shelves in shops, what my father would have called 'lowly' jobs. He was a bit of a snob – in the nicest way of course. Anyway, nothing ambitious. I'll make out I left school at fourteen, travelling with my family, but have worked as an apprentice in a load of outdoor trades like tree-felling and tarmacking. They should see I have more real-life skills and practical experience than most school-leavers and am used to grafting."

Kay shifted about in her seat. "I'm not sure about this, Jeremy."

"Why? Because you think I can't? Or it won't work?"

"I just … I …" she stuttered, unsure of her objections because deep-down she was excited by what she guessed he was plotting. "It could harm your prospects when you come to seriously apply for jobs or courses. You could damage your own reputation."

Jeremy's mouth fell open. "I can't believe you said that!"

"Oh, don't misunderstand me. I mean, because, when it all comes out of the woodwork – however you envisage that happening – you will be a self-confessed liar!"

"But I want to be a reporter, of some kind, ideally a foreign correspondent. Not that they lie – necessarily! No I don't mean that."

"I understand completely what you mean," said Kay, sympathetically. "Media coverage may sometimes distort the truth, often presenting the worst side. Thieving by Roma and child trafficking make good headlines, sell newspapers, healthy ratings. OK, all sections of society have a bad side but more often than not this is the only one we see … Anyway, sorry you've got me going now."

"Cool. You're right. But I've been looking at journalism as a career. I can write this up as an original article and, if it gets published in an actual newspaper, it'd be excellent on my CV! Wouldn't it? But, *more* than that I want to do something to expose all this prejudice. I mean, it's illegal to discriminate against ethnic groups, isn't it? So how can *I* be the bad guy in all this?"

Kay smiled and wanted to hug him. "You're right, Jeremy. I'm sorry, I was wrong to doubt you. Tell me how you are going to make this work."

"Well, as I said, I'll pretend to be a Gypsy, say I live on a local permanent site. By the way, could you give me the name of a Traveller you know there so they can forward stuff from any agencies and employers that's sent to me at their address?"

Kay reached for a used envelope and pencil to take notes. "I'll try. I'll have to explain to them what you're going to do, in case … well, I don't know, just in case." She shrugged, hoping his good intentions would not go sour or be turned against him in some way.

"I'll apply for six jobs as a Gypsy, then another six – as similar as possible but with different employers of course. With the second lot I shall be myself – just say I need to earn some money and get some work experience before deciding on a long-term career."

Such an approach could be off-putting for employers, thought Kay to herself, but perhaps not for casual work with a high turnover. As Jeremy went on to set out his intentions, she felt confident that something would be achieved from his idea, but not sure what that something would be.

15

Ruby-Ann had just left Dunstan for Ireland, after a farewell that was more bitter than sweet.

"It was so great to see you," she'd said, giving him a last kiss on his cheek, "but you were right. We've changed – well, Dunstan you more than me. Perhaps you don't realise how much. Proper *Gorjer* you are and that's for sure!"

Dunstan felt his jaw clench and heart pump hard as she said this. The accusation, 'Proper *Gorjer*', harshly emphasised and sounding different from her lips, hit a nerve and he glared at her. Deeply interred emotions slid back to a school playground, taunts for being a 'Gyppo' echoing in his head. They both stood, as sitting down had not seemed necessary for a quick goodbye.

"Don't you be looking at me so fierce!" she then said. "I can't see much of the old ways in you at all. And you've no children to pass on the way of life so you, well, Dunstan, you've betrayed us all, in my view. If you and I had married in the first place, like we should've, then my children would've been yours to pass things on to, but you threw it all away!"

"Ruby-Ann …" Dunstan began softly, looking down to avoid her staring eyes, feeling he should say something, "You *know* my reasons for leaving the family. If all that hadn't happened, I … I'd've *probably* stayed and yes, we *might*'ve been married and all you say, but please try not to *blame* me." Against his will, his voice rose and he paused to look her straight in the eyes. "If I hadn't *taken* the blame and run away, then for sure Presley would've been locked up, leaving Mother and Father with no one to help them. You know that."

She folded her arms and rested back on one heel.

"Did you ever think of the shame I felt?" she said, raising her chin.

"You were fourteen!"

"Old enough to know my own mind! *You* could've stayed!" shrieked Ruby-Ann, pointing an accusing finger at him, her eyes flashing with anger.

"With Presley in the nick! *I* wasn't old enough to support them," shouted Dunstan, feeling something snap inside. "And you remember my father with his broken leg and his bad back, he could hardly hobble along nor lift a thing. Mother couldn't have managed with no one to bring in enough money for food. Oh, Ruby-Ann, how people forget."

"Others would've helped out."

Dunstan shook his head. "They would've tried, but times were hard enough for everyone then! Presley *had* to stay with them and *wanted* to! But I knew I would manage going it alone." He thought of how he had planned to send them money, but it didn't happen for a long time. "I could see a way, whereas Presley, if he had run off, he would never have coped without family. I know he wouldn't. I was right in that. And if he had been caught then he would've been in even greater trouble."

But he could see this woman's scorn was not to be easily doused by words.

"You could've come back to us," she stated, flatly, reaching to the nub of the matter. "We never went back to that place anyway."

Dunstan went quiet. He was tempted to say that if he'd come back to them he may have been found and charged with causing grievous bodily harm, but he knew that was improbable. He was not worth police time. There was some truth in what Ruby-Ann had said and he felt guilt stir in him, uncomfortable feelings that he had learned to keep tucked down, neat, out of the way.

He recalled how they had begged him not to leave them, unable to see what would happen, not willing to see that one day he would have gone anyway.

After Ruby-Ann had left for her return journey to Ireland, his little home was so peaceful he could hear his own muted sobs as he lay with his head in his arms and gave vent to the distress he felt at this reminder of what he had done to his family. As a young man he had known he would not be forgiven easily. To go back was never going to be easy. To look Mother and Father in the eye, as he did eventually …

After splashing his face with cold water he turned on his computer and began to type.

In case I read my story when I'm senile I need to rewind a bit and explain that when I was nearly sixteen years old, Presley had been getting into some kind of bother with the police. Our entire family of some thirty or so people claimed it was not his fault. He was innocent. I was not witness to what happened but was told he and two cousins were barred from a certain village pub. The landlord said there had once been a brawl (they say it was ten years before) and ever since local people objected to Gypsies or Travellers being in the bar. They would say 'NO GYPSIES SERVED HERE.' Our two cousins, even Duggie who was sometimes quick to put up a fight, decided not to make a fuss. They left and tried a pub down the road where a local drunk picked on them. With bad feeling already brewing and a few too many beers inside him, Duggie then lashed out. He was already known by the police for his temper, never having actually broken the law, and Presley stepped in and took the blame. He convinced the police that it was actually him that had landed a punch on the drunken *Gorgio* and was given a warning. So Presley was kind of on probation and must not put a foot wrong or he could be up before the Crown Prosecution Service.

Then, thought Dunstan, the memory causing his pulse to quicken, a year or so later history repeated itself. It was another scene, a different situation, but the pattern of what took place was much the same. Presley was the one to have lashed out, without witnesses.

A group of young spivs spilled out of a village hall 'hop', a weekly dance held every Saturday, showing off, arms draped about the shoulders of girls teetering on high heels. They began name-calling across the street to Presley and Dunstan. Presley watched them silently, teeth grinding, jaw clenched. He saw them peel off in different directions and the one who had called out, "Dirty Gyppos" took off down an unlit alley. Dunstan held back but Presley, a brawny young man, saw his chance and seized it.

Dunstan took the blame. The bodily harm this time was bloody and he knew he would have to keep in hiding away from his family for some while before it blew away. For some while his family, apart from Presley, believed Dunstan to be guilty.

"It makes no difference to me," Dunstan had lied to Presley. To leave his family was the single most challenging thing he'd ever do in his entire life.

"You can't do that. I can't let you," Presley protested feebly.

"You're a bloody *dinilo*. You gotta get rid of that temper of yours. But what is done is done. Now, you've got to live with them so make out you didn't do it. Make life easier for you." Presley soon agreed, knowing how big a debt he owed his younger brother.

What he had never quite worked out conclusively was how many years' absence it needed and how many years he wanted? It was a slippery grey area that he could not grasp firmly. How long should he stay away from all the people he loved most in the world? At some point in his story, he would have to face this squarely. Now he must return to Seamus and his family back from Stow on the Wold. He poured himself a generous whisky and took several gulps before typing on.

Maybe it was their tattered tents or perhaps it was their Irishness, but whatever it was, some *muskerros* passed by and stopped to take a closer look.
This happened a few hours before we got back from Stow, four days after we'd left. The harassment Seamus' family – his parents Doreen and Aiden, grandparents Mick, Irene, and Maisie, brothers Tubs, Jimmy, Sean, and sister, Flora - suffered was hard to believe but they were ordered, practically pushed and manhandled, off the site. Uncle Ned, who had not travelled to Stow, feeling unwell in some way, stayed behind to wait for us, together with a few older ones with horses and wagons. Ned told us that it had been a right to-do, with their littl'uns screaming with fright. The police stamped on the fire and knocked over a pot of broth they were having for dinner and told them to leave. They meant for everyone to go. So, of course, my uncle and his crowd were thoroughly disgruntled by the whole rumpus. They all had to up sticks but we knew they'd leave us secret signs for the route they were taking. We'd see them before long, we knew that, and we did, not far away.
Mother and Father felt bad on all counts. They pitied Doreen, Aiden and their family and felt guilty for encouraging them to join us, leaving the whole group now with nowhere proper to spend the coming days. Some of them'd had good work lined up in the nearby village, tree lopping and other gardening jobs, mostly.
Once we'd all met up again, Father decided to call everyone together, "We got to stick together. That includes the Irish for it ain't their fault. In no way are they to blame. 'Tis anybody's fault but theirs, including our own, and that we must live with. Now, we pack up peacefully and *jal the drom* soonest."
He had to persuade our people to squeeze the Irish family into our wagons and trailers. There were some families who still had bow-top wagons and horses, which made travelling difficult, them being able to average no more than three or four miles an hour. Sometimes we would have to leave them for a few days and then come back and pick them up.
Hungry and tired, we had to get closer to towns to find work, often different work from what we'd been used to, but

it was even harder to find a place to stop, and when we did stop we were more conspicuous than we had been down country lanes. The rougher areas in towns, left after the war, were being cleared for smart, modern blocks of flats and we stood out more. Thinking back, I can see our ways of living did not blend in so well.

Anyway, Father's word was heeded for he was well respected. Over the next few months life got harder. It was a taste of things to come. Work was getting scarcer in the countryside and we had no time to find it, being often sent on our way. Most days I went out with my father, following his methods to find *Gorgios* most likely to give us work and learning how to make the most money we could out of them as best we could. A welcome smile was a rare thing in the towns where we stopped and I noticed it began to make Father gruff, moreso than before. Sometimes, travelling through villages, we would have stones thrown at us. We ate hedgehogs, rabbits, snails and nettles, with potatoes when we could get hold of them. Two babies were born and three older family members and a child died and were cremated with wakes to follow in the Romany way, bringing more distant family and friends to us to pay their respects. Some of them stayed with us so we grew in numbers. It gave us strength to stand up for ourselves.

There was little time to settle, rest or have regular meals, certainly no time for school or books or learning of that kind. I learned other things though. How to stick up for myself, to say what *Gorgios* wanted to hear, to avoid getting into trouble and to take what we felt was rightfully ours, a place to be on this good land that belongs to no man, but is God's own earth.

Dunstan closed his eyes as tears stung them, bitterness burning inside him. His hand formed a fist as if of its own will and thumped his desk hard. He took another slug of whisky, scarcely aware of its heat as it slipped down his throat.

16

Kay had spent the last few days working in the garden, digging, hoeing, raking and spreading manure. She could feel tension in her lower back and knew it was time to stop, aware that there was more work than she could manage alone. She cast her eyes over the plots of ground, once neatly divided by grassy paths now grown straggly and unkempt.

Moreover, she would produce far more fruit and vegetables than she could ever use herself. Her previous arrangement with Dunstan had taken care of the excess as he had outlets, clients and customers who bought it from him. It had all worked so well. Now the garden was becoming something of the proverbial albatross, and for what? A mountain of stuff with nowhere to go. Her freezers were filling up with this year's rhubarb and early raspberries. She would need to start making jam and preserves; friends were becoming almost burdened with broad beans and soon would be in receipt of courgettes and spaghetti squashes. Perhaps she should set up her own market stall!

After putting away her tools in the shed, taking care to lock it securely, and peeling off her gardening gloves, Kay made her way back to the house. Her landline was ringing, a sound that these days made her heart race. It could be her firstborn, Claudia, who was now heavily pregnant and so far away from her it made her heart ache. She would drop everything and rush up to Solihull if she was called, but Claudia always assured her she was 'fine'. She seemed to be learning everything from baby care books, but once her daughter held a crying infant in her arms Kay was sure a mother's experience would be required. To be a grandmother! This was a wonderful thought and she hugged the idea of this new life soon to appear with utter delight. Or, she thought, quickly prising off her muddy gardening boots, it could be Suzi, Millicent, one of the Farlows most probably Jeremy, or someone else from the village. There again, it might be Billy or her poisonous pen-pal.

Once inside, she rushed to pick up the phone with trepidation. "Kay! It's me! Natalie!" came an excited voice. Kay took the handset to one of her soft, squashy sofas in the conservatory.

"My dear girl, how lovely …"

"I was so glad to get your message. How are *you*?"

"Good. Where are you Natalie?"

There was a giggle. "Ah, you've caught me out. I'm in the bath!"

Kay laughed. "Oh Natalie, which part of the globe?"

"Oh, I'm home – well, you know, with Mother, but only just. I've been in Europe mostly, studying groups of Roma. Doing a Phd now – started on research for my thesis."

"Really? You stuck with your original passion, then?"

"I guess I did. We must meet up some time. I bet you've got loads to tell me."

"Indeed I have," said Kay, wondering how much she could confide in Natalie. "I was …er … wondering how your father was too. It's so long since I heard from him. Is he well?"

"Oh, yes he's fine. I went round and saw him last night as a matter of fact. Him and his new woman."

"Oh!" Kay physically jumped when she heard this, actually causing pain to her back which had begun to seize up from being at rest. "Well, there's a surprise!"

"He seems full of the joys of spring."

"So, come on. How did they meet and all that?"

"Oh, through Max – we're still friends when I'm around, Max and I, but there's no way we could keep things going as they were. I'm away too much. It's not fair on him, well on either of us really …" Her voice faded and Kay held on until she could continue. She wanted to hear more about Ted and his ‘new woman’. Natalie went on, “Anyway, get this! Elizabeth Hodgeley-Smith works for the council, well to be fair she’s quite high up I think. But not my type at all. Full of pomp and paperwork!”

“Oh dear – what a shame. Not someone you can see as a possible stepmother then?”

She could sense Natalie shuddering. “Oh, no way. Even worse than my real mother! Sorry, I shouldn’t have said that … Look, it was such a total bugger it didn’t work out between you and Dad. Imagine! I would’ve called you … No, well, anyway, how is the delicious Dunstan?”

“Oh …” Kay paused. “Look, let’s meet up some time and I’ll tell you.”

“You’re being very cagey! It’d better be all good. I’ve never seen such a heaven-sent coupling.”

Kay nearly choked. “Coupling?! Hey, steady on.”

“Darling Elizabeth was very interested in you, when she found out my father was still pining for you.”

“Oh no! Don’t be ridiculous, Natalie. Now this is nonsense, do you hear? He was never pining for me. Was he? Did he feel spurned?” She didn’t want to make it sound as if she cared but she did need to know the strength of his feelings. Might it have driven him to seek revenge?

She heard Natalie’s attempt to stifle a chuckle. “I think not so much ‘spurned’ – what a lovely word, as never really in the running. He knew that and was quietly resigned, despite the fact I do believe he had what he would quaintly call ‘serious intentions’ towards you.”

“Oh Natalie,” protested Kay.

“He’s not one to bear a grudge really and he seems quite happy with darling darling …they’re away on a three-week Baltic Cruise at the moment, as romantic as honeymooners.”

“Oh! Lovely,” replied Kay. “When did they go?” What she really needed to know was when Ted would be back.

“They’re about half-way through I think.”

“Lucky them.” She then moved on to fix a date for lunch a couple of weeks away and they said their goodbyes.

As Kay pottered about restlessly that evening, swaying between TV, radio, the Internet and books, she became less certain on what to do about Ted. She did not want to exacerbate the situation. If Elizabeth Hodgeley-Smith, whom she would privately refer to as Liz to save time and energy, was already jealous of the attention Ted had once given her, then it would be foolish to suddenly invite him for a tête-à-tête, even on the pretext of discussing the recent Gypsy-related report in the paper. But she needed to see him, to test him out. The more he entered her thoughts, however, as a human being and friend, the more preposterous grew the idea of him being the letter-writer. But there again, there were two sides to him. Her memory stepped back to when she had first heard him on the radio publicly accusing Natalie of stirring up trouble. That was strange to say the least. His own daughter! And it was he who had written harsh words against Gypsies and Travellers in the local paper even though he later showed great diplomacy. He was indeed an odd mixture of a man and could not be ruled out, she decided.

As she turned off the TV before retiring to bed, she made a startling connection. She'd had no letters for a while. Well, of course, Ted was away in the Baltic! It all added up.

Feeling quite disturbed by the weighing up of evidence, she would sleep on it and see if a good night's sleep might help. Sometimes dreams could solve problems, she reflected, hopefully.

Jeremy appeared the next morning with an update on his project.

"I've registered with two agencies for temp work with a basic CV – all lies!" he announced with mischief in his eyes. "Had to fill in a form. Put my ethnic group as Romany Gypsy and gave the address you told me. In the first one, the woman there, about your age, gave me a funny look, but she knows the law."

Kay nodded. "I imagine no agency would *openly* discriminate. They could be sued. Reputation ruined."

"The babe in the second place – she blushed! Actually I think she has the hots for me, you know …"

"Oh Jeremy! Stay focused, young man!"

"Anyway, *she* said she would put me forward for about six different things – I just said I'd do anything. Shelf-stacking, sweeping roads, washing-up, filling envelopes … *Anything*! But I did make it clear I had experience of garden maintenance. She suggested I try the Job Centre, but they'd see through me, wouldn't they, ask for proper ID and stuff?"

"Mm. So you're waiting to hear from both the agencies."

"Yeah. Couldn't give me any promises – what with the current unemployment rate and all that. Not the best of times to be job searching if you ask me. I guess I shall have to do this for real soon."

"You could get yourself qualified in something first. Perhaps the country will have recovered by then," suggested Kay, offering him some chocolate brownies.

His eyes lit up. "Wow! I've never had this Mumsy home-cooked style you know. I think I could move in here and be happy for the rest of my life."

"What a lovely thing to say," replied Kay, "even if for a rather shallow reason."

"Never say food is shallow." Jeremy laughed. "It's more vital than sex in my book."

"Are you like your mother? Do you remember her or …" Kay had heard that she died when he was a baby.

"I've seen photos, but no. 'She gave her life for me', as my father so often reminded me. It seemed to give him pleasure to say it." He looked down and there was a slightly awkward silence for a moment before he went on, "I am like my father apparently – my *natural* father, that is."

Kay's heart gave a little thump. "Oh! Oh dear, I'm sorry, I feel as if I've been prying."

"Don't be soft. You only asked me if I'm like my mother. As it happens your question is more loaded than you could possibly know. My father was Asian. I believe his family originated from Delhi but he lived in the Midlands somewhere. I'm the product of an affair she had with this man – whom I've never met, before you ask."

"And your mother died giving birth! Oh how altogether tragic …"

"No. No. She committed suicide."

Kay put her hand to her mouth. "Oh, no," she murmured sympathetically, feeling doubly shocked.

"I guess she was hoping I'd come out blond and blue-eyed like Imogen and Tim – living proof of their paternity. I was a point of shame my father could not get over. OK, she messed up, but Imogen can just remember when she was little, her father just used to ignore our mother. She describes it now as mental cruelty."

"Jeremy, I'm so sorry. What an unfair burden for you to live with. And certainly, well, obviously not your fault. Actually," she said, her eyes filling up a little, as she reached across the table and squeezed his hand. "I think it's made you a very special, caring person. You have empathy and feeling for others and a burning need to do something to help. That's a very good thing, you know."

Jeremy's chin wobbled and he got up awkwardly from the table, opening and closing his hands, unable to speak. He wordlessly stepped out of the kitchen and Kay let him go. He had probably not talked about this to many people, if any, thought Kay. Now she understood. She would guess he had been the victim of racial abuse and bullying at some point during his schooling and all with a distant father with a heart of stone, she surmised. She had already heard that Mr Farlow had always been away on business. She knew that. It all tied up.

Jeremy wandered back in after about five minutes. "All right?" asked Kay. "Coffee?"

He nodded. "Thanks. Anyway, must stay focused." Kay returned his smile, acknowledging that he wanted to move on, go back to the plan. "Two other agencies, I registered as myself. And I've applied direct for about half a dozen jobs from the paper."

"So now we sit back and wait," said Kay.

"That's about it. Meanwhile, I'm going around with Nathan. You know, the Gypsy gardener who did work for us. I had to work hard at this, but finally he let me visit where he lives."

"That's great. Which site?"

He described where it was, unable to remember the name. "I met his family. They were having a party and he sings, plays the accordion and guitar – not all at the same time. His grandmother is a great character. She makes things. You know …" He waved his hands around, apparently searching for words.

"What? Clothes pegs?"

"No, no. Really clever stuff. Can't describe it, but out of bits of cloth. Pictures and all framed and everything." Despite his admiration and enthusiasm, Kay could see him struggle to enter a world miles away from that of a modern nineteen-year old male.

"Collage? Appliqué?"

He shrugged. "If you say so. She sells them. And embroidery – smocking she called it. And Nathan's uncle, he looks a bit gruff, but he never stops talking – all about his day and the jobs he's done, how him and his mates felled and split eight trees, and found a nest of snakes … it's another world. So cool."

Once Jeremy had left her, with her head churning over his revelations, Kay was no further forward in making a decision about confronting Ted, once he got back from the Baltic Cruise he was sharing with Liz, his 'darling, darling'. How can she get him on his own, she asked herself, now there is another woman in his life? And how would that look? He might misinterpret her intentions and she could do without that.

"Oh Dunstan, where are you? Why are you being like this?" she suddenly heard herself say aloud, concluding that she must be going slightly insane.

17

Dunstan was making himself porridge, for it was a cool, grey day, disheartening for midsummer. He planned an overdue tour of his gardening projects today; there were some he had not checked on for a month or so.

As his van rounded a bend leading into a straight stretch of road where Kay's front hedge became visible, he slowed down. Should he stop? What would she make of it if he suddenly turned up? He had begun to realise that she probably did not realise the cause of his absence all these weeks, for he had kept his anger tight within. His foot lightly depressed the brake as he noted the box hedge was in need of trimming. He shot a wary glance up her garden path towards the house. There was no sign of activity, but it was still only eight o'clock – she may not even be up yet, or she might be in that cosy kitchen of hers buttering toast, or scrambling eggs. He smiled. Would she be dressed for her day, he wondered, or still in that bright robe thing she sometimes potters in around the house? As these fond thoughts turned over in his head, his van passed and continued on towards the village of Appley Green.

His day proved to be more physically demanding than expected, so much had been left undone for too long: laying concrete paths; trimming trees that had grown too tall; and vegetable plots, planted but neglected. That evening, after a day that left him with tight tendons and tender muscles, he grilled himself a chicken breast and fried up fresh young courgettes with chopped onion and cooked potato slices. Not as tasty as Kay's version, he decided; she would have added herbs.

Sipping coffee now, he struggled to remember what happened to the two groups – his own family and the Irish.

Though tired, he eased himself across to his computer table, switched on and read back to himself his last entry.

When Minny runs off with Sean

Minny was a troublesome little girl. Always stepping in deep puddles, running around making the dogs bark and teasing the boys. She was, however, beautiful, with dark almond eyes and long lashes, smooth skin the colour of an acorn and full lips that drove young men crazy with desire. She was too young to be kissed or loved in that way. Once she was of the right age, there would be a queue a mile long, of that Ada and Fortune were sure. Her parents guarded her, protected her and looked forward to her finding a good catch!

She was just sixteen when she went missing. Then it was rumoured that Sean, Seamus younger brother, had also not been seen for a day or so. At first people were dismayed, unbelieving; word got round and many young men were angry and disappointed that they had been outrun. Ada and Fortune made out they were distraught and angry with Minny and, most of all with Sean, but looking back I would say they were secretly delighted with the match. Sean was a good young man, helpful and respectful, although they knew Minny probably had her luscious eyes focused on his square jaw, broad shoulders and other attractions!

It was no surprise when Minny and Sean soon returned to us for the wedding and a big party. This really sealed the bond between the two groups.

Dunstan stopped for a moment to look in the box of photographs. He was sure there was one of the marriage. After a moment, he pulled out a group photo. As happy faces smiled back at him, his lower lip trembled. People from those days, decked out in their finery, smart garments replacing their everyday roughish clothes. Girls' and women's hair combed, tied back, braided and beribboned in the older fashion, or loose and curled, all looking stylish. Men in suits. That was a fine day, indeed, when the sun shone and everyone was happy. Minny and Sean with their arms linked, gazing at each other, not the camera, after their escapade to spend some private time with each other. That done, of course, a wedding was the next step!

He was reminded of other parties, the musical evenings they would have, with step-dancing, the old accordion and fiddles in full swing. Seamus and his family could launch into the most haunting Irish folk ballads and, knowing the times they had been through, everyone stopped dead still to listen, without making a sound or movement until they had reached the last note. His fingers flew as he put all this into his story.

Signs of times to come

The best times were when we went picking strawberries, cherries and hops in Kent, just like previous generations. Sometimes there were *Gorgios* from East London there too and we would all rub along together fine. And we had somewhere good to stay. We were welcomed by the farmer and everyone.

But there was a year when we went back to various stopping places at the end of the season, and we began to hit problems. Normally we could stop up in the forest, there was always plenty of space, hidden away and we'd have little trouble in finding our bit of turf we carefully placed over our rubbish, like a lid. One of our spots had been taken up by a group of Irish! Another was common land that had been bought up by the local council; we tried stopping there but were given two weeks' notice to get off. Apparently it was no longer common! Then there were some empty buildings we knew of – I think they were Nissen huts – that provided good shelter, but 'hippies' had gone into them, with their parties and flowers in their hair! Not our kind of people. We always found somewhere but we could no longer take it for granted that we would. We tried splitting up in smaller groups for a change, to make ourselves less noticeable but we were quickly shoved on.

Some years later, after I had left, it was explained to me that the wider family all got together, decided to pool their money and buy a piece of land. This they did, believing they would then have the right to park their wagons and trailers on it. The vendor led them to believe this would not be a problem, thus ensuring he got a fair price for his land! They knew nothing about planning permission, indeed in those days it was barely necessary, and they felt sure they had found their haven. It was neat, tidy and safe for their children to play. It was out of the way – quite far from schools, hospitals and shops of course, and everyone was content enough.

Much later they were told they would have to apply for planning permission which was then turned down; they had to remove their homes from their own land. They had invested hard-earned money and sweat into that patch of earth, but were forced to leave, now with nowhere at all to go.

The overall group then became larger than before, far more people than during my childhood when families would travel, work and live together happily enough. When I was a teenager, we were being moved on and we heard about evictions around the country. We would move to the outskirts of a town in order to find work and the residents did not want us there. They shouted threats at us. Police and various unfriendly *Gorgio* officials would arrive unannounced. The places where we pulled up were rough, too, bomb sites some of them, places where buildings had been demolished, or ground awaiting development, sometimes next to refuse tips or gasworks. In the days of horses and wagons, being close to railway lines was no bad thing as the track verges provided us with a good path to follow. Many folk parted with their horses once they had a motor and trailer and that was heartbreaking for they were like family! But there was always a ready market for horses which is why horse-dealing goes on to this day.

Now Duggie was making a bit at the bare-knuckle fighting and folks would come along and lay bets. People would lay a bet on anything. Could be on two flies crawling up a wall! The hat would be passed round for the fighters but more money was made – and lost – by those gambling on it. Presley had taken to bagging potatoes and manure – not in the same sacks! He would go round door-to-door and make a fair bit of *vonga,* proving himself to be a good provider for Mother and Father.

Mother would look worn out – gone were the fresh cheeks and twinkling eyes. Always the gentle smile, but most of the time I remember her as being exhausted. (I wonder now at how she stayed with her man and never once spoke about returning to her own natural family, although as I understand it, her people were pretty much split up and would not have been able to take her in.)

Due to ill health and lack of work, cousins of Father were forced to leave us and move into a council house. That was a sad day for all of us. The tears, everyone clutching each other as they said their goodbyes, you can't imagine, for it amounted to being put in prison, away from family and friends, with little prospect of work. Unable to read or write, they would have to face all the humiliation of applying for welfare support. Which was worse, taking charity or being confined within bricks and mortar amongst strangers, I wouldn't like to say. But they had to face both these horrors.

We would see them from time to time as we passed by their place and heard how local people turned them away from their shops and pubs. The children were bullied at school and were not free or safe to play outside in the street or parks. Then their young men would get into fights.

It wasn't long before large, almost permanent compounds began to show up and a new era began where old traditions were lost. Everyone closed in on each other, and some families did not get on due to past feuds. Police were not helpful.

Dunstan was feeling drained as he turned off his computer and retired to bed. With all these memories swirling in his head, he promised himself a visit to Copper tomorrow. It was a while since he had seen him. He would take that photo with him and perhaps a few of the others he had come across in the old tin box, like the one that had the old *vardo* behind the group of relatives. Copper would love that.

18

Having woken up with the dawn chorus, Kay sat at her kitchen table drinking coffee and reading the paper, when she began wondering how many more years she had left! She put down the paper for a moment of quiet reflection. This was not something she normally dwelled upon, usually too busy getting on with life. But just lately, too much of her time was spent worrying and this was not a good way to go at her age. She should shift her attention to her imminent grandchild; her social life in the village; Jeremy's project; planning a holiday and going back to Richmond to see old friends – the rich and positive aspects of her life.

So, she began to make a list of her problems and how she could make them go away. There was the phone call from Billy, claiming that she was partly responsible for his brother's death. She had heard nothing more from him but, until she spoke to him again, she would forever feel uneasy. So she must seek him out and lay this ghost to rest. Some would say this was crazy talk but, no, it had to be done to dispel the vague but weighty threat he posed.

Then there were the letters; she felt fairly sure she had that particular irritation buttoned up but it had to be seen through. It had taken another fortnight before the thought struck her with great clarity that it was not Ted who had written the letters.

Liz was the culprit, not Ted. It made complete sense: the language used in the letters and motives both political and personal; Natalie did not regard her as an altogether nice person; and there had been no letters for three weeks – whilst Ted and Liz were away on a Baltic Cruise together. When Natalie had mentioned this to her, it had led her to pin the blame on Ted again, but now her suspicions had swiftly swung round in the direction of Liz. It must be her. And she would need to be confronted, without involving Natalie. It would not be fair, she decided, to make her complicit in any way with this battle; so she sent Natalie a text: `sorry – cancel lunch for now. Will be in touch soon. K :)`

As for Dunstan, she could hardly bear to add him to her list. It pained her deep in the pit of her stomach to face that there was nothing she could do except try to forget him, impossible as that was. To have him at her side would mean more than anything, or at least on a par with holding that grandchild in her arms.

Then there was the Gypsy site; she would walk round there now to see how things were. The Irish Travellers had soon moved out of the area; where to, she had no idea. Now the Romany Gypsies who had been living there were due to move on too. They had been busy offering services to local households; their children had made a brief attendance at school and now she wondered where they would be heading.

Molly-Marie was busy struggling with paperwork when she arrived at her trailer, the interior of which was immaculate, with cream carpet and upholstery; anything that could be polished gleamed in the sunlight streaming in through the windows.

"Hey there, Kay! How's you? Sit yourself down now. Will you have a cup of tea?"

"That'd be lovely – how's everyone? Got some place to go?"

"I can stay here, part of the job. But the families have no place lined up. The permanent sites are full up already, of course, and there's no other official transient sites anywhere within reach. So – I guess they'll just have to park up and cause trouble somewhere."

Kay closed her eyes. This was bad. It was true what Max had said to her. This one small site was nothing more than a 'kind gesture'. But she would not be dispirited. Talks were going on. Things would improve, but it would take time. She was determined not to let the situation add itself to her list of personal problems. She could not keep these troubles as her responsibility any longer.

On her way back home, she had a call from Claudia's husband, Jim.

"Waters have broken, pains every ten minutes." He sounded breathless and she could tell he was driving. "On our way to hospital now. Sorry, must go."

She stopped in her tracks. This brief nugget of information filled her with delight and anxiety in equal measure. "Shall I come up?"

"Don't trouble. No point until they're home really Kay," he assured her.

This knocked her back. Surely Claudia would want her to see the new baby, in hospital, as soon as possible. Feeling rejected, she resisted arguing with her son-law and sent a text to Claudia: `thinking of you darling, keep me posted, or say if you want me to come up now, much love Mum XX` Claudia would pick it up at some point.

Life must go on. She made a call to Liz and gained an appointment more quickly and easily than she had imagined possible, for midday. A meeting had been cancelled, apparently. She could just about make it if she put her foot down. Keeping her mobile firmly switched on, she seized the opportunity but had her bag (packed with small knitted garments, baby-suits and a baby's first book) ready to shoot off to Claudia at a moment's notice.

The meeting with Liz was at her office and Kay was going on the pretext of interviewing her for a press article. Surely Liz will have heard about her columns in the local newspaper and she would be glad to give her two penn'orth on the subject of Traveller sites in the borough.

How to broach the subject of the letters would be tricky. She would employ the stratagem she had planned to use with Ted.

They shook hands, and she could see Elizabeth Hodgeley-Smith's gaze take her in from head to toe. There was a fixed smile that she thought would quickly drop once she whipped out the letter that related to the incident in the antique shop. She would show her the article first.

"What a pleasant office," said Kay, looking around the light and airy room with a view across a car park, all the while wondering if she was a grandmother yet.

"Thank you. I'm usually out and about. Endless meetings," she replied, with a 'what can you do?' expression. "But how can I help you, Mrs Brackenbridge?" OK, thought Kay, we'll be formal. Suits me very well.

Liz had tilted her head slightly, hands resting clasped on her desktop blotter.

"What's your view on issues relating to current site allocation for Gypsies and Travellers in the borough, or indeed, the county?" asked Kay.

"Big question." She answered fairly, giving a reasonable assessment of the problems and proposed solutions for the future. She outlined the national picture too. With great efficiency and preparedness, she passed her copies of various reports. Kay took notes and thanked her.

"I wondered if you saw this article in the local rag?" Kay then went on to ask.

The smile did not change. This woman did not seem so bad as she helpfully leaned across her desk to take the cutting from Kay.

"Oh, no, I don't think I did. Must have missed this. So much to read!" She put on a pair of glasses and read the article carefully, a small frown appearing. She looked up again, pushing the glasses down her nose. "That's very sad. I mean, the way people are sometimes. But I can only suppose there was an element of misunderstanding. Stems from mutual mistrust, perhaps." The smile now seemed genuine. Kay could imagine Ted and Liz having civilised conversations over dry sherry and smoked salmon blinis. "What do you make of it?"

Kay felt unsure now, but she went ahead, pulling the letter from her bag, then pushing it across the desk towards her blotting pad, staring intently at Elizabeth.

The smile faded, but not in a guilty way. Her grimace rather showed concern. "This is frightful! What is this garbage? Did it come out of the blue? Do you have a clue who may have sent this?"

"I have an idea, but I'm not sure. They seem to have stopped coming now …" Kay did not take her eyes off her, by now hoping she did not seem extremely rude.

"They? You've had many such letters?"

Kay nodded.

Elizabeth looked appalled and something told Kay she was not the culprit. "What do the police say?"

"I … I haven't told them yet. I didn't see the letters as life threatening. Malicious, yes, but …"

"I think they should know. This person could be dangerous. I don't like the personal attack on you. It's … quite vicious. Are you not afraid?"

Kay's heart sank.

After this productive meeting, that had taken barely half an hour, Kay was walking back to her parked car, quite lost in thought. Her mobile vibrated in her pocket and she snatched it. A text from Claudia's phone : `All well. Should have result v soon! Jim.` So now she couldn't communicate direct with her daughter! Her reasonable self reminded her that poor Claudia lying spread eagled in some delivery room would be in no fit state to send texts and Jim had probably had to slip out of the hospital to send her this quick reply. He was, indeed, a fine husband. She told herself to return home and be patient.

At lunchtime there was still no further news from Jim or Claudia and, feeling somewhat redundant, Kay decided to confide in Natalie about her encounter with Liz. Perhaps she should tell the police, as Liz had urged. But what would they do? What *could* they do?

"Do you want to know what I really think?" said Natalie, after Kay had poured out her story on the phone, including her initial suspicions of Elizabeth.

"Please. I'm weary of trying to untangle life for myself. I truly am." Kay sighed, all the while staring at her mobile, occasionally picking it up, willing it to ring or buzz. "You think I should tell the police?"

"No, I mean, I think I know who's behind this."

Kay sat up straight.

"It'll be my mother."

Kay's eyes widened. "Your …?"

"Yeah … she's actually done this kind of thing before. I remember. It was years ago but Dad found out she'd been calling up some woman, anonymously. Mother suspected he was seeing her, you know."

"But I don't know your mother! We've never met – not that I'd ever met Elizabeth either – and, as you know, Ted and I have never … well …"

"She knows all about you, though. And once I was telling her how fantastic you'd been helping me – well taking over from me really – in the Gypsy campaign. She heard about how Dad had intervened that night and practically saved your life – as rumour had it around the village."

"I'm lost for words! You really think?"

"It's a dangerous allegation. I mean, my own mother. Terrible! I know that, but I also know how vicious she can be."

"But she was the one who left Ted, wasn't she? For someone else? Years and years ago."

"Yep. She was." Kay could hear Natalie's voice wavering and there was a pause.

"I'm so sorry. I didn't mean to upset you with all of this." She heard Natalie sniff.

"No, it's OK. Not your fault, is it?"

"I shouldn't have bothered you …"

"Glad you did, Kay. Whatever I think of my mother I wouldn't want to see her pursued by the police, which …"

"No," Kay agreed. "And she's stopped. I mean, the letters do seem to have stopped coming. That's why I suspected first your father – I'm sorry how ridiculous that seems now – and then Elizabeth …"

"Aha! It does all tie up. My mother went ballistic when she heard Dad and Elizabeth were going away for this three-week cruise. It spelt commitment to her in big letters. Up until then she thought they were just friends and still believed Dad hankered after you, but what hurt her most, I think, is that I made it clear that I was genuinely fond of you and would've been happy to see you and Dad together … "

"Oh, Natalie …"

"Oh I know, it's all rubbish, but I guess one day I opened big mouth. Both feet in, you know how it is sometimes."

"It does seem to make sense. But are you sure?"

"I really am."

"I'm so relieved to have it solved, I can't tell you. What did she hope to achieve by the letters though?"

"Just to bring you down and stop you being so bloody good at everything."

Kay forced a laugh. "Hah! Natalie, if only you knew. My life is in tatters …" except, she thought, for one thing, her imminent grandchild. What if her run of bad luck had extended to Claudia and something tragic had happened in Solihull?

"What do you mean? Tell me."

Kay hesitated. "I … I had a vile call from a chap called Billy. He's the brother of Gary – you remember, who … fatally stabbed my husband, Marcus, before I came to Appley Green?"

"Oh my God! After all this time! What did he want?"

"Gary died in prison. I don't know how and I won't rest until I do know, to tell you the truth. I hope it wasn't suicide. Billy was blaming me for his brother's conviction because I picked up that knife as a precaution …"

"That is completely out of order! Has he contacted you since or been near you? I mean what's he planning to do? Do you know?"

Kay shivered. "No. No." She felt close to tears, and shook her head even though Natalie could not see her. "But you've no idea what a relief it is just to tell someone. I've kept it to myself."

"What about Dunstan?"

There was a long pause. "What about Dunstan?"

"Oh! I …"

At that moment, her mobile rang loud and clear and Kay hastily said, "Just hold on a sec Natalie. Don't go …" Maybe she was thinking if this was going to be bad news I need you there, Natalie. I need someone to wail at down the phone.

"Kay!" shouted Jim. There was a good deal of background noise.

"Jim …"

"All good. Took a while. Lots of pulling and pushing. Poor old Claudia, but she's fine and yes, you are the proud grandma of a bouncing boy, a bit tired but perfect in every tiny detail …"

"A boy! Oh that's wonderful … congratulations," said Kay down the phone, a sob in her throat. "Wonderful. Give her all my love and ask her to call me whenever she can." She wished with all her heart that Marcus could have lived to experience this moment; it was overwhelmingly sad that he was deprived of sharing her joy.

"We've already got photos and I've sent them to you from my blackberry – check your email."

"But when …"

"… and Claudia says to tell you he's going to be called Dunstan. Unusual, eh? Which is what we wanted, but not too weird, and she said you'd be pleased. I hope so. If two Dunstans in your life is not one too many?" Jim laughed, confidently anticipating her surprise and delight.

"How lovely. Oh I'm so very happy for you both. Give him … er … Dunstan, little Dunstan, a kiss for me."

"Now, go see him on your computer ..."

Kay put down the phone and remembered Natalie left hanging on her mobile. She put it to her ear. "Hello? Natalie?"

"Hello Granny? Yes, I got the gist. Congratulations."

"A baby boy. A boy. I've never had a boy."

She briefly Googled Dunstan to find out what the name meant. Jim was right, it was unusual. There was a St Dunstan's Hospital wasn't there? Perhaps that was where the man, Dunstan, was born. She found a reference to St Dunstan 'patron saint of armourers and gunsmiths.' She chuckled. Actually his surname was Smith, so maybe it did make some sense. Oh, now this is interesting. Dunstan became Archbishop of Canterbury in 906: 'He lived in Canterbury, delighting in teaching the young and only rarely troubling to involve himself in the politics of the realm.' Of course, she was thinking of Dunstan the man all the time she scrolled through the text, until she gave herself a pinch and considered how the name might in some way suit her grandchild. For sure it suited the man to a T ; the uncanny parallel sending a shiver down her spine.

19

Dunstan was in high spirits at the thought of showing Copper the photographs; they would jaunt joyfully together down memory lane. There was no one else left now with whom he could feel the same amount of shared pleasure.

Though reconciled with his close family as a middle-aged man, Dunstan felt that many other friends and family members had become distant. That strong feeling of connectedness that came with living the Gypsy life was frayed at the edges, for he was generally regarded as a traitor by those who did not understand he had left in order to save Presley's skin. They simply felt he had rejected them and their way of life. He knew that his long absence, so many years, could not be easily explained away, even to himself.

Throughout his life, both before and after he left his family, Copper had always been there for him, though they were not blood-relatives. On the road Dunstan's family group would meet up with Copper's folks and then on one such occasion, Copper proudly announced he had bought a scrap metal yard. His own business! He couldn't stop smiling! Dunstan recalled how everyone clapped their hero on the back and shook his hand, pleased. His own scrap-metal business, so people would be supplying him! It would help his community and he knew that. He had taken that big step and Dunstan put him on a pedestal. He looked up to Copper and turned to him in his early teens when he had a hunger for the wider world that his father had no feeling for. Some time he would need to write all this up.

Copper would remember the wedding of Minny and Sean as clear as day and would know most people in that group. Dunstan ended up with half a dozen photos ready to show Copper. No one of his acquaintance owned a camera in those days but *Gorgios* would pass by, see the pretty scene and want to take a picture. Sometimes they would offer to give them a copy, or by pure luck a family would chance upon a photo of themselves, maybe years after the event. That was rare but exciting. Photographs were precious.

Copper did not answer his mobile phone, so Dunstan sent a text, unsure if Copper would pick it up. He was probably driving or just plain busy at the scrap-yard. It was early Friday evening, the time of the week when he was most likely to be at his shack, though this was always unpredictable. "Family wants me home Saturdays and Sundays, 'course they do," he would tell Dunstan, "and workin' all hours between, it ain't possible to come down 'ere much now." If Copper was not in his rustic retreat he would drive on to his large country home. It would be good to see his family as well and they would be interested to see the photographs, he was sure of that.

After checking on Mrs Hardy's fruit cage; the Rollinsons' new poly-tunnels; and problems two of his lads were having with a client, whose privet hedge they had mistakenly trimmed too far, Dunstan returned to his mobile home to get washed and changed. He whistled, feeling brighter than he had for a while. His next project, after seeing Copper, would be to call on Kay. He was determined now. Never mind a reason; he would just do it! Life was too short to bear grudges and this whole thing was way out of proportion. His life story had sweetened some of the sourness of his spirit, by simply allowing itself to be spilled out onto the page.

Soon he was bouncing his way up the rough lane to Copper's place, the bushes so overgrown they were practically encasing his camper van. As ever, he grumbled as the vegetation brushed against the sides of his vehicle. It was soon obvious that Copper was not there. No Bramble, no car. He tried again to get hold of him on his mobile; there was a risk that he might be on his way over, so if Dunstan set off to his other home they could miss each other.

A voice answered this time, but it was not Copper's. It was female. "Hello, Dunstan. This is Sheila. Just saw the message you left earlier … sorry, I …" Dunstan knew then that something was wrong. This had never happened before; another person answering Copper's phone. Sheila was one of his daughters.

"I'm at the shack now," said Dunstan. "How's you? Is he with you there?"

"Well, he is, but … oh, *dordi, dordi* Dunstan, he's left us." Dunstan almost stopped breathing. "God bless him, my Dad passed away just an hour ago – peaceful in his bed." She stopped, trying to muffle her sobs.

Dunstan felt the blood drain away into his boots. He swayed, his legs giving way, sat down on the ground, hand to his forehead, struggling to take this in. "No. No. Can't be. Tell me it's not true …" he muttered.

"I wish I could. I wish I could, Lord love him …" The sound of Sheila crying was clear now, unashamed grief. There was a medley of voices in the background, calling out to her.

Dunstan took some deep breaths. "I'm just … so shocked, I … as much as you all must be." His voice was hoarse as he forced the words out.

"I know."

"No, it won't go in. Sheila, I can't believe it. Doesn't make sense. A fit man …"

"He was getting old, bless him. Fit for his age, yes. But … doctor said his heart stopped, sudden like, so quick. Best way to go …"

Dunstan paused. "Yes. I suppose."

"Yes."

"Please … tell everyone I'm thinking … you know … let me know when the funeral will be …"

"Course I will. Bye now Dunstan."

"Goodbye Sheila my dear. Bye, for now."

For an hour or more Dunstan sat in his van, unable to even think of driving off. He sobbed, swore, thumped the steering wheel then sat perfectly still gazing at the decaying shack, the old black kettle prop, a pile of logs, various pots and buckets strewn around amongst wood-shavings, the hazel tree already beginning to produce the first nuts of the year. He could visualise Copper sitting in one of the plastic chairs, laughing and joking … Maybe he would never see Copper's special place again.

When he finally switched on the ignition and turned his van around in Copper's yard, Dunstan knew what he must do. It was not a matter of feeling obliged. No, he wanted and needed to head off to join Sheila and all Copper's family. Once they knew the funeral date, friends and relatives would be travelling from all corners of the British Isles to sit up and share their grief with each other, then celebrate his long and wonderful life. On the way, he pulled over into a lay-by to call Presley.

He could remember as a child, without any kind of phone, word of mouth would ensure that news like this spread from one group to another faster than you could blink.

"Pres? Copper has gone. Yes. I know. Pass it on. Tell everyone. Ruby-Ann will want to come back. I'll let you know funeral day as soon as I know myself."

Clear memories flooded back of him as a *chavi* walking slowly in a line of people filing past a coffin, holding his mother's hand, unsure of who was lying inside stiff and stone cold. It happened throughout his childhood, sometimes in the woods, sometimes in a trailer, everyone dressed in black.

Copper's funeral would be huge, such a massive event for a family to cope with in their fragile, emotional state; with women kept on their feet to provide quantities of food. Dunstan had seen this many times before; it was always a priceless comfort to have the community come together. As he drove along, his vision blurred by tears he dashed away with the back of his hand, he wondered what would happen to Copper's vast estate and belongings. His sons would carry on working the scrap-metal yard, and now run it, but he had a beautiful house, home to so many family members. Not a simple matter of burning his clothes and setting fire to his trailer as custom would have it, but Copper for sure would want a traditional send off with a big fire going and everyone around it.

As the driveway to Winkfold Manor came into view Dunstan swallowed. He wasn't sure he could take this without crumbling in a heap.

He was greeted warmly by Copper's family and taken inside.

Dunstan thought his heart would burst as he entered the room where Copper lay. He stood alone by his side, bottom lip trembling, and stroked the old man's hair, laying the photograph of Minny and Sean's happy wedding day upon his chest.

20

Kay was aggrieved at not being asked up to see the newborn but did not want to impose herself. Surely a grandmother should not need to be invited! But things were different these days from when she was a young mother. A couple of days after Claudia and Suzi were born, Marcus had returned to work so she really needed her mother to help cook wholesome meals, sort out the gruesome nappy bucket and do the shopping. Now Jim would probably have paternity leave, they would use disposable nappies, order food online or by phone and have it delivered. Everything had changed. But that aside she wanted so much to hold that precious wee mite who was one quarter her genes, or however it worked out. "Shall I send the little jackets and things …or … ?" she had offered. Small garments she had made over the years ready for this day had steadily accumulated; it was old-fashioned, maybe, but gave her pleasure and she knew that Claudia would love them. And there was the lacy crocheted shawl handed down from her grandmother. "Er … no, no," said Jim, after a slight hesitation as if afraid of sounding ungrateful. "There's no rush. He's got so much, honestly." It was hard.

Suzi was coming over to see her this evening and would stay for a couple of days. They could have a proper talk about it. She would tell her to stop being soft.

Jeremy came round early that afternoon on a surprise visit, providing a welcome distraction. Once she had spilled out to him the news of her new status in life, she could focus on what was on his mind.

"So how many jobs were you offered in your Gypsy guise?" asked Kay, smiling at him as she placed two mugs of tea on the kitchen table.

"Turned down flat for all of them except one. Other applicants were 'stronger', had a 'full education' or 'more relevant experience', but remember, Kay, stacking warehouse shelves and the rest did not need either education or experience."

"OK. So you got one? That's not so bad."

"Ah no, well, listen up. Offered an interview, right? For a job doing filing! Didn't know offices still needed filing clerks like in Charles Dickens's day! So I called them, recorded the telephone conversation which I'll play to you some time …"

"I'm impressed," said Kay, offering him a plate of brioche buns, thinking how she had been filing clerk on many a student holiday job. "You've read Dickens."

He pulled a face. "Mm. Thanks," he said, taking one. "Went for an interview – just a quick chat with an office admin woman – not too demanding obviously for this kind of unskilled work. Need to read, though, with this job so they gave me a written test. I may be wrong, but I thought maybe they were hoping to trip me up. But I completed it so-so, not *too* well, so as to not arouse suspicion." He paused to finish his bun.

"So – did they seem friendly towards you?"

Swallowing, he nodded. "Yeah, they were OK. Offered a one-week trial."

"What about the other applications, with you as yourself?"

"Aha! Yeah. The control group! Well, wouldn't you know I got interviews for all of them – again just brief chats."

"Have you had them already?"

"Sure I have. I've been a busy boy!" He grinned mischievously. "They all asked me why I wanted the job. Bit of a no-brainer really. Money possibly? Knew what they were getting at though. Lowly jobs, right? Anyhow, said I was thinking about what I really want to do, and needed work for quick cash. Could've been a put-off for them even if these jobs do have fast turnover. Better for them to have someone keen who'd stick with it. But, whatever … I was offered five of the six jobs."

Kay sipped her tea, then nodded slowly. "Mmm. Says quite a lot, doesn't it?"

Later Kay walked alone around her garden, surveying its unhappy, sodden state. The predicted 'barbecue summer' had so far not materialised. In fact the sky was turning black again as if heralding the end of the world and she heard a distant rumble of thunder. As she strolled around before the inevitable downpour struck, she gave herself a chance to take stock. Her life was beginning to turn itself around, for the better, wasn't it? Actually, she thought, not entirely. The arrival of little Dunstan, whose photographs she turned to many times a day, had lifted her out of the bleak mood that smothered her so often in recent weeks, although her joy was marred by the physical distance that lay between her and her grandchild. The poisonous letters had stopped; she was confident of that but, deprived of an apology from Natalie's mother, felt somewhat short-changed. But there remained Dunstan and the uneasy threat of Billy. What could she do to bring these two very different matters to a head? The only way to dispel such problems was to confront them.

She could find out Billy's contact details somehow, through her solicitor, maybe. He might have something archived. Data Protection would not permit release of those details, but perhaps he would forward a message on and then Billy would contact her. Yes, that was doable.

As for Dunstan, she would try again to contact him. It was a while since pride had stopped her trying. It was, indeed, many weeks. If he was with this other woman, the one from Ireland, then perhaps he was too embarrassed to face her. But that did not stack up. Dunstan was a decent sort. Why had he just given her the cold shoulder? It was hurtful and perplexing.

She peeked inside a cold frame that she and Dunstan had planned together the last time he was here and caught her breath as she spotted a plump little baby aubergine. Her first!

A crack of thunder overhead made her jump. Thick, heavy drops of rain fell like shrapnel. She scurried back towards the house and, as she did so, heard a voice calling round the side. Was that Suzi? She was due later this evening but perhaps …

Suddenly, Claudia and Suzi, like some kind of mirage through the rain, followed by Jim holding a baby-carrier complete with baby, were coming towards her. Suzi was doing her best to hold aloft an enormous golf umbrella to shield some of them some of the time. Kay put a hand to her mouth.

"What? Oh. Oh, why didn't you tell me? What devilish conspiracy is this?"

Claudia rushed over to Kay, laughing. Everyone hugged each other thoroughly but briefly – as attention was directed towards baby Dunstan, even though they were by now getting soaked. They all made their way to the back door and were soon in the kitchen.

"We thought we'd surprise you," said Claudia, pulling off her jacket. "If we'd warned you, you would have fussed – cooking feasts."

"You know what you're like," added Suzi, nudging her mother.

Kay gazed into the little face, still blissfully sleeping. "He's just perfect. Beautiful. And you're well? Getting enough sleep? Fit enough to travel already?"

"Oh, mother. I'm fine."

Jim had been hanging back quietly, Kay assumed to allow grandmother, daughter and grandchild to have their emotional reunion. He was a good man. Kay gave him a special hug.

"And how is Dad in all of this?"

He shrugged, smiling weakly. There was something wrong here. Kay could sense it. She made no comment, but switched on the kettle.

They moved through to the conservatory to sit in comfort and Kay felt blessed.

“You must’ve thought it odd we didn’t drag you up to see us,” said Claudia, once they were all sitting down.

“I know. You think I’m getting on a bit for long drives on my own …”

Claudia laughed loudly. “As if! Far from it. No. There’s something else.”

21

Goodbye old friend

Yesterday I went to Copper's funeral. I could not write a word this week, waiting for the day. Because his death was 'sudden' there was a post mortem. Conclusion – heart failure. Yes, a good way to go, in your home with family all around. He had suffered from no lingering illness.

I am still shaking from the day. My hands won't stop. Once poor Copper was brought back home in his coffin, the night before the funeral, people flocked to sit up with him, to take a turn for the 'awake'. We had a few beers, his sons, Presley, Seamus and I. Got a bit maudlin, to be honest.

Come the day, I was back with near a thousand people, I reckon; some I knew, or knew of, but most did not know me and looked at me a bit blankly. They did not recognise me or had forgotten I ever existed, maybe. That was hard. I cannot lay the blame for that at anyone's feet except my own. I suspected that some people thought I was a *Gorgio* come along to spectate.

The coffin was in an old-fashioned, glass-covered, horse-drawn hearse fully rigged out with velvet, pulled by four majestic black horses, their coats gleaming like satin. The flowers! Well, you've never seen so many. There was one wreath shaped like a coffee pot, made of flaming orange flowers – chrysanthemums and dahlias. He would have laughed out loud at that! A great crowd followed the hearse on foot from Winkfold Manor to the local village church. Not too many vehicles, just a few black cars for some elderly folk, but for the rest, we walked in solemn procession. All the roads were closed off to traffic and police were everywhere – even those in plain clothes, you could tell who they were. They were all pleasant enough.

The church could only hold a fraction of the mourners – I managed to get a seat inside with the family. After all, we'd been close, Copper and I, for so many decades and his folks knew that. People talked amongst themselves waiting for the ceremony to begin; the time came within the service and prayers for Copper's eldest son, Sonny, to say a few words. A bit younger than me, he is, and everyone in that church knew him. You could tell. I envied him! I did. I felt a deep-seated wish that I belonged, as Sonny did, to all these good folk who had come to pay their respects to my best old friend in all the world.

"My dear Dad, God bless him, known to everyone as Copper, was beloved indeed. We all loved and respected our Dad, not because he made it big-time," some people laughed and Sonny smiled, but that was all right, quite fitting, "not because he had a big house and all the rest, but because to all of us he was the best father, grandfather, husband, uncle, brother, cousin, friend. He could raise your spirits with his good humour, and lift your heart with his kindness and generosity. God rest you in peace, dear Dad." It went something like that. The handkerchiefs all came out, mine included.

They did ask me if I wanted to say something about those years before his firstborn came along, but I declined. I was afraid I would break down and then, in the church, I was glad I had not accepted the offer, for many people present there did not know my face or my name.

As the tension broke and alcohol flowed, so tongues loosened up and I found myself surrounded by people as it dawned that I was Dorothy's and Derby's son. When I first returned to Mother and Father the welcome was low key, for they did not broadcast the fact their errant son had put in an appearance. So now they were full of questions and Presley told them plain how it was I came to leave, for those who did not realise how things had turned out all those years ago. I was accepted and given respect and how good that felt, I can't even describe. It was a sense of belonging I had missed all those intervening years.

This was one of those moments when Dunstan stopped to once again wonder who was ever likely to read this. Who was he writing this for, and unable to pluck any kind of reply from the air, it begged the question why? Why was he writing all these words? For himself, he used to say, and yes, it had been good therapy, he realised that long ago. But he wanted more. He wanted to hand all this down to someone. The barrenness he felt at having no children of his own filled him with something close to despair. It was too late now.

22

"Jim's department has been closed down," began Claudia. She and Jim sat close together on a sofa in Kay's conservatory and she reached out for her husband's hand. Jim was in the manufacturing side of telecommunications; that was the extent of what Kay knew or understood about his work.

Jim offered a mirthless smile. "Couldn't have come at a worse time," he added, his gaze shifting towards little Dunstan, who was still asleep. "But there we are. So, no alternative jobs within sight. We're a bit stuck really."

"I'm so sorry," said Kay, shocked beyond measure.

"We've talked it through and through. Should I go back to teaching now and Jim look after the baby? Shall we live off the redundancy for a few months, stay where we are and hope that something turns up? Try consultancy for a while? Move abroad?" She shrugged.

Kay's heart sank. She tried not to betray any trace of alarm. "So, have you reached any conclusion yet?"

Claudia and Jim looked at each other as if braving a joint parachute jump. "Mum, there's more chance of Jim transferring his skills in London."

"I'll actually go back to what I used to do, before the Solihull job ..." put in Jim, nodding. "Network security – well, along those lines. Get myself up to date."

"He's found one or two possible openings already." The dark cloud in Kay's heart suddenly turned into something fluffy and bearable. "The problem is that London is so expensive and, for the time being, we wondered if we could stay with you until we find somewhere of our own."

Claudia biting her lip, Jim and now Suzi, exchanged looks and had apparently ceased to breathe.

"I can't think of anything I should like more!" cried Kay. "You half scared me to death then. I thought you were moving to Siberia or somewhere. For heaven's sake, of course you can."

"Oh, Mum." Claudia jumped up and gave her a hug. "We thought it might be a bit much."

"Give yourselves as much time as you like. Jim, you find your feet. Get a place of your own when you can, in your own good time."

"We'll have to sell up, and we could put most of our stuff in storage …"

"Lose a bit of money on that, unfortunately, but can't keep up the mortgage payments obviously," added Jim.

"Any chance of some tea?" asked Suzi. "And possibly, cake?"

Little Dunstan then gave a loud squall and Kay suddenly found herself the recipient of a hot, cross baby with fists, who needed changing and feeding.

The next few days swung by in a blur, a merry-go-round of activity. The largest spare bedroom was organised, then filled with baby clutter; Kay was content to mind baby Dunstan now and then and share her kitchen with Claudia who insisted they did not expect to be waited on.

Kay was still privately thinking about Dunstan, the man, and Billy, brother of Gary. She did not confide in Claudia, for so many reasons, although when Suzi had asked after him she came close to telling her about Dunstan's strange behaviour. It was about a week after the big arrival when Claudia announced they would be visiting Jim's parents who lived in a small cottage in Hertfordshire.

"It'll give you a bit of a break and we need to explain things properly to them, too. They'll cope with us for a few days."

A sudden silence reigned in Kay's house, in noticeable contrast to the recent domestic hubbub. Her solicitor had contacted Billy on her behalf and she did not have to wait long before Billy called.

"I got your message. You want to talk?" he asked.

"Yes. You seemed very … distressed when you called before." She chose her words carefully, avoiding ' bitter' and 'angry'. "Understandably, of course. I … I'd like to understand a bit more, you know, what happened to Gary and …"

"OK. Meet me, then. I'll tell you all I know. Everyfink."

Kay's heart was now thumping hard. His original call came flooding back, the words he had used: *You owe us, you do. Gary … never meant to kill no one and now, gone for good. No chance to make good. All fanks to you, you bloody, fucking bitch!* No, she certainly did not want to invite him into her home. This was not a social visit. She would agree to meet him perhaps in a public place, where there would be plenty of witnesses, in case …

"You could come to mine. Hackney."

"Er … no, it would be easier for me to come to south London. Perhaps a pub or coffee house somewhere near the river? Within walking distance from Waterloo?" Kay suggested, nervously. "I try and avoid using the Tube these days," she lied. She thought The Anchor pub was not too far from the station and gave him directions.

"Right. When? Tomorrow?" He's a bit keen, she thought. A bit too keen.

"No, I'm rather tied up for the next few days." She would prefer to have Claudia and Jim at her house so that someone would be aware that she had gone to London to … to meet a friend. Just in case … If she were to go while they were away no one might notice or particularly care if she did not return. Now she was being over-dramatic. This was just playing safe, she told herself, firmly. She had heard of lone workers who took such precautions routinely; people who went out to lonely, desperate places to see clients had to log their whereabouts at all times. It would be madness not to.

They agreed on a day and time. It would be coming up to lunchtime. Crowded. She would be quite safe. She dropped Natalie an email to let her know what her plan was; it helped just to share this with someone.

23

A couple of days after he had written up his account of the funeral, Dunstan was trying to sink back into his life story, to move on from Copper's 'sudden death'. But reverting to his teenage years was even more emotional now, his head whirring with scenes of yesteryear, still deep waters churned up by the gathering.

A faint tapping on his door, which he had left open to allow a warm breeze to waft inside, caused him to start and look around. Natalie was cautiously peering in.

"Hi Dunstan. I wasn't sure which one was yours! It must be years since I came here. When I was still at school, probably!"

He blinked and gave himself a little shake, as if emerging from a dream back into reality. "Then it's been too long. Come along in now. I was just feeling a bit lost and lonely, so it's nice to see a fresh, young face." He briefly filled her in on Copper's funeral as he made some coffee.

"You don't do things by halves, do you?" she said, smiling. "Your community, I mean."

"We know how to give an old man a good send off, that's for sure."

"Course I never knew you were of Romany blood, you know, even though I've known many who are ever since I was a child. But, I always felt there was something of the Gypsy about you. The distance you put between yourself and other, your ways … oh, I don't know." She shrugged.

"Well, by and large, I'll take that as a compliment. Now what brings you round here? Without sounding rude, I take it you had a reason for calling after so many years!"

"It's about Kay."

Dunstan felt himself being scrutinised. "Ah."

"Yes. It's none of my business. I don't know what's going on. And neither does she! She knows about this other woman, of course, what's her name? From Ireland?"

Dunstan opened his eyes wide. "What 'other woman'? Who?"

"Whoa! Don't shoot the messenger! Seamus showed her a letter – Ruby someone?"

His mouth fell open. "What! Oh bloody hell! Kay thinks she …? Oh, *dordi.* I should've gone to see her long ago, even though I sense she doesn't want me. I was about to, you know, then there was the funeral. Kind of threw me backwards."

"Anyway, I'm concerned about her."

"Is she ill?"

"No. She seems very well, but I'm afraid she has an uncanny knack for putting herself in danger." They exchanged looks but did not need to speak of the famous incident when Kay's husband had been murdered; or the time Joseph and his brothers, angry young men, came round to her house in search of the young woman she had kept in hiding.

Dunstan raised his eyebrows expectantly. "So what's she done now?"

"It's what she's about to do! It's no good me telling her not to. I have no right to do that, but I felt I should pass on something she told me. I don't think anyone else knows."

"Go on."

"She had a threatening phone call from the brother of the person who murdered her husband. Billy."

Dunstan paused to take this in. "Really? After all this time? Over four years now isn't it?"

Natalie nodded. "He called some weeks ago to tell Kay that Gary had died in prison – now she's anxious to know more details …"

Dunstan smiled fondly. "Curiosity killed the cat."

Natalie swallowed. "My God, I hope not! But I am a bit worried actually, Dunstan. That's why I'm here. She's now deliberately got in touch with him …" Dunstan stood up and began pacing, "… and they've arranged to meet. It's so obvious Billy's got an agenda. You know, some other motive. I mean, I sometimes think I'm naïve, but dear Kay is too trusting by half." She went on to give him the details of where and when.

"Tomorrow then?"

"I should have let you know before, but I wasn't sure if I ought to interfere in any way at all. Time just disappeared."

"Mm. It has a habit of doing that. As you say, quite pointless anyone trying to prevent her going. Huh! Least of all me." He rubbed his chin pensively, stubble rasping against his fingers.

"Should we call the police?"

"No. If she'd wanted the police to be involved she would never have set this meeting up. She'd have called them long ago."

"Mm." They both fell quiet for a few moments thinking. Then Natalie said, "What if we went along and … sort of spied on her?"

Dunstan nodded. "I think, in her best interests, that sounds like a fair plan."

Natalie then punched the air. "Damn it! I can't. I'm promised elsewhere, just remembered. Seminar. People coming from Eastern Europe. I have to be there."

"Well, don't worry. I'll go. I can postpone what I had scheduled for tomorrow. Just needs a couple of phone calls. Chances are I won't be needed but I can at least intervene or call the police if I see her being harassed in any way … and you'll know where I am, should *I* go missing. What's your mobile number, Natalie?" He gave Natalie a wry smile as he reached for his own mobile, denoting the absurdity of this notion, and punched in her number.

That evening Dunstan found it hard to stop thinking about what he and Natalie had agreed upon. He switched on his computer as usual after his meal, and his hand reached for the phone. He considered sending an email. Should he reason with her, be persuasive? How would that look after so many weeks? There would be a wall of silence, or of resistance. *Who do you think you are, Dunstan, telling me what I can and can't, should or should not, do?*

He would stick to the plan and meanwhile try to lose himself in his story. He looked back to where he left off before recounting Copper's funeral while it was still fresh in his mind. It would be difficult to go back in time again. Seeing so many people from his past had altered his perspective somehow.

He must explore his reasons for not returning to the fold as a young man sooner than he did. He looked out photo albums of his backpacking days where he had inserted brief travelogues; South of France, Sicily, Morocco, Turkey. This could run up a few volumes. He would have to skip a few years, the years after he had first escaped the law and assumed the identity of a *Gorgio*, finding casual work as a travelling student might – washing-up, picking fruit, waiting at tables. They had been good years, but at times lonely, despite all the short-lived friendships he made along the way. Once he got too close to people, then the awkward questions would begin, and he would move on.

When he came across Roma in Europe and heard about their harsh treatment and saw first hand their desperate plight, he did not know if he was tied to them in any way. Where did he belong? By the time he was twenty years old, there were times when he found life in some ways easier as a *Gorgio* and grew to like that side of it. *Finding life in some ways easier as a Gorgio* ... What was he saying? What the devil was he thinking? No, he was never a *Gorgio*, and never would be, but it was so easy to let words distort what you mean. No wonder Kay had not realised the impact of the words ***Gypsy Turned Gorgio***.

By living in a tent for four years, he had saved enough to be able to rent a flat on his return to England and fit it out with a bed, table, chairs and other basics. How unreal that felt! He could remember it so well. Switching lights on and off, locking and unlocking doors, post suddenly appearing through his letter box. The noises of strangers moving about above, below and either side of him. Sometimes a raised voice, children crying, TV on too loud, a party that went on until late. His flat smelled of former occupants. The harsh glare of street lights, the screech, whoosh and roar of buses outside as they braked and revved their engines kept him awake when he would lie and wonder what he was doing with his life. Traffic fumes polluting his space as soon as he opened a window. This was temporary, he decided, for sure. Would he go back to his family or get a job and work towards a successful lifestyle, *Gorgio*-style? He was torn. He was confused.

What could he do? What skills did he have? How could he make money, enough to maybe even buy a house? Did he want a house? Did he want to become a house-dweller? Splitting himself in half, he played with these questions. How would he know where happiness lay if he did not try something different? To be anything other than self-employed – it would be like reinventing himself! He could suffer that only as a stepping-stone to getting his own business one day, of some kind.

Thus he decided, sitting alone in that gloomy apartment, to 'get a job', work his socks off and see where it led him. Of one thing he was absolutely certain; if or when he returned to his family, he must re-appear as a successful man. To face Mother and Father, he would have to be able to hold his head up high and say, "Hey! Look what I did," and ply them with money and gifts. The Prodigal son, isn't that what the Bible says? For what other reason could possibly keep him away from family, if not to make money to send home? All that business with Presley would no longer wash. Of course not. He was not a 'wanted man'; not that important.

Dunstan could picture now the advert in what was then the Labour Exchange for a 'Trainee Welder'. He knew facts about metal just from listening to Copper for years on end, so he bluffed his way into it, without any practical experience, skills or knowledge of welding! He would listen and learn.

One day, after he'd been there about a year, getting on well, he got talking to a bloke called Christian and it all came out. He felt a need to talk about Copper and how his hero acquired his own scrap-metal yard.

"Some Travellers do make it, you know."

"Oh? Gypsy, like, you mean? That's interestin'. How'd d'you know him, then?" Christian seemed interested and sympathetic.

"Oh, always known Copper – since I was a nipper."

"How come then – they're a bit secretive aren't they, them pikeys?"

Suddenly it was out and all round the workplace, unbeknown to Dunstan, until his boss found out and made life difficult for him. He remembered when he had shared the truth with Kay, how difficult it was to tell her about being blamed for a crime he did not commit. For years this painful memory had filled him with fury and crushed him with hurt; it made his heart race. Although relatively petty it was enough for him to be given his cards without any hopes of a reference.

He would give just a brief account of this in his story; such bad luck would make miserable reading! And an even smaller mention of the work he finally got in that dark, dingy warehouse where desperate people worked. Two years ago, Kay had listened to all of this and it had felt so good to tell someone. She seemed to understand that he could not go back to his family a failure.

How I worked my way up

Once I was working in the warehouse, at the bottom of the heap, I saw this was my last chance. I strove to please everyone, co-workers and supervisor alike, and was polite to managers whenever they passed through. No way would I reveal my ethnic identity again! Meanwhile I saved and paid for a college course in bookkeeping and office administration. I could see this might lead to a way to earn more money and even then I wanted to be in a position where I could improve conditions for the workers. I wanted people to respect my word, my opinion. I was eventually successful in applying for a routine sort of office job there, did well at that, and after four years was promoted. After a further eight years – I was thirty-four – I was appointed Operations Manager, the job I'd had my eye on for years. I could go back to my family a proud man!

But what then? Leave my job that had cost me dearly in blood, sweat and tears? Working for other people, which went against the grain so hard? And without making those improvements I'd wanted to make for such a long time?

Not long after this, I met Margaret, the company's solicitor. We were forced to spend time together checking over contracts and other legal documents, often over lunch. Within six months we were married; she thought I was old-fashioned and kind of sweet, wanting to do things the proper way, but it was my roots. I was a gentleman in that respect!

Dunstan hesitated before putting in the next heading, but not for long.

Living a lie

Married, living in a three-bedroom suburban house with a garden. At last I had my 'bit of earth' and could keep it tidy and make it look colourful the way my wife wanted it.

There were dinner-parties, the golf club, holidays abroad. Margaret played bridge and drove a convertible sports car in the summer, wearing a silk scarf to keep her long wavy chestnut hair from flying around, designer sunglasses to protect her eyes, and sunscreen to save her skin from cancer. No babies came along – Margaret found there was a medical problem, but it did not seem to bother her. I tried to hide my excruciating disappointment.

No one knew, not Margaret, our circle of friends, nor people at work, that I had once lived in a bender tent; my grandfather was a horse-dealer; I still could not take to using a bath, always preferring a basin or shower.

One evening we were having a meal to celebrate our tenth wedding anniversary, giving us a rare chance to really talk to each other. Margaret had been telling me how she hoped one day to become a QC – Queen's Counsel. It would mean more studying, more qualifications. I looked across at her. She was wearing a black cocktail dress with light grey pashmina softly draped around her shoulders. She looked stunning and she gazed back at me with love in her blue eyes. We were surely unshakeable.

"I want to tell you something," I said, actually, and of course naïvely, looking forward to my revelations.

"Oh no, you're leaving me!" she teased. We both knew I would not do that.

"There's so much about me you don't know," I went on. I felt then that I really wanted her to know about my real life – all those things I've written about here. I'd always said my parents were dead and other relatives sadly had either died or we had just lost touch. She was never curious and was perfectly happy to have the quietest register office wedding you could ever imagine.

"I'm a Gypsy," I stated proudly, with a broad smile. She stared at me uncomprehendingly. "Of Romany ancestry. Half-Romany at least."

"Don't be absurd."

"Some would say I was a 'didakoi'."

She gasped. "Why would you say such a thing? Who on earth gave you that idea?"

I chuckled, still thinking she would warm to the idea, be somehow proud, intrigued.

"Yes! I want you to meet some of my family. Those still living, at least! It's time I went back."

She visibly shuddered. "Well!" she said, forcing a smile. "That'd be nice. Where do they live? What a secret!"

Maybe it was true that she had been having an affair all along, as she claimed a few weeks later. I'll never be certain. But if it was true, she had kept it extremely well hidden. I can only surmise that my close family and other relatives tipped her over the edge, throwing her world and social status upside down. Suddenly I did not fit the image she had in her head any more and one day I returned home from work to find a note to say she had left me.

24

Kay heard through Jeremy that Imogen had found work mucking out stables but was not earning very much. She had also started a hairdressing course with plans to work eventually on cruise-ships, the total package very nearly achieving her wild ambitions.

"But, hey Kay, look at this," he went on, opening up a window on his laptop.

She reached for her reading glasses.

"It's Nathan's blog and see this too." He moved to a Facebook page and Nathan's profile on Twitter, then various links into websites Kay knew nothing about.

"I'm stunned. So Nathan may be a hedge-trimmer by day but he also appears to be a political journalist!"

"Yeah. We're working on all this together, but he's the one with the ideas and views. And the real-life stuff, you know. That's what makes the difference."

Kay read a selection of what Jeremy was displaying for her and was moved. The words were well crafted, countering opposition but keeping impartial. "Good journalism," she remarked, but she could read between the lines. He was able to express the sentiments, the repressed emotion and often outrage, of his people so much better than she could ever hope to do.

She looked at her watch. "I'm sorry, Jeremy, I have a train to catch, but keep me up to date with this, won't you? I'll keep following this myself anyway. All great stuff. Tell Nathan." She felt she sounded patronising. Why should Nathan need her approval?

Before long Kay was on her way to meet Billy. Claudia and Jim believed she was meeting up with old friends from

Richmond, and Kay hoped they had taken it in that by lunchtime she would be in a pub by the River Thames in London. She mentioned The Anchor several times the previous evening, wishing they would note the name of her whereabouts, but they were preoccupied with their own plans.

"Funnily enough, we're going up to London tomorrow too," Claudia had said, as she held Dunstan over her shoulder, patting his back, before optimistically putting him down for the evening. Kay felt a flutter of panic. Now they would suggest meeting up for afternoon tea or something, to which normally she would readily assent. "We've so much to get through. Jim has loads of people to see. Appointments, you know, while Dunstan and I …," in a nanosecond of misunderstanding, Kay jumped at the mention of Dunstan's name, "… are going to do some research into London properties while we're there, although I think we shall be looking around here for somewhere to live, you know? I fancy the country, once we can afford to buy somewhere."

Kay nodded, relieved and selfishly delighted that she might have her daughter and grandson living within easy reach, unless they eventually settled on some place north or east of London.

"Everywhere's expensive I suppose," said Kay.

Claudia nodded with a sigh. "Weighing up commuting costs against living in London – it's all a nightmare and, as far as we can see, completely out of our reach, whatever we do." She threw up one hand in despair, whilst still holding the baby to her shoulder. Kay feared she might drop him.

"Well, don't panic, darling. Of course you want your own place, but you know you're welcome to stay with me for as long as necessary."

Claudia nodded and sniffed as she left the room cradling Dunstan.

As the fast train streamed through Woking and Surbiton, stopping briefly at Clapham Junction, Kay imagined how this meeting might go. She wanted to find out more about Gary's death, hoping he was not driven to take his own life. Whatever Billy's reasons for meeting with her, if he comes across as intimidating, she can always walk away. If he is threatening or actually violent, then she would call the police. There would be a crowd of people. Anyway, what could he do? Her pulse quickened and she smiled sociably at the suited businessman sitting opposite her, who had just closed up his laptop, wondering if fear was written on her face. To prevent her from simply walking away, Billy would have to assault her in public. She told herself not to be a drama queen and checked her mobile was switched on.

She allowed her reveries to stray into Dunstan the man territory. Presumably he was still working the various gardens in the area, whilst managing his teams of young men, all the while striving to sort out their chaotic lives and troubled minds. If he had become neglectful, maybe he would be stripped of his OBE! When today was over, she wondered if she should make another effort to find him, indeed the happy couple Dunstan and Ruby-Ann, to find out what was going on.

25

Dunstan woke early and could not get back to sleep. He felt confident that nothing violent would happen today in London but there lurked a feeling of unease at what he was planning to do. To be hiding behind pillars and bushes like a private detective! If Kay knew, he could imagine how her eyes would flash with fury at the sheer effrontery, the interference, the insult of being treated like a child suspected of misbehaviour! Well, he would make sure that she never knew, unless of course he was actually needed, but he discounted this notion almost immediately.

During a spare hour before breakfast he returned to his story. He wanted to wrap up this era of his life. Nobody would be particularly interested and it was no longer fulfilling the therapeutic function that reliving his childhood had provided.

Life after Margaret

Certainly the absence of Margaret, my wife, left a void that needed to be filled. Life became aimless. I returned to my family and that was a big day, indeed. Apart from one brief rather sheepish visit this was the first time I'd seen them properly since I left at sixteen.

Once I had located them again, which was not easy, there was much explaining to do, even more of a challenge. They knew about me taking the blame for Presley's fight and for that I'd become something of an absent hero, but of course, I can see now, better than I could at the time, that I had never conveyed to them my reasons for not coming home sooner. It was a matter of pride and I had to eat humble pie. They got impatient with all the analysing, although I think it all needed to be said. Mother threw her arms around me and sobbed at one point. Father punched my chest, unable to speak. I tried to imagine what course my life would have taken had I stayed with them; I was too young for them to be dependent on me. Presley would have been arrested; they would've been pushed to the brink and ended up in housing of some kind, away from family and friends and in the middle of an estate where they were not welcome. Unable to earn a living, most probably, Father may've been forced onto the state for financial help, knowing that the rest of their family group were coping without. They may have plunged into a downward spiral.

At least they were alive and, though old and not very fit when I returned to them, they were reasonably well for their age. As for me, I would not be the person I am today and there are pros and cons about that, I guess!

I could not give up the living I had then, but I was at last able to help them; so we continued like that for a while until they announced they and Seamus' family were going to Ireland because some Irish relations were in need of support. At their age, I was worried it would all be too much for them, but "Hey, we're all travelling people, are we not? A bit of travelling'll put new life into old bones, that's for sure," said Seamus. Going back and forth across the Irish Sea was something they had done all their lives.

Meanwhile, I noticed problems going on in the warehouse. There was a rapid turnover of workers because, no matter what you did, at the end of the day, carting around bags of fertiliser and chemical agricultural products was hell enough to make anyone flee as soon as they had a better offer. Changing things was no easy matter. Many of the low-paid, unskilled, young men in the warehouse who came and went were unstable, living chaotic lives ... with stories to tell. Some had run off from violent families or a failed relationship and were homeless; others were emotionally scarred from childhood abuse. There were drug addicts, and youngsters who had got in with the wrong people, then been in trouble with the police.

I decided to help, first with a charity for the homeless, then engaging them myself in gardening projects and setting up my own charity …

He knew he must leave this to catch the train, so briefly summarised.

In a way I was going back to what I'd learned as a young child – tree surgery, garden maintenance and all that, as my father and uncles did. That's how I came to be doing what I'm still doing to this day and the rest, as they say, is history. I found I was growing an excess of food so set up a fund to help the charity, by supplying local outlets. I was awarded an OBE but I kept quiet about that – until I met Kay.

He looked at his watch and, after toast and coffee, he left for London.

24

The wind was blowing Kay's hair into an unruly tangle as she crossed a road bridge by the Shell Centre building. She wended her way through a market full of garlicky smells she would normally have savoured with enthusiasm, and bypassed the Festival Hall and Hayward Gallery where in other circumstances she would have been intrigued to know what exhibitions or performances they had to offer. Soon she was by the river, passing the graffiti covered skateboarding area, and plane trees whose bark was for some reason swathed in red and white polka dots, making her feel slightly Alice Through the Looking Glass-ish. She had happy memories of this area from days with family and friends, and Marcus of course; visits to the Tate Modern and The Globe theatre. This stretch of Queen's Walk seemed longer than she remembered it, however, and she quickened her step, twisting her ankle slightly on a patch of uneven block-paving. Now past Gabriel's Wharf and the Oxo building, Design Centre … she looked at her watch and hurried on. She passed by some buskers who were making joyful music. They sounded and looked like Eastern European Gypsies but there was no way of being sure. She stopped to throw some money in their tin and they smiled cautiously.

The walk took her about half an hour, certainly longer than she had anticipated, but she was not late. Not early either. There were a few people in the sunny seated area outside overlooking the Thames. Was he perhaps already there, she wondered, watching her? Kay entered the saloon bar casting her eyes around for a young man who would be looking out for her. Already it was buzzing with humanity, what appeared to be working people, shoppers and tourists, a mixture of ages, races, suits and jeans. It struck Kay as busy and noisy for half-past twelve. Billy said he would wear a black and white tee-shirt with a skull on the front. Darkly appropriate, thought Kay when he said this, but at least it would be distinctive. Was this the kind of place where he would normally hang out, she wondered? She suspected not. She told him she would be sporting a cherry red jacket. It seemed enough for him to go on, although she did wonder afterwards if she had been insensitive, wearing a bright colour to face what was going to be a sombre exchange. She scanned the women within view to see if there were any other red jackets and she winced slightly as she spotted one; a woman about her age in a maroon leather jacket, with a group of women all sharing a joke at a table in a slightly raised area by a window.

To be less conspicuous, she stopped loitering and went purposefully to the bar to order an orange and passion fruit drink. With it being lunchtime, the young Australian-sounding barman seemed ready to take her food order, but she said she would leave it for the moment. The décor had a nautical flavour, as its name implied, with dark ship-like wooden fittings and reddish ceiling. Her stomach felt as if she were on a rocky boat. She had been insane to come here alone to meet Billy. He may have his entire family, a posse of brigands, brawny men, around the corner ready to surround and kidnap her. With the point of a knife poked teasingly into her back, she would be powerless. Threats might hang over her to eternity unless she complied with his demands. Only now did she think of these things.

She paid for her drink, took it and the change from the smiley Australian and saw a small table become free as a couple left. She walked up two steps to it, keeping alert as she went and, once seated, had a good view of the lounge area. The woman with the maroon jacket was moving to the bar with a friend following behind, carrying lunchtime menus. They looked ready to order their lunch. Then Kay caught sight of the skull and she felt as if someone had thumped her in the chest. A tall, slim man, neat in appearance, short hair and a piercing in one eyebrow, but so what, thought Kay, nothing unusual about that. He approached the woman waiting to be served at the bar who grinned good-naturedly and shook her head. Kay felt she must get up but her legs felt weak, unable to support her. Then he turned to swing a steady semi-circular gaze until it came to rest on her. She swallowed, her mouth dry. He was coming straight over to her. She took a sip of drink as he approached and found the glass was shaking.

"Kay Brackenbridge?" he asked, neither smiling nor frowning. He probably had some idea of what she looked like anyway, from the trial; though she could not recall him at all. At the time he would have been lost in a sea of faces in the courtroom.

She nodded and stood up, her gaze, equally non-committal, briefly lowering to his tee-shirt. "You must be Billy."

She expected him to suggest they move out. It all seemed too normal, to be eating and drinking at a table for two in a London pub, an unfit setting for the conversation that was about to take place. But he sat down, calmly reaching across to a neighbouring table for a menu.

"Have you ordered food?" he asked. Kay was stunned by his easy manner.

"Er … no. I thought I'd wait till you …" No way could she force anything down her throat still constricted by fear. "Well, wait a while anyway. Until we've had a bit of a chat?"

He shrugged. "OK. Right. I'll just get meself a drink." He stood up. "Can I get you somefing?"

She lifted her nearly full glass and shook her head. "I'm fine."

She tried to think through what she wanted to say. She was sorry about Gary. Had he been ill or …? Were the other inmates violent towards him? But, she kept thinking, he did actually stab my husband to his death in front of me and ran off like a coward. Let us not forget that. She felt anger and hatred for Gary, strong, unforgiving feelings, rise up inside her as stinging tears rushed to her eyes. No, don't break down now. This was not a good time. Trying to steady her nerves, she stared at the inscription on the menu cover, claiming a connection with a Dr Samuel Johnson quotation: 'There is nothing which has yet been contrived by man, by which so much happiness is produced as by a good tavern or inn.' It posed the idea that he may have had The Anchor in mind. On another day, perhaps, she could agree; it may be true unless you were a Gypsy a few years back, thinking of the 'No Gypsies Served' signs she had read about. Her mind was racing. She focused hard on the door and watched people as it repeatedly swung open and closed.

Then he was there, this man, this Billy, Gary's brother, now drawing up his chair opposite her, placing his pint on the beer mat. His hands did not look like working hands. Not rough, but smooth, quite pale and slender. He was clean-shaven.

"What do you do for a living, then Billy?"

"Journalist. Well, kind of."

Suddenly the agenda was rewritten; she wondered what kind. "What! You mean, you …"

He smiled, revealing a set of good teeth. Somehow this surprised her as she expected him to have a set of stereotypical drug-rotted teeth, because he was the brother of a dead drug addict.

"No!" He smiled awkwardly. "I can see what you're finking. Nah, not workin' at this moment, if that is what's going through your mind?"

"Too ready to jump to conclusions." Naive and gullible, too, so I'm told, she thought, warning herself against taking his words at face-value.

"I'm a telecomms journalist. ICT, networks. Techie stuff!" Same line of business as Jim, Claudia's husband, she thought briefly. "Mrs Brackenbridge …"

"Please call me Kay."

"Kay, the phone call I made to you before. I was pretty screwed up. Bladdered, if you must know."

Kay raised her chin. "Uh-huh?" She would let him do the speaking first.

"Yeah. The family had just heard the news. I'd never seen our Dad cry before – you know he's the one with the fists, not tears. And Gary's little wife, Sasha, she's a cute girl all right – only nineteen but she took him on, was determined to make him come good, you know what I mean? She was the only one who could reason wiv him."

"Gary was married? I didn't know. He seemed too young."

"He was twenty-four when he died. Yeah, he was young."

Too young to die, he meant. "Billy, he killed my husband."

"Wo-o-ow! We all know that. We're all *sorry* for that. Course we are, but …"

"But, if I had not picked up that knife …"

He nodded slowly, looking down into his beer, before looking up again and meeting her gaze. His eyes were filled with tears. She hadn't expected this.

"How … how did your brother die?"

"They were trying to get him to go cold turkey, you know? But he managed to get a supply of speed, amphetamines, and overdosed by accident. The drug he got was rubbish, impure, supplied on the street from outside. Made it worse. A cocktail of chemicals, they said."

"How do you know it was by accident?"

"He wasn't about to take his own life. We know that. Everyone who'd visited him just before says the same. He was talking about plans for the future, if only he could come off the old smack. He would do 'is time, however long it took, behave and get out, start afresh. I was going to put in a word to make sure he was put on one of their special programmes, to get him off gently, but for good. He wanted this, too. He wasn't a bad lad, Kay, not really."

Kay tensed. "You'll forgive me if I can't agree with that."

"Mm. Understood. But he had a tough time as a kid. We both did, but at least I had a Mum for a few years. She scarpered when he was just two years old. What kind of mother'd do that? I was ten. Now Dad ain't no mother substitute! He's … he is everything you wouldn't want in an old man. I don't need to spell out what I'm on about to you, do I?"

"No, I can imagine what you mean."

"Thirteen he was, the first time he decided to try and make it on his own. Ran off… anyway, ended up with a gang. It's the old story."

"And what about Sasha, then? How did they meet?"

"He was in a hostel and …"

As Billy went on to fill in all the gaps and detail about Gary, his wife and his two children, one born while he was in prison, complete with photographs.

"Oh, Billy …" she gasped when she saw the two small doe-eyed faces staring back her. Ivan and Bella, the proverbial picture of innocence, were held by their mother who looked about fourteen. "They're beautiful." These were real people, young lives shattered.

Then she uttered the words she never thought she would be saying today. "How can I help?"

Billy shook his head sadly. "There's nothin' you can do. I'm not demanding, not expecting anything from you. I just wanted you to know a bit more about Gary. That was all, and why I was so pissed off. I needed someone to blame and for a bit, sorry to say, that someone was you."

"How is Sasha managing?"

"Badly, but she knows nuffin' better. Young single Mum, council flat, poor area, just as her Mum was before her. At least her two kids have the same Dad, even if he did die a druggie in clink!"

"I will do something for them. I'd like to ..." *I'll set up a trust fund for them* … she almost went on to say. No. Billy might not take to charity, to being patronised. *And they can come and stay with me. We'll* … she was off into some kind of daydream. No. She stopped herself. It wasn't going to happen. This was too bizarre.

Billy clasped his hands on the table and leaned forward. "I didn't come here with a begging bowl."

"No. I know that. I see that now, but …"

"You fink it'll make you feel better to give money?" he said, regarding her with a cynical smile. Had he read her mind?

She paused, twisting around in her seat, hand to her mouth. "You're right. Yes, it would make me feel better, but I do want to help Ivan and Bella."

"Well. No reason for me to say no to your offer. But I ain't gonna be involved in this. OK? Here's Sasha's mobile number." He wrote the number down on the back of a beer mat. "But … she'll likely be a bit awkward about having help from you, of all people. Gary's crime weighs heavy wiv her – if anything she'd want to help you. She's a real good girl …" He shrugged. "I dunno. You can sort this one out between you." He gave her the beer mat and left.

Kay wandered off in a daze after he had gone. The meeting did not come close to anything like she had imagined it would be. She sat on a bench and looked out at the Thames, staring at riverboats and buildings across the water. People on the paved embankment passed by in a blur. She sat limply, tears rolling freely down her face, uncaring if anyone noticed. So drained was she, that she could not even be bothered to pull a tissue from her bag.

A man sat down next to her and she turned to see Dunstan. He held out a neatly folded handkerchief.

25

On the way to London, it occurred to Dunstan that Kay could be travelling on the same train. He had taken care to dress in clothing not typical of his style; he was usually a rough casual or smart suit kind of man. He found a pristine, white, polo neck sweater of thin synthetic fabric that someone had given to him once and he had never worn. This, with sunglasses on a grey summer day, was enough to change his persona, he believed. Of course, Kay would recognise him in a heartbeat if face-to-face, but possibly not from a snatched glimpse. For now he was also wearing a light jacket that Kay knew well and he decided to take this off, fold it up and slip it into his rucksack. Trousers? Well trousers were trousers and would blend into the background.

If she noticed him that really would scupper everything. He began to feel he was on a serious mission of espionage to uphold national security, or perhaps track someone's wife suspected of infidelity. He decided he would not make a very good private detective. But hiding behind a newspaper gave him time to think about the possibilities of the day.

He could not second-guess what might happen but he must think through the scenario that he and Kay might actually meet after their long separation. What must she be thinking of me, he wondered?

At Waterloo, he stepped off the train and scanned the people around. This was stressful and confusing. On the one hand he was looking out for Kay, on the other he did not want her to spot him; and there again, he wanted them to see each other very much.

This guy, Gary's brother, what the devil was he up to? Dunstan strode out in what he sensed was the right direction after leaving the station, checking a location map when he found one. Natalie had referred to Billy's phone call to Kay as being 'threatening' and it took place some while ago, but other than that it all seemed vague. It would be extortion or blackmail of some kind, he suspected, but what could he threaten with? The case was closed. Nobody was hiding any evidence were they? Yes, she had picked up the knife in a moment of panic, but she had harmed no one and had paid a heavy penalty for her error. Her husband, Marcus, was brutally murdered by a desperate drug addict and she suffered injuries so painful from her fall downstairs to reach a phone that she blacked out and was temporarily disabled. This was his understanding of the incident which she had described herself in the local newspaper article two years ago.

He checked the exact whereabouts of the pub by asking a couple of people, both of whom spoke little English and had no inkling. It looked simple on the Internet map he had pulled up last night, not worth printing off. He gazed to the left at the choppy waters of the river as he strode on. Leaves were already falling off the plane trees and jumping about in the fresh breeze, a sign that summer was nearly over. He stopped briefly to watch a relatively large vessel plying its course laden with waste containers. Soon he heard live music and threw some coins to a colourful band of buskers as he passed by.

The pub came into view; and he was early. He veered off. She might come this way at any moment; she could be here, right now. After five minutes or so, from a vantage point a little way back from the river, he spotted her. She was wearing a neat fitted jacket he had not seen before, over a black and white dress. Trim for a woman of a certain age, he could not help but note, and felt his stomach give a little flip. She had grown her fair hair a little longer than when he had last seen her; it looked lustrous and feminine. He resisted an urge to rush over and take her hand and stop her from going any further. It was intervention she would not appreciate; he knew her well enough to be certain of that.

He watched her go into the pub. So far so good. But now what? He would not recognise Billy because he had no clue what he looked like. Hoping in vain for some improbable sign, like someone calling out, "Hey Billy!" or for a man to stop and answer his mobile, "Hi Billy here." or for him to inadvertently drop his driving licence … He gave himself a little reality shake. Right. He would allow Billy some slack and then risk poking his head into the pub. How else could he determine what was going on? Unless he just waited until Kay emerged from the pub either alone or with Billy; then he could follow her or them. He weighed up and decided to compromise. He would wait a little longer, maybe ten or fifteen minutes, then slip in and take a discreet look.

It seemed an age, as if time had slowed down, as he checked his watch every couple of minutes. Then he pushed the door and glanced around. Yes! There she was, sitting with a guy and they appeared to be chatting amicably. He was showing her something, a piece of paper, card, maybe a photograph. She was completely unaware of his presence in the room so he hung on for perhaps a minute, watching covertly, apparently sauntering slowly towards the bar. She had her hand to her mouth and looked tearful. Oh, so this guy was playing with her head, was he? Emotional blackmail? He felt angry and protective and felt like rushing up and splitting his head open, but no … he turned and left, ready to bide his time until they were done.

26

For a moment Kay felt her head swim, as if her brain had come loose inside the skull. She was in London by the River Thames, with people rushing by going about their business and Billy had just left her alone, feeling distressed, thoroughly at odds with herself and the world. Dunstan had just sat down next to her.

She could see him, she felt the light touch of his fingertips as he passed her a handkerchief, which she took silently, feeling her pulse notch up a gear. She waited to hear his voice to be sure that this was not some kind of dream or hallucination. *Why are you here? What happened to you all these weeks? You think a handkerchief could ever make up for you abandoning me when I needed you? I hate you!*

Still Dunstan said nothing – like a ghost. What did she want him to say, if anything? That *he was sorry*; that he had missed her and there was nothing going on with the other woman from Ireland, that he would be coming back to her house for breakfast, lunch and dinner, and be working in her garden just as before. But no Kay, she told herself, the mist in her head gradually clearing, that was not going to happen. You can't just turn back the clock.

She swallowed to moisten her throat. "Dunstan."

"Yes." He had turned to face her and smiled tentatively, but it was a proper smile, showing teeth! The blood rushed to her cheeks. The nerve. Couldn't he see she was upset?

His rough, manly hand had reached to enclose her softer hand, instantly triggering distant sensory memories; it felt warm like woollen gloves from the airing-cupboard when bare hands are frozen blue from playing snowballs; like when her first boyfriend had held her hand on the way to the pictures, sending a fluttery sensation right through to her groin.

"Billy's gone," he observed, simply. She turned towards him, eyes wide now. "I'm just relieved you're safe." Yes, they must deal with the present situation first, before explanations of the past.

"Billy. How did you know?" Kay's mind was racing. Who else knew? Not Claudia. Nobody, except Natalie.

"Never mind."

Fair enough, he would not want to betray the fact that Natalie had informed him. She waited a while before speaking again.

"Gary left a young wife and two little children, one just a toddler. Sweet." Her voice cracked and she put a hand to her mouth as her bottom lip trembled. After a few moments, she went on to tell him about Sasha, Ivan and Bella. "Sasha may not want my help, but I feel … incomplete, somehow, by not supporting her. She will struggle on her own, I imagine." Dunstan had taken in what she was saying and was giving it some thought. He was always a good listener. "What do you think I should do?"

"There are so many inner city children who need things – not necessarily material things, but experiences, time, fresh air, love … at least these two have the love of one parent, and from what you say, it sounds as if Billy will be a support. To focus on just this family, whose father did you such a wrong, may not be the best way forward. But of course, it's up to you, entirely."

How she had missed his sensible way of assessing things. "I'll give it some more thought," she replied. One day Ivan and Bella would ask questions about who she was, what the connection was; Dunstan was probably right.

"Natalie was worried about you." So she was wrong in her generous assessment of his delicacy; he had little hesitation in dropping Natalie in it! "We decided to look after you." She could see he looked doubtful, watching her reaction, of course knowing he was treading dangerous waters. But this was no bad thing.

"It's good to have friends who care," she said. "And you miss them when they're not around …" She tossed him a meaningful look.

"Ah! Yes. I think there was a misunderstanding. At some point you believed I was about to abscond with Ruby-Ann?"

Again Kay turned to him and gasped. "The gossip that goes on … tsk."

"She was the pursuer and she's gone now. I was the pursued, or pursuee," he stated plainly, then adding, " but my reasons for ... er, well, disappearing, really lay elsewhere."

"Yes?" she asked, really wanting an explanation now more than she had ever wanted anything in her entire life. *It had better be good.*

"It was the title of my diary, my life-story, you know?"

"Of course I know."

"The title, I mean. You remember?"

Kay racked her brains. The title had genuinely gone from her memory. She turned down the corners of her mouth, trying to think.

Dunstan put his head in his hands. "Oh my God," he was saying. "You really never knew did you?"

"What? What was it? No, I don't remember. Yes I do. You were calling it *Dunstan's Life-Story.*"

"You wanted to call it something else."

Kay frowned. "Oh, now let me think. This is so long ago. I scribbled an idea, what was it? I thought it needed a bit more … oomph. Gypsy who left …? Changed to become like a *Gorgio*? I can't …"

"*Gypsy Turned Gorgio*!"

"Did I say that? Well, if you're a Gypsy you can't actually become a *Gorgio*, but you did become a settled person, you joined *Gorgio* society. You told me yourself."

Dunstan closed his eyes. "Of course you understand. Why did I ever doubt you?"

"You mean, you went off in a huff because …? But, Dunstan I clearly remember you saying to me much the same thing …"

"Then it was my fault for explaining things badly. I'm sorry, Kay." These were the little words she had waited for. Happiness surged within her, as a parched plant must feel when rain falls. "How's the garden?" he then asked, ever the practical man.

"Could be better," Kay replied, narrowing her eyes, giving him a look of mock-anger.

"You found another gardener, though?"

"No, I did not."

Dunstan looked puzzled. "Oh! I thought …"

"How's your life-story going? I'm so looking forward to reading it, you know. There'll be things I know nothing about, I'm sure. A whole new world."

Dunstan leaned forward, hands clasped, elbows resting on his knees.

"Have you finished it yet?" she asked.

He shook his head, seemed unable to speak. Kay waited, giving him time.

"I decided to just … keep it to myself."

Kay felt bewildered again, just when she felt they had found some sort of middle ground of understanding. Yet, just twenty-minutes ago, she was still hating him! At least she had moved on from that unhappy place.

"Oh," she said, in a tone that was enough to show her deep disappointment.

"Have you eaten?" asked Dunstan.

"No."

"Well, would you like to? You know, a bite somewhere else?"

Dunstan was sensitive enough to guess she would not want to go back into The Anchor now, however tempting its menu might be. Kay did not admit straight away that a ferocious appetite had replaced her earlier nausea that could do justice to four courses, but she nodded as they stood up.

"Dunstan, I hope this doesn't sound a trifle pathetic, but you know, are we friends?" She was sounding like a child in the school playground and felt the colour rise to her cheeks. "This is all rather confusing."

"Kay," he said, wrapping an arm around her, in broad daylight with strangers still passing by. It was a long time since she had felt that degree of comfort. "I hope we are more than 'friends' by now, if that's all right with you, of course."

27

Over a long, late, Italian lunch Kay and Dunstan caught up on events of the past few months. She realised that when you love someone whose absence robs you of happiness, forgiveness is easy. But true forgiveness should be founded on understanding, not falsely brushing grievances down or away, out of sight.

She explained Claudia's situation and showed him a photo of her first grandchild, quickly moving on as she thought it best not to share the baby's name with him just yet. It might seem a bit presumptuous, since her daughter had taken his name when they were estranged. She diverted to the Farlows and their various exploits, especially those of Jeremy, and Dunstan listened intently. Then they somehow moved on to the prevalence of misunderstandings in life.

"I've always been good at jumping to the wrong conclusions," confessed Kay.

Dunstan reached across to squeeze her hand. "You can't go on beating yourself up like this for ever, you know. From what I see, you go out of your way to help other people. Remember it's only people who never try anything who don't make mistakes. It's an old one I know, but it endures, doesn't it?"

She shrugged, her mind still on how things can be misread, usually through ignorance or seeing things through blinkered eyes.

"Communication is altogether troublesome," commented Kay, with a sigh, as she put down the fork and spoon after her last mouthful of seafood linguine.

Dunstan tilted his head and smiled at her. "Kay's saying of the day! Finding the right words and putting them in the right order, this is what *I* have trouble with. More than that.

Memories are disorderly and so … emotional. The problems of recall are huge."

"But the title – ***Gypsy turned Gorgio***? This was enough to jeopardise, to destroy, our friendship?"

Dunstan reached across the table to take Kay's hand, then gently caressed her cheek. She could see that his eyes had filled with tears. How she wanted him to hold her tight; more than that.

"Not really. It was me. Things going on inside my head. Why I did what I did, and how important my roots and my people are to me. I got completely entangled in myself, my own past."

"Did it restore your sense of cultural identity, or make you more confused?"

He nodded. "The former. But it all got out of proportion. I … I would like you to read it, Kay. Then you may see. Although, I'm not looking for an editor!"

"What about publishing it?"

"Definitely not."

A waitress came to clear away the table.

Dunstan looked at his watch. "Well, it's about time for afternoon tea. Shall we head on somewhere else?"

"Tea and cake. Oh, why not? Let gluttony rule the day!"

They sat side by side with arms linked on the train that evening in late August, feeling replete and content to the core of their being. About halfway, it began to feel hot in the carriage and Dunstan removed his brown linen jacket.

"I'm not sure about this white jumper," said Kay. "Is it new?"

Dunstan smiled. "I can only apologise. It won't happen again."

Later that evening after they had shared a light supper in Dunstan's mobile home, courting privacy, Kay, followed by Dunstan, rose from the sofa where they had been sitting and he, like a bear, drew Kay into his arms so she felt herself disappear into the coveted warmth of his chest. He said, "Now I have you back I am reluctant to let you go."

Kay could feel her heart pounding against his midriff, as if she had just run a marathon.

"Well, I could …"

He placed a finger over her lips. "Kay, dear woman, will you run away with me?"

28

Dunstan took a walk outside alone in the moonlight after he had driven Kay home. It was a fine night, the clear sky peppered with stars doing their best to put on a show despite the light pollution of nearby towns and distant cities. Without thinking he spotted the Great Bear up there and his ears tuned in to an owl calling. He had grown tired of pacing up and down, inside his small home, feeling caged in with his pent-up emotions. He must wait twenty-four long hours for an answer! How could she do this to him? But he realised he deserved to be thrown into a state of abject misery, of desperate uncertainty about his fate. And there was a real chance she could turn him down.

He had explained to her what he meant.

"Run away with you?" she'd exclaimed. "What? Where to? Do you mean, abroad?"

He had to cradle her face in his hands and kiss her forehead, her cheeks and finally her lips before she realised that this was a proposal of marriage. It would be an elopement, a secret. When it dawned that he was living out the old Romany tradition, she infuriatingly, put her practical head on.

"But Claudia will worry! She'll think something has happened to me, if I just disappear."

They compromised. If, and only if, she agreed to 'run away', that is elope, that is marry him, she would leave a note conveying some indication of when she would return. Who she was with could remain a secret without telling any actual lies. She would be lying, but only by omitting the full truth. "I can live with that," she said.

The fact she had thought it through, with lightning speed, said enough, but still she had not said that little word, "Yes." It was hard to bear. The key to a different world, a new life: the key to Kay! He chuckled to himself as he strode back through a field of horses towards the motor home park. What a party they would have when they got back!

29

Kay could not sleep after her eventful day. She lay floating in some kind of other world, smiling, hugging the duvet, crying with happiness, mascara streaking the white pillowcase like some wilting romantic heroine.

"Of course I'll make him wait!" she whispered to herself, as all the tensions melted and she drifted off.

The following morning she awoke and took some deep, steadying breaths, deciding to allow herself some readjustment, time to ease herself into what was happening to her, to her life. She would introduce some normality, whatever that was. She would say nothing about Dunstan to anyone else until he knew her decision.

Over breakfast, Claudia and Jim reported on their day in London. "Nothing definite for Jim." Claudia reached across the table to her dejected looking husband and gave his arm a squeeze, which suggested that he had been knocked back. Kay hoped the strain of being unemployed and homeless with a new baby would not be more than their marriage could bear. She was optimistic. They were loving and supportive of each other; she felt confident they would come through the other end of this, somehow, and be the stronger for it.

"Just have to keep trying," said Jim. "Anyway, these things take time."

"I'll look for a teaching post, maybe some supply or something, to keep the boat afloat," said Claudia, cheerfully.

"But what about little Dunstan?" asked Kay with some trepidation. She would never have dreamed that the prospect of being a full-time nanny could possibly fill her with something akin to horror.

Claudia gave her a look. It was one of those questioning looks that required no words, conveying love and gratitude, whilst asking for pity and mercy. The tilt of her head, raised eyebrows, the funny forced smile with teeth clamped, managed to express all of this.

"Darling, you can't count on me day in, day out. I'm sorry. Much as I want to help, it's too much of a commitment," she said firmly. There was no point leading her up a rose-scented garden path. "I mean, now and then, of course. You know I'd be delighted. But that's not what you would need."

Claudia gave a little toss of her head. "No, no. Of course not Mum. I wouldn't dream of it. Jim will do a share, I can find a nursery that takes … infants, little babies that is … and … we'll manage." Her smile through the tears tore Kay apart. Why was the route to happiness so fraught and convoluted? She thought of Dunstan and the life that lay ahead and was immediately comforted. Call me selfish, self-centred, self-absorbed, but nothing was going to stand in the way of that, although he did not know it yet.

"How did your property search go?" asked Kay, thinking it best to move on to other, probably equally depressing matters.

Claudia put her head in her hands. Baby Dunstan woke up and began crying. "I'll tell you later. It was completely bloody hopeless," she added, as a taster, before flouncing out of the kitchen to fetch him.

As she was about to allow herself some thinking time on Dunstan and their future together, Kay had an unexpected visit about elevenses time from Jeremy and Nathan.

"Hi. We thought this was probably a good time to catch you." Kay wondered why, but was pleased to see them anyway. "You remember Nathan?"

Nathan extended a hand quite formally. "I wanted to thank you for that time you stood up for me, well for my people, really, when we came lookin' for work at Jeremy's house."

"Made a bit of a fool of myself, really. As if you need my support!"

"No, it helped. Thank you."

"I heard you did a good job of work – that is what helped, more than anything I could say or do."

"Most of us try to please, when we get the chance!"

They sat down together at the kitchen table. Kay poured them coffee and found some chocolate chip cookies. Nathan outlined more of their plans to lobby MPs; write political articles and letters to influential and known sympathisers; initiate more events where Gypsies and Travellers could interact with the general public to help break down mutual mistrust.

"This is all wonderful."

Nathan shrugged modestly. "There's a lot of activity goin' on out there."

Kay nodded. She knew what he meant. "But I feel you are taking the Appley Green campaign to a new level."

Nathan shook his head. "No use working just locally. You saw what happened with your transit site. It's gotta be a co-ordinated approach with all the authorities involved. But where you helped was in raising awareness with *Gorgios*, like yourself."

"Well I hope so. We certainly need to try and counter the relentlessly negative newspaper reports and TV documentaries." Kay felt great relief at what felt like handing over the baton to a much faster runner. "And now Jeremy, you told me about Imogen before. So what are *your* career plans at the moment? More coffee? And Tim? What's *he* up to?" She knew she had to hurry things along but did not want to appear rude.

"Tim has joined forces with some flash entrepreneurial type who is into buying large houses for conversion into residential homes – homes for the elderly being a growth market," explained Jeremy, frowning, avoiding eye contact. A sensitive young man, reflected Kay; probably thinking that this topic was delicate for anyone over the age of fifty. "Trying to buy up at the right time when prices hit rock-bottom."

"Mm. Difficult to predict that, but sounds like a fundamentally sound plan," replied Kay enthusiastically. "Big project though. Huge investment."

"Guess so. Tim will be more on the business side of things. Part of a team."

Kay bit her lip, thinking back to Tim's lacklustre performance when the water tank burst. "So long as he doesn't take on the house maintenance side …" she muttered.

"And you, Jeremy?"

"Me? Well, I've applied for a journalism course. Doing freelance stuff already."

"Well done you! You've made things happen. I'm proud to know the Farlows!"

"Wow. Are you really? That … that means a lot, actually. I'll tell Imogen and Tim."

But Jeremy looked hesitant as if all was not quite well. His brow was now quite furrowed.

"Something wrong though?" asked Kay.

"Well, the bloody horrible outcome of all this, with Imogen likely to be travelling, me not yet exactly a big-earner, Tim's business buying up large houses … it all points to the fact that we need to sell up. We'll have to sell The Cedars, which is hard for us really. It's our home and all we have left. We should have taken care of our finances, but we were young, we were stupid. I know, I know."

"Oh you sound so old and wise now," teased Kay. "But that is really sad, of course it is, and I do sympathise."

"And it's not a good time to sell to get a good price, *obviously*," added Jeremy.

"But there again, most young people do leave home to become independent, you know."

That afternoon the house fell quiet as Kay began sifting through her several wardrobes. Where would they be going? What clothes would she need? She was so excited she found herself singing to herself very loudly: "Dream the impossible dream …"

She stood before a full length mirror to examine her appearance. Would there be time for a trip to the hairdressers? She decided not, running fingers through her hair which, she thought, was looking wild and felt like straw. Almond oil conditioner should soften it. Touch suddenly became important, the first time since … well, she thought, since Marcus. What would Marcus make of all this? She turned to his photograph by the side of the bed and gazed at his face, the silver-haired scientist taken from her before his time. "Marcus," she whispered, to him, "are you OK about this?" He would be glad, she felt sure, that she had found another source of happiness.

She slid open the bedside drawer to pull out her manicure set ready to give her nails a service. Mm … hair removing cream. Surprises could be enchanting, mysteries magical but truth be told she would not be averse to knowing some of the practicalities. Would she need a passport? Sunscreen? In a way she hoped not. All she wanted was to be with Dunstan and get to know him, up close, intimate and personal. She took deep breaths to help cope with some of the images that were racing around inside her over-active imagination. Airports and all the hassle they tended to entail, were not on her wish-list just at that moment. Something simple, somewhere peaceful. It was a waste of time and energy trying to guess what he had in mind.

One step at a time. Focus on basics. Returning to her wardrobes stacked with many years' worth of hoarded clothes, she rammed the hangers from one side to the other, back and forth, pulling out this and that, deciding finally she had nothing to wear. But that, frankly was ridiculous, even she could see that. She thought back to comments Dunstan had made about what she was wearing and realised they had never really dressed up to go out together. Maybe he was happy to see her in normal, everyday clothes. Jeans would be pushing it, though. She sighed.

What was she wearing the first time she met him? As she ran a bath, she thought back to the day he had arrived to be 'interviewed' for the position of casual gardener. He had looked strikingly smart in a suit with white shirt and a silk tie. The tie was brown and turquoise. She could visualise it, clear as if he was there now. Probably the slickest outfit he had ever sported in her presence. She thought back. After *he* had finished asking *her* questions, they took a walk around the garden. A picture arrived in her head like a scene from a film. Pencil denim skirt, a pink dotted shirt with scarlet trim. Red beads and sandals. She still had these items. Were they clean and respectable? Her hands plunged back into the rail of miscellaneous clothing and soon pulled out what she was looking for. She looked at her watch. The skirt was fine but the crumpled shirt would benefit from a wash and iron. There was time.

They had planned to meet on the village Green at half-past seven, weather permitting, not to 'run away' as such, but for her to give him an answer.

Claudia, Jim and little Dunstan were visiting friends in Oxfordshire and would be back late. She had written a note for Claudia, ready to leave on the kitchen table at the appropriate time, to say she had gone away for a few days, not sure how many, to see an old friend. It was a sudden invitation.

That was the deal and if her answer was yes, they would run, run away, she knew not where. It was a golden evening, the sun sinking in a pearly-pink sky and as her feet in red sandals stepped out towards the village, she felt as if she were about seventeen.

25

Dunstan knew he only had the day to pull together his plan before they met on the Green tonight. He would have to proceed on the basis that Kay would accept his offer of elopement but, with so many unknown factors, she must be bursting with questions that would have to be answered to her satisfaction. Subject to her agreement, tomorrow would be the big day.

He debated with himself, maybe I should wait until she reads my life-story before throwing her into the deep end. Am I doing this all the wrong way round? If her face falls when my surprise becomes visible, then … where do they go from there? Maybe this would indicate they were not meant to be after all …

He sat thus deliberating over mushrooms and sausages, now finishing with toast and marmalade. He looked at the jar labelled with one of Kay's handcrafted stickers. It was almost empty and was the last pot she had given to him. He smiled to himself thinking he must be sure he does not give the impression that this is a union of convenience. Perhaps he would stand to gain more than she would in that sense, for she loved to feed and care for people. It was her nature. And, she had a fine house and large garden she would never leave, he knew that. What was he going to offer her, apart from his undying love?

Help in the garden was no basis for marriage. A handyman good at fixing things was no substitute for a husband. What had Marcus been like, he could not help but wonder? This conjecture was painful. They had been married for thirty years or more, he understood. A happy marriage, the perfect couple with two lovely daughters; a husband for whom she had grieved long and hard, for whom she had fought a seemingly endless emotional battle since his bloody death.

And me? Well, she will understand me better when she reads my life-story. Dunstan felt frustrated now, afraid that this life-story was becoming the key to unlock the door to their future happy life together. It was assuming too much importance. Could he not just tell her the story, in the true Gypsy way? What had happened to that great 'oral tradition'?

Was his plan a selfish one? For him it would be the most wonderful fantasy perhaps. But for her? She might prefer a holiday in Barbados! Well, they had the rest of their lives for sun-drenched holidays if that was what she would like. But then if that were the case, maybe they would not fit hand-in-glove. If she was truly horrified with his offering, then she was not right for him. He felt deep-down that she would at least approve. She might even be excited, delighted, euphoric! But it was impossible to be sure.

"The shack has been tidied up," Sheila had told him, sounding strong now, for the grieving was over. "We've had to sort out much of Copper's things and burn them. It's what he would've expected. But we kept plenty of keepsakes too. People are a bit more practical these days, so we only put the rubbish on the bonfire!"

"So, you've got a likely buyer then?" This is what she had hinted at before, as none of Copper's family wanted to keep it, or perhaps all of them did and this was a way to save disputes. She didn't explain and Dunstan did not ask.

"Yes. Very keen couple. Just sorting out their finances. Of course it's in a good location. A nice spot. They'll knock it down but there, that's life. But anyhow, Dunstan you're more'n welcome to go stay there for a bit, and it's all been spruced up for the viewings last week."

"Great. I just want a few quiet days there, but don't tell anyone, Sheila. Can't be doing with a hoard of visitors, just want to remember old Copper." He felt himself blush, in the knowledge he was not telling the entire truth.

He was waiting to hear back from someone he had found on the Internet, since he did not have the right personal connection himself, who provided Gypsy horse-and-wagon rides. Meanwhile he threw a few items of clothes into a small bag and checked his supplies of practical ironmongery and equipment necessary for survival, as well as scented candles, books, CDs and deliveries of food and meals organised. He hoped he had thought of everything. The only problem now, really, was if she were to say "No."

Dunstan sat on a park bench on the Green. It was dedicated to Ted Devonish's father, local landowner who had been a great benefactor to the parish, particularly in the years after the Second World War. This reminded Dunstan of a rumour he had heard, must be well over a year ago, possibly two, that Ted and Kay were an 'item' as the village would say. What happened there? He couldn't quite recall, but he hoped that it had been her wish that the relationship did not ripen and not his, for otherwise she could still be harbouring feelings for old Ted.

Feelings of insecurity suddenly took hold. He had grown used to the idea now that she and he were going to spend the rest of their lives as a couple. He could imagine no other future without that basic framework and he just wanted them to fill in the picture together.

Looking up, feeling tense and nervous now, he could see her, a distant speck up the road, just passing by the village school, swinging her arms like a much younger woman. He did not want to appear as if he were staring at her so pretended for a minute or two that he had not yet spied her, to allow her time to approach. At the appropriate moment, he stood up and ambled thoughtfully towards her, feeling an irrepressible smile surface. He could tell at a glance what her answer would be and felt like leaping towards her, sweeping her right off her feet, swinging her into the air, shouting out for all the village to hear.

She, too, was smiling and as they approached each other, her step quickened. Words seemed superfluous as their arms locked around each other and, regardless of who might be watching, how many net curtains might be twitching, they kissed each other until forced to come up for air.

"When do we go, then?" she asked, her eyes twinkling as he gently guided her towards a quiet lane leading down to the common where there was a patch of springy turf famous for its sunset views and, Kay had heard, the site of many furtive conceptions.

Dunstan could not stop the smile, as if his face had frozen into some kind of contortion. "Tomorrow morning. I'll come and pick you up on foot at half-past five."

Kay gasped. "What, no vehicle? You really do mean run away! You must tell me a few things, though …"

Dunstan knew there would be questions. "Of course."

"That's quite early. Do I need a passport, or swimwear?"

"Tsk, tsk. Too many clues. OK. Fair enough. No, neither. Toiletries, a few clothes, camera if you want. Pack a small bag. I think everything else'll be taken care of."

"I'm very excited," she admitted, biting her lip guiltily, like a child desperate to know what her birthday treat is but not wishing to break the spell.

As they reached the viewpoint, the sunset such a romantic cliché, they had to laugh aloud.

"Well, I may as well complete the scene," he growled, getting down stiffly on bended knee. "Just to be clear on this, because as someone said, 'communication can be troublesome', Kay, will you be my wife, to love and to cherish?"

"I certainly will, Mr Dunstan Smith, for better or for worse."

Together they uttered the words, cautiously, "Till death us to do part."

26

Two black and white horses and the colourful Gypsy wagon, more beautiful, and grander than any Kay had ever seen in museums or pictures, or even imagined, were waiting for them at the same spot on the common where they had tentatively exchanged their simple vows. It was early, barely light, and the sight opened up gradually as she and Dunstan approached on foot. A cool breeze brushed her face and birds all around were announcing the sunrise.

She felt a fizz of sheer joy, something spiritual that transcended the normal spectrum of emotion. As Suzi would say it was 'off the scale'. Now it was there in front of her, she could not think how she had not anticipated this all along. But it had not crossed her mind and she was glad of it, for the blissful surprise was pure gold and far exceeded anything she could have dreamed up.

A man jumped off the wagon and waved his goodbye to Dunstan. He pulled a bicycle off the back and rode away.

Transfixed she stood, still unable to believe her eyes, utterly enchanted. Then a horse gave a short harrumph, impatiently pawing the turf with a hoof and the other left its mark from behind. The smell that wafted across brought her back to her senses.

Dunstan had put their bags in the wagon through the small door at the front behind where the 'driver' sits. Climbing up, Kay peered inside to gain an overall impression of neatness, luxury and pride, a wealth of ornate decoration – horses' heads, bunches of grapes, loops and swirls, lace and velvet, brass hinges and an old, slightly musty smell of polish and tea …

"I'll give you a short guided tour later," said Dunstan, double-checking the horses were hitched up correctly. "The *grys* are ready to pull off. Are you fit to go too?" He held her shoulders gently but firmly and looked deep into her eyes, as if searching for an answer beyond words.

She paused and he appeared to be holding his breath. "I've never been more ready for anything. This is just …" and her eyes filled with tears, "wonderful." She had no idea where they were going, but she trusted this man, more important than certainties.

"Oh, you bloody perfect woman, come here." She felt herself then being crushed and kissed in no uncertain terms. "Just hope the weather holds," he then added, with a note of precaution, but not enough to burst the bubble.

She decided not to ask where they were going. Maybe he just had the wagon for a day.

"Where did you find this wagon and horses? It must be very old."

"It's just from a company that hires them out commercially, usually with a driver, but I said I wanted it without."

She wondered what would happen if they had or caused an accident but then had a stern silent word with herself.

"You never lived in anything like this, did you, though?" she asked, rather afraid if this might be insulting. It probably came from his grandparents' era.

"Sure I did, except the one we had, where I was born in fact, was top of the range, a Dunton Reading, really more of a Showman's wagon. Can't think how my Grandfather got it in the first place, but anyhow …"

Then she heard a little of his very early life, which prompted a string of questions as the horses clip-clopped along down the lane, the iron wheels rumbling and clattering as they sped round. Ahead she could see a fairly steep hill.

"My goodness, poor horses. Will they make it up there?"

"Sure they will, so long as they don't stop," and he went on to reassure her that if they did there was a special mechanism that would stop the wagon from rolling backwards, pulling the horses down with it. She now understood the basic principles of a scotch-roller!

Before long they were on a main road, with noisy traffic streaming past, passengers waving and some drivers thoughtlessly hooting. She was aware they were quite a spectacle, better than being in a limousine any day! Kay felt like royalty!

"Won't be long here. Try and keep to the quiet roads," he said, shouting above the din. "Not fair on the *grys*,"

As they came off the dual carriageway into a peaceful back road, the sun came out in full force.

"Perfect timing," commented Kay, linking her arm through Dunstan's. "It's all going too well."

He gave her a bemused look. Perhaps, she thought, they would stop somewhere for a brunch soon, as neither of them had had any breakfast to speak of before leaving at the crack of dawn.

"Did you pack your autobiography? Is it in your bag?" she asked.

"It is."

"Would there be time to read it today?"

He shrugged. "Who knows? Depends," he replied laconically.

"I can't wait to read it."

Maybe this was more than a token journey, a symbolic 'running-away'. What did he really mean by 'elopement' she began to wonder more and more? Clearly not a marriage service, unless they were heading for Gretna Green, which could take months! Only one thing was certain, she felt. They will be sharing a bed. The desire between them was palpable.

They stopped now and then for the horses to graze, or *poove*, as Dunstan called it, supplemented with some hay that the hire company had provided. At the first stop, he unhitched the horses and tethered them to a plug. Then he disappeared inside the wagon for a moment soon to re-appear with a black cast-iron kettle and prop. Quickly gathering some kindling and sticks, he lit a fire, all very efficiently, as if this were second nature to him.

"This must take you back," remarked Kay, wanting to help but not sure how.

"It surely does. I was a teenager the last time I held the reins of a horse pulling a *vardo.*" Dunstan paused to study her face. "But are *you* OK with this, Kay?" he asked, anxiously, now presenting all the ingredients for a perfect English breakfast and a sizeable pan. She loved the way he dropped in the odd Romany word; deliciously romantic, but he wasn't suggesting they spend the rest of their days together on this wagon, was he? Surely …

"Absolutely," she assured him, wondering what lay ahead for the rest of the day, but content to let it take its course. Trust is a wonderful thing, she told herself.

27

It was only mid-morning when Dunstan turned the wagon right off the road into the wilderness leading to Copper's shack. He felt a lump in his throat as the sights and smells all around called up a disturbing range of emotions. This place represented his emotional past, memories he would never allow to fade, and he had at his side the woman who was his future. Two lives coming together. Kay would understand better when she had read his story; it would be difficult to explain all of that. Something his people would never agree on, probably, but his printed words might be better at conveying the complex drama of his life.

With sideways glances, he discreetly scrutinised Kay's face as the horses forged their way ahead down the overgrown track. Foliage brushed the sides of the wagon but did not touch where they sat. She was leaning forward, a hand on her chest, mouth slightly open, eyes wide, but saying nothing. He was surprised at the lack of questions today; she seemed remarkably compliant.

Once the wagon and horses drew up beside the shack, the yard seemed to shrink as they nearly filled the space. Dunstan unhitched the horses and led them through a gate to release them into the small, adjacent field where he knew they would be safe. It was a paddock with lush grass and a water trough, where Copper had for years kept a couple of piebald Gypsy cobs; Dunstan had known the landowner for years, sharing many a pint with him and Copper in the local pub.

Kay stepped down from the wagon, looking decidedly uncertain and Dunstan was now concerned. She was unhappy. She had changed her mind and wanted to turn around and go home.

"Is there something wrong?"

"No, no," she replied, with a shake of her head, as she took in her surroundings. "Well, this is a rural hideaway and no mistake," she added, her gaze swivelling round. "But, Dunstan, how long … I mean, how long will we be here for?"

Then Dunstan realised her worry. "For a couple of days, and," he replied, then raising his eyebrows and taking her hands in his, he added, "a couple of nights. Mm?"

Instantly her mood changed and no more was said about it. Poor Kay, he thought turning away to smile. Surely she did not think … Communication, or rather lack of it, is certainly troublesome.

"I expected you to ask long before," he said, passing by her with the bags.

"Two days will be total perfection," she said, wandering around to take in her surroundings. "So, we won't actually be … sleeping in the wagon? And eating? Shall we cook outdoors, or on the stove in the wagon, *vardo* I mean? And anyway, do we have food? And is there somewhere to have a shower or bath? And towels? Oh, I haven't brought towels. Who owns this little cottage? Oh look, have you seen?" she exclaimed finally, as she pushed open the door and went inside like Goldilocks.

Her final question brought home to Dunstan just how much she did not know and how much she would actually enjoy finding out.

"Do not worry about meals. Or, anything. Relax, Kay. We shall eat like a king and queen. Trust me."

Kay turned to face him, now both inside the small cottage living-room, with two chairs, shelves, a wood-burning stove and a few knick-knacks. "I do, Dunstan. I trust you more than anyone I've ever met, actually." Apart from Marcus, she thought, but felt mention of his name might be bad timing.

"What? A Gypsy?" he asked, tongue-in-cheek.

"Nothing to do with it. You're an individual, a person whom I trust. It doesn't really matter what ethnic group you belong to."

"Doesn't it? Well, perhaps, after we've consummated our 'elopement'," he murmured slowly into her ear, "you'd like to recline on a sun-bed with my story. I think a few things will make more sense when you've done that."

28

Kay's head was rewinding to the bit about 'consummated'. How quaint he was! How sweet. Suzi would mock, Claudia would snigger, but he suited her very well.

"Sounds good to me. You've sorted out the priorities then?" she teased.

After a wickedly sublime hour of intimacy in the cosiest love-nest imaginable, where they had both rediscovered what touching and passion were, for after all, it had been a long time for both of them, she wondered dreamily if she could possibly love him more than she did. Now she settled herself on the sun-bed with the pile of papers feeling wayward and hedonistic, enjoying every minute.

She could hear Dunstan filling a kettle as she finally put down the manuscript, having reached the point where Dunstan left off writing. She wondered if he would ever bring it completely up to date; maybe he thought this unnecessary.

He had been loving and attentive throughout the two hours she had been reading. "Are you warm enough?" "Is the sun in your eyes? Thirsty?" "You don't have to if …"

But she had wanted to very much. What it felt like to be drawn into the past life of the man you loved, to feel his sorrow and joy, was too overwhelming to put into words. It was an emotional, spiritual experience like slipping into another dimension. She felt privileged to have reached through to the very core of his soul. Nobody else had flown and nestled inside his head and his heart as she had. Now she lay back in the early evening sun, closing her eyes to let the pictures in her head run across at will like a slow motion film, frame by frame.

Questions popped up too. What about other people in her life? Most of them had yet to meet Dunstan and will be totally surprised to have him introduced and presented, apparently bursting into her life, as her … well, what husband? Partner? Common-law husband? Was there such a thing these days? Did Dunstan now regard her as his wife because they had finally made love?

She could hear the soft sound of his footfall as he came closer and then feel the warmth of his presence next to her. She opened her eyes.

He was smiling, holding a tray like a waiter. "Tea?" he asked.

"Wonderful." She sat up, blinking in the low evening sunlight. "I finished …"

"I know. I can see. So?" He put the tray down on a table and drew up a chair to be next to her.

Kay reached out for his arm, just to make physical contact, to reassure herself that he was still there, vital and strong and not just a character she had been reading about in a book. "I feel I know you through and through now."

"You can never know everything about a person, though, can you?"

She smiled. "No," she agreed. "But something like this certainly helps. I mean for a couple like us, coming together late in life. You know."

He poured the tea into finely decorated bone china cups and passed her one.

"So this was Copper's place," she went on. "What will happen to it?"

"There is a buyer, pretty much confirmed. They'll probably pull it down."

She frowned. A place filled with so many memories? He was watching her face again. He had been doing a lot of that today, she had noticed. A sign of true love; it felt good to be the object of such fascination, despite a saying attributed to Antoine de Saint-Exupery, 'Love does not consist in gazing at each other, but in looking outward together in the same direction,' which Kay normally regarded as more purposeful.

"Such a shame," she reflected, pensively. "A waste. Does nobody want to preserve it – for posterity?"

"Apparently not."

"Is it a direct sale – or through estate agents?"

Dunstan said he had no idea.

Their brief romantic break passed by, remote from the real world, like a blissful dream. They talked and strolled; ate and drank; made love; listened to music; read books, looked through the old photographs and even played Scrabble. Dunstan did a bit of pruning and wood-chopping as if, thought Kay, it was his own little abode. On their last evening, they laid plans for the celebrations on their return to Appley Green, agreeing that they would need to allow a couple of weeks to stand any chance of people actually coming.

"People live busy lives," said Kay, "and get booked up, but at least summer holidays are nearly over." Although, she thought, many of her mature friends would never dream of going away during school holidays.

"Days gone by, you know," Dunstan had said, rather wistfully, "the marriage and all the celebrations would be quickly arranged by the parents, the family, but in our case … well …"

"We'll just have to do the best we can. It'll be great! And we can throw a small supper-party for you to get to know Suzi, Claudia and Jim as soon as we get back."

A few moments' silent contemplation followed. Kay pictured Suzi, Claudia and Jim, one or two cousins she had not seen for years, friends from Richmond – people who had known Marcus, and newer, now close friends from the village. She would look forward to seeing Millicent's jaw drop. Molly-Marie, Natalie and her father, Ted, would be invited to the party. People would assume that Natalie's mother was not there to save the awkwardness of a divorced couple having to face each other socially. Even though she had never met the wretched woman, she might have extended an invitation to her – had things been different - simply as Natalie's mother. For Kay, just the simple act of deliberately excluding her would be a mild reprisal, even if it did fall far, far short of what the woman deserved. So, her world would be coming together with Seamus, Presley, Geena, Copper's descendants whom Dunstan had described to her in detail, along with a multitude of extended family members and friends who had scattered far and wide and would need to be 'rounded up'. Many he had seen at Copper's funeral.

"You see, word'll get out. Not invitations exactly. Be prepared for a big gathering. Is that OK?"

Kay nodded but she was unsure about some small but important aspects of their union. "Dunstan, I'd like a ceremony, wouldn't you? That'll take longer, won't it?"

He drew her close. "Whatever you want, dear woman. I seem to be getting my own way most of the time! You want a marriage in a church? Or somewhere else?"

"I think just somewhere nice, but proper vows and everything with a few people we know, not a huge crowd."

Thus they agreed on a celebration, which Kay would term an engagement party to show the world they were quaintly 'betrothed', but which to Dunstan would be as rock-firm a commitment as any formal exchange of vows, for "After all, with that many witnesses, how could we possibly wriggle out of it?" he pointed out. Then, when it could be booked, they would fix a venue for a 'wedding-day', a smaller event. Meanwhile the supper-party … and another, rather crucial discussion on where they should live together.

The next morning Dunstan was up at dawn. Kay lay back in the small double-bed tucked away in the tiny cottage bedroom. The window was open, fine lace curtains lightly fluttering. She listened contentedly to the crows cawing in nearby treetops, the cooing of wood pigeons and more tuneful birdsong, thrush and blackbird, possibly others.

Dunstan would know and be able to name all of them. How lucky she was to have him as a soul mate in the autumn of her years. She was so excited at the prospect of her friends and family sharing her happiness and meeting Dunstan properly, who until now had been rather a well kept secret.

29

Dunstan brushed down the cobs and led them through to the yard where they stood patiently waiting as he prepared for departure. He had already double-checked the windows were fastened, everything inside was all secure and packed down, something women would normally do, but he could hardly expect Kay to know all the ins and outs of this to the required standard! She seemed to have done a pretty good job, however, and he nodded approvingly. She had also proficiently stamped out and damped down the remainder of the fire that had heated their breakfast kettle of water.

Kay was standing back now, observing, with arms folded.

"Thanks for your help," he called across to her. "You can climb aboard now."

She clambered up the wooden steps, and he then pulled the harnesses off the cratch, below the window at the rear end of wagon, and stowed the steps away in their place.

Soon the *grys* were gently backed between the wooden shafts to be yoked up, the traces hooked on and breeching straps buckled. Kay held the reins while Dunstan, on foot, led them from the front to the track, with one hand firmly under the leather harness.

Once he was back at her side and they were again trundling along the tarmac, Kay expressed her relief.

"Dunstan! You left me in charge, holding the reins. What if they'd bolted?" she cried.

He chuckled, knowing he'd had them firmly under control. "These cobs are too experienced and reliable to do any such thing!"

"I somehow knew that," replied Kay with a smile. Dunstan knew what she meant. Just as a good pair of horses are worth double their weight in gold, her restored trust in him was worth more than anything money could buy.

30

Claudia and Jim were the first to know about the 'betrothal', since they were in the kitchen when Kay and Dunstan bowled in, full of fresh air and smelling of horses. After a brief exchange of greetings, Dunstan discreetly went off to the village grocery shop to allow Kay some space.

Claudia's utter astonishment took a while to abate, for although she had heard the name and liked it enough to pass it to her baby son, she had known virtually nothing about Dunstan the man.

"Your gardener. A Gypsy. Look, Mum, I'm trying to understand, but this is all a bit of a shock. And you're 'kind of married'. I mean, what?"

Over many cups of tea, Kay explained as best she could. To try to summarise Dunstan's life history was impossible.

"You look very happy, Mum. That's enough for me."

"Mm," put in Jim. "Radiant, I'd say. Congratulations, Kay." He squeezed her shoulders affectionately as he passed by her chair on the way to the sink.

"Thank you Jim," said Kay, "that's nice."

"We'll be off to Solihull to clear and close up the house. Just as well we're away for the next few days isn't it?" said Claudia. "Give you two love-birds a bit more time together on home ground."

Kay sent out simple invitations she designed herself.

INVITATION
Informal Supper Party
on Saturday, 12 September at 7.00 pm.
Kay and Dunstan request the pleasure of the company of
....
at The Birches

They prompted a ceaseless peel of phone calls.

Natalie was the first. "You – and Dunstan?" she shrieked. "It's all on again, then? Oh wow! That's fantastic."

Suzi next, gabbling, and offering little chance for Kay to answer her string of questions. "Mum, what's going on? Does this mean something? This is the Gypsy gardener? Right? I mean you've never done anything remotely like this before since … well, you know."

"We're engaged to be married."

"Oh my God! Not just a supper party then …"

It took a while to sink in.

Seamus. "That'll be nice. So Dunstan will be joining us for the craic? That'll be champion." He would need a while to accept Dunstan's cruel betrayal of Ruby-Anne.

Molly-Marie called. "Is that Dunstan Smith, who left and came back and all that carry on and does the gardening and so forth, helping out the young men, is it that Dunstan?" she asked, as if there were an entire tribe of Dunstans roaming the county. "And you and he are celebrating something are you? Is it a birthday or something? Should I bring a gift of some kind, a cake or a card maybe? Ah! Do you know, I can't? I have to be at my daughter's for the weekend, but thanks so much anyway …" Well, thought Kay, the wedding party invitations would be going out soon anyway and she'd be sure to come to that.

A few days later, guests began to arrive eagerly for the supper party bearing a variety of offerings: lager, wine, champagne, chocolates and flowers. Kay and Dunstan stood side by side at the front door to greet the three Farlows and Seamus. With Suzi, Claudia and Jim there were seven guests in all, just able to sit round the table along with the two of them. Presley and Geena were unable to come due to suspected flu.

Kay had decided to keep the meal a master-class in simplicity. A substantial salad platter with hunks of crusty homemade bread to start with; people could choose what they liked and leave things they hated. A huge Greek lamb-in-the-oven dish with potatoes, lamb, rosemary and thyme all drizzled with olive oil in one big dish – two big dishes actually to take the quantity. This was to be served with green beans, peas and roasted peppers. All this was followed by a choice of cold puddings: self-assembled Eton mess; a cheesecake with a choice of raspberries, warm sweetened tayberries or a compote of gooseberries; and a blackberry and apple crumble with thick cream.

They gathered for drinks in the sitting-room first of all and soon conversation buzzed. Dunstan and Kay were the focus of attention and wonderment and Kay was certain that if people were not actually talking to her they were most assuredly talking about her and her man. Details about their 'elopement' spread very quickly around the room.

Dunstan was trying to clarify the situation with Seamus who, with the help of a few pints of Guinness, was at first grudgingly mollified and then became exuberant in his enthusiasm.

"So this means you'll be man and wife living … well now, where will you be living? Here I suppose, and that's for sure, I can see that as clear as day. There's no hopes of Kay living in that tin trailer of yours now is there, Gypsy lad?"

Dunstan laughed. "No hopes whatsoever!"

Kay overheard and added, "He can keep his mobile home as a bolthole for when he grows tired of my cooking! Or we have our first row."

Dunstan pulled her close and kissed her cheek. "I don't intend for us to row at all," and everyone went "aah." "As for the cooking, well …" he teased and she thumped him affectionately.

"He could keep it in the garden!" shouted out Suzi.

"Sure. I'll move in there and take it off your hands!" put in Seamus rubbing his hands together.

"And what about the camper?" asked Jeremy, for he knew Dunstan's vehicular status probably better than most. "And the Ford trucks?"

"Nothing will change that much," said Dunstan. "The main difference is that we shall be together. It's not a revolution!"

Kay kept thinking about Copper's shack. How complicated it all sounded.

Kay asked Tim and Jeremy to check there were enough cans of lager and bottles of wine in the spare fridge and to replenish stocks from the cellar if necessary. She chuckled to herself quietly. No, she thought, soon ushering everyone through to the dining-room, where the table had been extended to its full length and laid with a white and red check table cloth, chunky candles, cutlery and glasses, she and Dunstan could not live in his trailer. At least he had the sense to see that.

He was a good man. For all she knew he would prefer to continue living in his mobile home, just as many Travellers chose to live in trailers, houses seen as wholly uncomfortable abodes. True most of her house was unused most of the time, but she was too accustomed to the feelings of space and storage to give it up now. Others might think it would be an easy choice for Dunstan, but she appreciated that it would be a major change for him. House-dwelling would have unhappy associations too, of Margaret and their rather sterile married life. Then, further back there was the flat, his first experience of bricks and mortar.

Kay made sure everyone was included in the table chat.

"So Imogen, how's things with you?"

"Not bad, Kay, not bad at all," she said, piling her plate high with lettuce. "The hairdressing will combine with other beauty and health spa treatments. Lots of different stuff. I can try and join a cruise ship once I'm fully qualified and have some experience. I did do some training when I was at school, so they've fast-tracked me at college."

There were sighs of envy. "But you'll miss your brothers. And we shall all miss you."

She shrugged, putting on a brave face, Kay felt. "Well, it's not going to happen for a while yet."

"And Tim? Your venture going well?" He nodded and explained round the table briefly what this was.

"Of course, I expect Jeremy has told you, we shall need to sell up," he said, swallowing, abstractedly pushing cold meats into the courgette chutney on his plate, but not raising it to his mouth. "Yeah. Imogen sailing off wherever, Jeremy needs to be in London, I can't keep the place going alone, so there we are! That … is going to be … tough. But …" He took a slug of lager. "The hardest thing is I feel we've let our father down, really. He'd be devastated if he knew the family home he worked so hard for all those years has gone out of the family."

Kay noticed Dunstan was quiet but listening and watching intently. There was a lot for him to take in.

Jeremy chipped in, "Perhaps your business partner could buy it for one of the old folks' homes!"

Tim shifted uneasily in his seat. "I don't think we'd get a fair price to be honest. Not just at the moment, the way the property market is. We need to wait a while before we put up the For Sale sign."

Claudia then commented on the dire state of housing. "There are bargains to be had out there at the moment, for sure, but if you can't get a mortgage, it's all hopeless. I think we shall be living on the streets!"

Kay wondered if she meant that now Dunstan was on the scene, they must surely move out.

"You know you can stay here for as long as you need to," she said softly to one side so only Claudia could hear.

It fell quiet for a moment and the sound of a baby crying could be heard. Claudia sighed heavily. "Oh Dunstan, not now!"

Dunstan and one or two others not in the know, looked puzzled. What had Dunstan the man done?

Kay and those who knew, Jim, Suzi and the Farlows who had been round enough times to the house to meet the baby Dunstan on several occasions, all shrieked with mirth.

"Does poor Dunstan here not know?" cried Suzi. "Mother! Didn't you tell him? Dunstan, did you not realise you have a namesake?"

Dunstan looked astonished, then a little flushed and ultimately pleased. "No. I did not. I knew there was a baby of course, but … Now see here, wifey … wife-to-be … how many other surprises do you have in store for me?"

Kay thought about the shack, but kept quiet on that one. Soon baby Dunstan was brought downstairs to meet his new Grandad, his cries subsiding once held securely in a pair of gentle but capable arms. Kay saw the eyes of Dunstan the man fill with tears. She knew how much it meant to be granted posterity, even if this child was not a blood relative. How well she knew this man, she realised. How blessed she was.

Once the baby was given a placatory feed and put back to bed and Kay was clearing up the first course plates, conversation boomeranged back to property.

"How on earth do people find a plot of land in the country? That's what I'd like to know," said Claudia. "We thought we'd like to do this and build new, do as much of it ourselves as we can. But the price of plots, or of some crumbling old ruin that you'd have to knock down … It's absolutely the only way to get planning permission, though."

"It's pretty much flogging a dead horse. I think we'll have to give up on that though, unless I suddenly get a ludicrously lucrative job offer!" said Jim, with some false note of cheer, Kay sensed. "At the moment there's nothing in our price bracket." He reached across to Claudia and squeezed her hand and she smiled back at him understandingly.

Suddenly Dunstan sprang up from the table. "Look everyone. I have an idea. It's called a hunch, inspiration or something, I'm not sure, but how about this?"

Forks were suspended in mid-air, mouths fell open, Seamus dropped a knife and table napkin simultaneously onto the floor but failed to notice. Kay's heart gave a little thump. Whatever was he going to suggest?

"First The Cedars. Imogen, Tim, Jeremy. Is it possible you might consider renting out this property until the market price rises?"

They nodded in unison. "Of course." "Yes" "We could."

Dunstan then began pacing around the room. Kay thought he was about to suggest that Claudia and Jim could rent The Cedars, but he had no idea how vast and completely inappropriate it would be for their needs. Converting the shack would be better for them, but then surely Dunstan's needs were greater. This was already posing a dilemma for her in her quest to please everyone. She had already enquired about the cost of the shack from an agent dealing with it. Dunstan did not yet know but the buyers had in fact pulled out due to mortgage difficulties. She was keeping this little gem of information as a surprise for later.

"OK. I've had a project in mind for some years," he said and now everyone was hanging on to his every word. "In line with my other work with adolescents, juveniles, mainly lads, who come to me as damaged goods. Well, no, that's hardly a fair term, but ..."

"Do you all know this man has an OBE?" interjected Natalie and those who did not sat up straight.

"Well, the point is that if they had some guidance, some different experiences as young kids, they might've turned out differently."

Everyone nodded, not interrupting. It was indisputable. He went on, "What I'd really love to do is to set up a place where inner city kids could come and get a taste and flavour of the countryside. Maybe for a week, or even just for a weekend. It would need to be a charity but we could establish links with local authorities."

Kay's heart gave a little thump. He was thinking of Gary's two children, Ivan and Bella.

"Would it be like a petting farm?" asked Imogen, leaning forward, her eyes bright with interest. "With ponies and donkeys, rabbits and goats?"

"Could be. Could be anything I … we … make it. It could also show kids how to grow stuff, specially food. You may think everyone's into growing their own these days, but believe me there are a lot of children who barely know where peas or spuds come from!"

Kay thought back to his runner bean at school and his longing for a 'little bit of earth' like Mary in *The Secret Garden*, his attempts to grow vegetables when living on the road, against all the odds. He had already done so much for others, helping rehabilitate young men who had gone the wrong way and now he wanted to go on to do more; to effectively help nip social problems in the bud.

She got up from the table and took his hands. "Dunstan Smith. You are a wonderful man."

"But I'm not finished! I have some funds I would gladly invest in this scheme. It was put by for something else, but The Cedars project is the future and I would rather invest my money in that."

Kay raised her eyebrows questioningly. "Copper's shack?" she whispered.

Dunstan returned her steady gaze. "Mm. But, you know Kay, that is the past. There's no future in clinging on," he responded softly to her alone, before coming back to the table. "There are opportunities here. I know it's not your line of work, Jim, but like these young people here want to sensibly wait until we come out of recession before selling their house – and who knows maybe they will not need to do that now – you might do best to bide your time until the job market improves. In the meantime, you would be doing something so worthwhile it would look good on anyone's CV! Jim, would you consider helping run the enterprise? I know that with your computer skills and working in a team you could do this! It needs to be a going concern – you know, actually self-supporting but with charitable status."

Jim looked momentarily flummoxed. It was a big ask. But Claudia was staring at him, clearly willing him to agree.

She stepped in to negotiate. "On condition that we could have one large room to rent in the house – this house of many large rooms I've heard so much about. You'd need someone in residence for that kind of project, wouldn't you?" Kay was thinking practical things like CRB checks, but she trusted this man so much. He would make it happen. "And by the way, I'm a qualified teacher. I've worked in the inner city too. You can count me in. Music would be good as well. Choirs are very much the thing. Rap, rock, classics …"

"And there's local women who are brilliant at collage and appliqué," put in Jeremy, impressively. "I mean, they could teach … there would be girls as well, wouldn't there?"

"You'll need to do fundraising," said Suzi, allowing no time for an answer. "I can design tee-shirts and other merchandise. We could do a fun-run!" Kay looked at her face, lit up with enthusiasm along with the rest of the company around her table. It pleased her greatly to hear a softer side of Suzi, her successful money-making daughter.

"And at last my veg' and fruit will really have a home to go to!" added Kay.

Dunstan clapped his hands, as his cheeks turned pink. "This is getting very exciting, people!" Then he sat down, to collect his thoughts and calm down. "Anyway," he said, with a little sigh, as he reached towards one of the large casserole of lamb and potatoes. "It's just a thought. Just an idea."

Jeremy piped up again. "It's not just an idea. It's effing fantastic! And I'll tell you something. This could be an amazing way to bring different parts of the community here together. Nathan – he's my Romany friend, has many friends and family who would like to help with this, for sure."

Seamus was nodding vigorously. "And don't forget us Irish Travellers."

"They use computers too, of course they do, but many are good, practical, hard-workers, not like us soft creatures! Ground maintenance, building outhouses, tree clearance, bagging manure, putting up fences, spreading out tree-bark, handling horses … I mean, honestly, the list goes on and on and on and …"

"OK, Jeremy," cried everyone else, "Enough!"

"A toast!" said Kay, raising her glass, and hurriedly glasses were filled. "A toast to Appley Green and all who live here – or tarry awhile!

"To Appley Green and all who live here – or tarry awhile!" came the echo.

Glossary

Atching tan	stopping place, campsite
Chavi	boy
Chavies	children
Chop	to part-exchange, to sell
Chore	steal
Diklo	neckerchief or scarf
Dikhs	sees
Dinilo	idiot
Dordi	oh dear!
Duhvi	God
Gavver	policeman
Gorgio (Gaujo)	non-Gypsy person
Gry/grai	horse
Hoben	food
Jall the drom	travel on the road
Juval	woman
Lil	letter
Lova	money
Muskerros	police
Mush	man
Poove	allow horse to graze
Rakli	girl, young woman
Stir/stirapen	prison
Tatti tatti	baked potato
Vardo	wagon
Vonga	money

Note: spelling of Romany words is variable.

Bibliography

Books used by the author for background information in writing *Gypsies Stop tHere* and *No Gypsies Served.*

Romany culture and Gypsy identity
Edited by Thomas Acton and Gary Mundy
Published by University of Hertfordshire Press

We are the Romani people
by Ian Hancock
Published by University of Hertfordshire Press

Gypsy politics and Traveller identity
Edited by Thomas Acton
Published by University of Hertfordshire Press

Moving On – The Gypsies and Travellers of Britain
by Donald Kenrick and Colin Clark
Published by University of Hertfordshire Press

A false dawn
by Ilona Lackova
Published by University of Hertfordshire Press

Incidents in a Gipsy's Life
by George Smith
Printed by Parchment (Oxford) Ltd

Historical Survey of The Gypsies
by John Hoyland
Published by the Romany & Traveller Family History Society

Gypsies and Travellers in their own words
Compiled and edited by Peter Saunders, Jim Clarke, Sally Kendall, Anna Lee, Sakie Lee and Freda Matthews
Published by Leeds Travellers Education Service

Gypsy Jib – A Romany Dictionary
by James Hayward
Published by Holm Oak Publishing

Smoke in the Lanes
By Dominic Reeve
Published by University of Hertfordshire Press

Beneath the Blue Sky
By Dominic Reeve
Published by Five Leaves Publications

Bury Me Standing
By Isabel Fonseca
Published by Vintage

On The Cobbles
Jimmy Stockins with Martin King and Martin Knight
Published by Mainstream Publishing

The Last Bastion of Racism
By John Coxhead
Published by Trentham Books

Here to Stay
By Colin Clark and Margaret Greenfields
Published by University of Hertfordshire Press

Stopping Places
By Simon Evans
Published by University of Hertfordshire Press

Dreams of the Road
By Martin Levinson and Avril Silk
Published by Birlinn Ltd

Room to Roam
England's Irish Travellers
A Research Report by Dr Colm Power (June 2004)

Gypsy Politics and Social Change
By Thomas Acton
Published 1974 by Routledge and Kegan Paul.

The Secret Garden
By F Hodgson-Burnett
First published 1911

Gypsies Stop tHere

by
Miriam Wakerly

Will uprooting herself from London to live in the country help Kay escape guilt-ridden memories of her husband's death? Far from finding a quiet life, she is caught up in an age-old village conflict where passionate opinions on Romany Gypsy Travellers divide the local people.

A young woman, Lena, enters her life, unwittingly putting Kay's plans on hold as Kay struggles to not only come to terms with her emotional past but to resolve Lena's problems, those of the village and the Gypsies.
And another relationship blossoms that she would never have dreamed of …

This novel, set in UK 2007, is written from the viewpoint of a non-Gypsy woman who has her own intriguing tale to tell. It also brings us up to date with where Travellers are in the 21st century and shows a balanced understanding of the problems they still face. Romany Gypsies, who have been with us for over 500 years, are an ethnic group that even today suffer open racist abuse and discrimination in the UK.

Available from bookshops or online from:
www.strongmanpublishing.com and Amazon

What People have Said about Gypsies Stop tHere

Extract from review by Michael Smith (Veshengro), Editor O NEVO DROM, The Romani Magazine by Romani for Romani

"... should be in every public library, in every school ... I can definitely give this book full marks."

Review by Kay Green. Full review on www.booksy.co.uk Readers' Recommendations

"When issues are put into a personal story, they suddenly get a whole lot more complicated and endlessly intriguing ... Cliché it may be to say it, but Gypsies Stop tHere is a real page-turner ."

Book Review, Voice - Winter 2009, magazine of South East England Regional Assembly

"...gives an insight into the history of Gypsies and Travellers, the prejudices they face and some of the issues surrounding where they should live."

Ann Wilson (Romany Gypsy) Community Development Worker, Surrey Community in Action

"... well thought through ... a lot of up to date issues included in the story. I believe the story will help people with some of the real problems and prejudices that Gypsies and Travellers face. A good entertaining story to read. Enjoyed the book immensely and looking forward to the sequel."

Bernadette McLean, Principal of Helen Arkell Centre and non-executive Director of Barrington Stoke Publishers

"...a good read, this story provides an entertaining way of understanding a very important social issue ... A recommended read for book club members who wish to have a story that is thought-provoking."

About the Author

Miriam Wakerly has had short stories and articles published in magazines. Combined with bringing up three children, her career history includes teaching, public relations and marketing in the IT industry; and community work. Now retired from work other than writing, she lives in Surrey with her husband.

Miriam Wakerly has a BA Degree in Combined Studies (English, French, Sociology, Politics) from Leicester University. She is a member of the Society of Authors.

Find her on Twitter and her blog, Miriam's Ramblings.